Destined for You

SARAH GERDES

RPM Publishing

Seattle, WA

Copyright © 2016 Sarah Gerdes

All rights reserved.

ISBN: 1539460983
ISBN-13: 978-1539460985

Library of Congress cataloging-in-publication data on file

Printed in the United States of America

First American Edition 2017

Cover design by Lyuben Valevski
http://lv-designs.eu

Destined for You

CHAPTER 1

When Danielle stepped off the metro, she felt the morning breeze brush her face, the air from Lake Zurich already warm. Her heels clicked on the pavement, the steady sound keeping pace with her heart. On her first day back to work since having Monroe, her anxiety was balanced with enthusiasm and joy. She felt buoyant knowing Andre supported and encouraged her to find fulfillment on every level possible; family, career and her watersport of choice, sailboarding.

The streets were full of other well-dressed professionals that separated into distinct lines streaming into the steel and marble buildings. She joined them, holding her right hand loose at her side, feeling the heavy, diamond bracelet Andre's parents had given her. It was a piece of jewelry that happened to match the eternity ring on her fourth finger, given to her by Lars, her managing director and former love.

Past and present, she thought. As her late father often said, "Remember the past, live in the present and look towards the future." A future that included marrying Andre in exactly six weeks.

The elevator moved up quickly and silently. She was soon at the imposing double doors, gripping the handle and saying hello to the receptionist. Jacqueline Lader came up and welcomed her back.

"Nice to be here," Danielle replied. The head of human resources shook her hand, the formality of the environment unchanged in Danielle's absence.

"We will need to go through the security process again but

your office is ready and waiting."

On the walk down the hall, she experienced déjà vu as the other traders at their desks looked up, smiled then went right back to work, just as they'd done on her first day at the company. Ulrich, her trading desk manager, stopped by her office as she placed her purse in the wardrobe.

"Good to have you back," he said, gripping her hand. "I hope it's not impolitic of me to say this, but you don't appear to have had a baby."

Danielle smiled. "Compliments of any kind are good form."

"I'll let you say hello to the others and get started. The accounts are online and waiting."

Johanne, who had been waiting in the hallway, gave her a hug upon entering her office. "Ulrich was completely lying," he murmured. "Your blessings are nearly popping out of that top." Only her peer, the other gold trader in the firm, could get away with that.

"Wha..?" she half-gasped, turning away from the glass wall and self-consciously looking down. The buttons on her Chanel suit were secure, although the center one did reflect a bit of tension. "Nothing I can do about that now," she muttered, turning back to him. "Other than wait until they recede like the air out of a balloon."

"Don't worry about it. Anyone who doesn't know about Monroe will just think you got the standard, overdone American boob job while on break."

"Johanne!" she quietly exclaimed, looking beyond him into the hallway. "Have you been bottling up all your sassiness until I came back or what?"

Her co-worker and peer ran a hand through his ear-length hair and adjusted his metal-framed glasses. "Yes and no. It's stress that's been building since you left, like a wine that's been a century over-fermented and is ready to go rank."

Danielle shook her head, sitting down. "That's a lovely visual. Can't Dario help you with the stress relief?"

"Nope. While you were off giving birth, we hit the rocks and not long after I delivered your baby gift we broke up. I don't think it's permanent. More irritating than anything." He went to the door, forestalling any more questions. "Oh, hey, did you hear the other big news? Lars is engaged." Danielle was unable to stop from lifting her eyebrows. "Yep. You'd think it would put him in a permanently good mood, but he's the same. No change."

"What do you expect from the managing director?"

Johanne shrugged. "Business. Not marriage."

Danielle was sorry to see her friend and colleague go, but exploring other subjects, including her former lover, on the morning of her first day back to work weren't appropriate. A flashback of the two of them on her couch, the snow falling, and her crying in his arms when they ended their relationship appeared in her minds-eye. They'd discussed marriage before learning the baby she was carrying was Andre's, conceived at the end of that earlier relationship. The tears and breakup occurred because Danielle had refused to cut Andre or his parents out of a relationship with his unborn child. Lars was adamant. He didn't want to share her, or the baby she was carrying, with anyone. No back and forth between dads or grandparents, or running to someone else when things got difficult. It was heartbreaking for both of them. But it was right thing to do, she'd told her dying father. The only thing to do.

Weeks later, when Danielle's father had passed on, Danielle reunited with Andre at the funeral. From that point, their relationship had quickly renewed itself, like a flower gone dormant and left for dead in the winter, but springing alive with the warmth of spring. The engagement party had been held at Andre's parent's home, and Lars had attended. He'd known Andre's parents professionally for years. It was his firm that managed most of their money. Danielle would never forget the moment when her two loves, Andre and Lars, had been collegially talking, looked at her and shook hands. Two men but only one baby, and that made all the difference in her world.

Danielle closed her eyes and mind to the scene. She needed to get trading.

At a quarter past ten, the inevitable occurred. A two-tap knock at her door, the first flipping her pulse into overdrive, the second batting it back down.

"Good morning," Lars said.

"Hi Lars. Nice to see you." Crisp, genuine, professional.

"Is everything in order?"

She gestured to her desk. "It's all perfect, as if I never left. But you, well, new look?" For a moment, he appeared perplexed and she pointed to his chest area. "I didn't think a managing director could work in Zurich without a tie." She'd meant to break the ice by teasing him on her first day back to work after giving birth, but instantly realized she had erred. A man like Lars, who loved his ties and thought they were the must-have accessory for the well-dressed executive, would only make a change to his wardrobe because of an outside influence. *Like a woman.* "Well, thanks for allowing me to come back to work on a part-time basis," she continued. "I appreciate it."

Lars had the good manners to smile.

"I can say on behalf of the partners, we are the ones who are appreciative." Danielle gave him what she thought was an acceptable smile and attached the headpiece to her ear. She saw his eyes dart to the fourth finger of her right hand, to see the ring he'd given her the night they had broken up. The gift came with a request. Never to take it off, because if she did, it would be a sign she no longer cared to remember what they once had.

"Thank you," he said. The comment could be considered a natural addition to his prior statement about the appreciative partners. She knew better.

"Of course." They were mature adults, occupied in other significant relationships and working in a highly functioning environment, but she could still remember what once was without pain or regret, and, to her complete surprise and gratification, a little happiness for his newfound state.

Danielle traded until noon and checked her returns one last time. Her numbers were in the double digits. Not once during the morning had she allowed her mind to wander back to Lars. He simply wasn't a part of her emotional life any longer, a fact her unconscious self must be okay with, because she had no conflicting emotions as the elevator door shut.

Just as it should be. Past and present, she repeated. They could coexist.

CHAPTER 2

Danielle arrived to find Layda rocking Monroe.

"How was your first day back?" asked her soon to be mother-in-law.

"Great," Danielle answered, sitting down in the corner love seat. "With the expected twinge of guilt for not being home with my daughter."

Layda shook her head, flipping back her perfectly coiffed shoulder length white-blond hair. Monroe was cradled in her arms, her small face pressed against Layda's chest, just above the embroidered monogram on the pocket, the little fingers of one hand clinging tight. "You shouldn't have worried a second."

Danielle reflected on her relationship with Layda. Her initial, off-putting formality had been a front for a woman who was both shy and private by nature. Danielle learned Layda was also scared of becoming too close to Danielle too soon. The last woman to become pregnant by Andre had aborted the child, alienating Andre and devastating Layda.

"Has she been out of your arms at all?" Danielle teased.

"Well…" replied Layda, happily exuding contentment. "I did follow your instructions and put her on her blanket. She's doing her best to roll over but it won't happen for some time yet." Layda recounted the day. It was uneventful and typical for a five-month-old. Danielle imagined the little girl receiving all the attention a grandmother can bestow.

"I did need to supplement what you gave me with some formula. May I boldly suggest it may be time to start her on soft foods soon? I could puree some food from my kitchen garden."

The revelation came with a bit of melancholy. "You aren't being bold, and that would be welcome. Any hesitation is coming from me, personally. I'm in new-motherhood denial." It had gone by so fast, yet Danielle was grateful she was there to experience the firsts months.

Layda slid a finger within Monroe's open palm. "You've taken to it so easily, I never would have known you didn't have nieces and nephews. Most first-time mothers express so much anxiety."

Danielle slipped off her shoes. "Did you?"

"No, but I had two older sisters and a much older brother. By the time I was a teenager, I was babysitting for my cousins. I felt more than prepared when Andre came along." Danielle watched grandmother rock granddaughter.

"Do you wish you had more children?"

"We tried," Layda admitted. "It just never happened. What about you?"

Danielle was pleased Layda felt comfortable enough with her to ask. "I don't have a philosophical issue against more than one. That said, I don't think I'm ready to have a litter of four either. The doctor thinks it's a very remote possibility to have another, since Monroe was a meteor hitting the Earth type of rarity." She warmed from within at Layda's smile of encouragement. "I can see you being very content with a group of children running around that you can spoil rotten."

"Well, please don't feel any pressure from me. This granddaughter is meeting all our hopes and expectations."

"Any pressure I feel is self-inflicted and involves fitting into my wedding dress. If I reduce my nursing schedule, between now and the wedding, I can't guarantee I won't need another one or two appointments with the seamstress."

Layda waved her free hand in the air. "My dear, if you have one a week, it won't bother me. I've waited Andre's entire adult life for this event and I'm happy to pay for whatever is necessary to make everything perfect."

"You are too much, thank you. Oh, here. I thought you'd like to see what your hairdresser has created. Lani was my stand-in for the test up-do and sent me pictures." Danielle took out her phone and showed Layda the photos Lani had texted.

"Very elegant, but it will look better on you," Layda said with a conspiratorial wink, glancing at Monroe now asleep in her arms. "And I'm glad are going to be a part of our family. That's all we have in this world, don't you think?"

"I do."

She took Monroe from Layda, who left shortly after. Danielle gratefully took off her top, slipped into a camisole and had just finished nursing when Andre called. She gave him the simple version of the morning: her numbers were up, Ulrich was happy and Johanne was temporarily single.

"A typical first day then," Andre commented. Danielle imagined him sitting at his modern desk in his large office overlooking the lake, his father's office across the hall. She thought he sounded happy, and the fact he didn't ask out about Lars struck her as encouraging.

Just before six p.m. her fiancé walked through the door. Danielle's hips moved in time to the beat of the music on the radio as she closed the distance to him, her apron still on.

"That's definitely not Bach," Andre observed with dry humor. The dance music came from the kitchen, loud enough to make her happy but not so much it would wake Monroe. Her hips kept going as she embraced him, working in circles against him as her arms went up his back, her fingernails scratching him gently.

He hummed. "Work has evidently done some you some good."

"We need to get out dancing sometime. I think I can fit in my clubbing clothes again." She nuzzled his neck, breathing on his warm skin.

Danielle slid her hand under his chin, feeling the stubble of his dark facial hair within her palm. He might have traded jeans and leather jackets for slacks and a sport coat just before Monroe came into this world, but his beyond-sexy five-o-clock shadow had remained. Being a father had made Andre more attractive to her, not less, something she thought impossible.

"Do you think this will end after we get married?" Danielle murmured as Andre caressed her neck with his lips.

"You mean married, in the official way, versus the having a baby and living together type?" She nodded, her lips curled up into a smile. "Before Monroe, I never imagined myself as a corporate guy. Did *you* ever think I could have done this?"

Danielle's eyes were still closed, the tickling sensations moving up her legs at odds with the seriousness of the question. "No."

"I hope I've been doing a good job."

Danielle gently pulled back, staring straight into his eyes. "I'm sorry you have to even say that. Every day, every moment I'm more impressed. You're amazing."

The joy her answer gave him evidenced itself in a hard kiss, their lips parting together, searching one another as eagerly as if they'd just started dating. A giggle started to build as she gently, but firmly, pushed him back.

"Let me guess," Andre half-groaned, loosening his tie. "More things to do from my mother?" Danielle nodded, a closed-mouth smile on her face.

"She left me with a list of items to review. Engraved silver spoons. Monogramed chocolate initials. Typical wedding things, I think, having never been involved in one before."

He picked up a handkerchief with the date of their marriage embroidered on it. "You are handling my mother with grace and dignity," he complimented, inspecting the item with a quizzical look on his face. "She's in love with you almost as much as I am."

"Because I say yes to most anything she suggests." With her own parents deceased, Danielle thought it was a direct gift from God Andre's parents were living, and that he was close with them.

"No, you also agreed to live nearby," he said. He put the handkerchief down and pulled her into her arms.

"Two blocks up and one over is hardly next door," she murmured.

"Can I suggest we go through the list later, when Monroe's awake? I have a better idea for our free time right now."

Danielle was still holding his hand as they went into the bedroom and closed the door behind them.

CHAPTER 3

Finding a balance between career and home was easier than Danielle imagined. Because she was only working half days until her wedding, she went to the office from six a.m. until noon, ate lunch at home with her daughter, conducted research while Monroe napped then took it easy until dinner time, alternately playing on the floor, reading and making dinner. The week officially ended Friday afternoon when Andre commented that her appearance and demeanor was like breathing in fresh air.

"Do I need to apologize?" she asked him.

"Not at all. But I will say you are such an intellectual and driven woman, staying home wasn't doing for you what I think it does for a lot of other women."

That night, she took a bath, slipped on her purple lace lingerie, and called out to him, asking him to bring her a cup of tea. When Andre entered the bedroom, he saw her, smiled and put the cup on the dresser. He began loosening his tie with anticipation. She never imagined Andre as a dashing corporate executive, but here he was.

"Do you miss it?" she asked abruptly. "Your previous life, that is."

He approached her, unbuttoning his shirt. "Being out on the water with smoking clients? Or spending Saturdays at the bike shop selling thousand dollar jackets?" Danielle smirked. His shirt was already on the floor, and he'd gone to his belt buckle.

"Either." His pants dropped down and he kicked them off.

"Yes. Terribly." She smiled seductively, his answer rendering other questions unnecessary.

Saturday was spent relaxing at home, sitting on the couch with Andre going through more wedding details, having lunch at his parents and their first outing to the jazz club since giving birth. Sunday, she encouraged Andre to go for a ride on his Ducati motorcycle while she worked and napped with Monroe.

On Monday, Danielle woke full of the eagerness associated with being mentally and emotionally fulfilled. She fed Monroe, then pumped enough milk for another bottle, putting it in the fridge when Andre came in.

"A snack?" Andre said with a laugh, taking a drink of coffee.

"Taking milk from your daughter will give you an express ticket to the dark side."

"Might be worth it," he quipped. "You go. I'll finish with her."

"You sure? This is awfully early for you and it's only my second week back."

"Our schedule is working for me," he said with a mischievous smile. "Mornings will be my bonding time with our daughter."

"And evenings with me. Perfect." She gave him a long kiss before she left.

Two times during the week, Johanne stopped by her office, giving her accolades for her returns and asking about her work load. She thought of the extra accounts he was managing that were technically hers until she returned full time. His not-so-subtle hints culminated on Friday, when he stopped by her office just as she removed her headset. He sat down, the sheen of his blue, button down shirt contrasting nicely with the steel grey slacks he wore.

"Do you have a set of glasses to match every outfit you own or do those change color in the light?" she asked him.

He sat back with the posture of a man who had something more on his mind than his appearance. "I have many," he said gingerly. "So, after two full weeks, what do you think?"

Danielle held his gaze. "I think I'm surprised you waited this long to ask."

Johanne's foot twitched, his voice as bright and confident as a mother encouraging her daughter in a beauty pageant when he spoke. "I bet you wouldn't even notice the extra time at the office between now and the wedding."

Danielle shook her head slightly. Lars walked by and must have seen the perplexed look on her face and been curious, because the next moment he was at the door.

"Good numbers today," he said to them both. His tan suit was lighter than his skin color, the warm brown contrasting with his dark eyes. Today he wore a tie of a darker green with a slight pattern. She liked it. She momentarily wondered why it had returned, dismissing the notion. He was more elegant and commanding with a tie on, not off.

Johanne tilted his head towards Danielle. "I'm trying to convince her to work more hours."

"I'm not financially opposed to the idea," Lars said.

"In contrast to the morally-opposed kind?" she responded with a wry smile.

Johanne spoke before Lars had a chance to. "Do you think Ulrich and the partners would approve of Danielle taking over more of her old accounts now, rather than after the wedding?"

"It's a legal question, not a preference," Lars began. "The conflict of interest issues only change when Danielle is married. Our practices are meant to keep us from being sued, not to manage your personal intentions."

Johanne pulled one side of his mouth to the other. "Four weeks."

"Well, at least one other person is as excited as I am," she quipped.

Lars displayed no humor when he spoke. "If the partners approved the account transfers before her marriage, it would require personally calling each client and getting written consent from each one before the accounts could be handed off to Danielle."

"By we, you mean you?" Danielle asked. Lars nodded. "Is that even possible?"

Lars pursed his lips, tilting his head. "Anything is possible, within legal boundaries. I can't guess at the outcome, but that's only because I haven't ever been asked to do such a thing. Only back two weeks and you continue to pose all sorts of scenarios we've never had to deal with, Danielle."

She lifted her hands in a mea-culpa. "Typical American problem-maker."

Lars continued. "If you're serious about taking back the accounts and working full-time, I'd need to get the documents together. Before I go to the effort and expense, are you sure you want to return full time?"

She glanced at Johanne. "I'm not sure."

"It's only three more hours a day," Johanne replied, in a 'what's-the-big-deal type of way.'

Danielle dropped her head back and laughed, feeling the tickle of her shoulder length hair move from her neck to her back. "Seriously, it's a little more than that."

Lars held her eyes for a moment then addressed her colleague. "Johanne, you may not know this, but the way Danielle works is she's here physically for eight hours, but then she'll trade the other markets after hours, the same as she did before."

Johanne's eyes went wide and his jaw slacked. "You traded the east coast markets? You Yankee dog," he muttered.

Lars continued, clasping his hands and leaning against the credenza, the posture of a statesman closing a deal. "So that adds up to a whole lot of time here and at home that she's not with her twenty-two-week-old daughter or soon to be husband."

Johanne was silent as the words sank in.

14

"Now that we have my life sorted out," Danielle interjected, feeling slightly unnerved and flattered that Lars was so easily able to recall Monroe's age, "I do need to keep to my schedule, at least for today." Johanne rose, deflated. She came around the desk and touched his arm. "I'll talk it over with Andre and see where we land, okay?" She looked at Lars, who nodded.

"I'll go through the diligence on my end just in case."

Johanne lingered after Lars left. "Danielle, I'm sorry. I don't mean to pull you back here. I just…"

"I know. I get it." He wanted to unload some accounts and see if he could salvage his relationship with Dario.

Danielle was a block from home when she impulsively stopped by the flower mart and picked up a bouquet of lilies with carnations and juniper. The scents were strong and compelling, reflecting my life, she thought to herself. The image of Lars came to mind, and she felt no change in emotion or pulse rate. Her interaction with her former lover was easy and professional. It had been nine months since they'd last been romantic, a veritable eternity of time given the changes in her life.

She put the change in her pocket and walked out of the store. *I'm happy his life is moving forward as positively as my own. I don't feel even a twinge of envy.*

As Danielle crossed the street, she saw Lars getting into the waiting car outside the office building. *Well, maybe a little twinge of envy.*

CHAPTER 4

Over dinner, she and Andre discussed her returning to work full-time and Andre encouraged her to go for it.

"I think you're ready," he said, gripping her hand. His face shone with pride in her skills and confidence in her abilities. "As Johanne said, it's only three more hours a day, and of course Lars made no objection because he knows you can handle it."

Danielle was a little taken aback by his cavalier attitude. "You do recall how I operated pre-baby? Research during the evenings and on the weekends?"

"Yes, and you have my mother who is a ready and willing babysitter for the foreseeable future." He could tell she was reticent and took her hand. "Look, we have the morning routine down. I'm here until nearly eight when you are out the door by six. You get home by four or just before."

"What about my evening trading?"

"I'll hold Monroe, read to her and sing songs in the background when you are the computer. You can stop and put her to bed if you want. Don't worry. She will be slathered with love and attention by three very capable adults, not including my father."

Danielle sighed. "We do have nights and weekends."

"And millions of children with two working parents who seem to turn out okay. Neither your work nor our little girl will suffer."

Danielle bit her lip in a momentary burst of insecurity. "What if I don't meet client expectations?"

"You and failure in the same sentence is an oxymoron. Besides, your returns will outshine Johanne so quickly the clients will be celebrating."

"He's not doing badly," Danielle said, defending Johanne. Neither Lars nor Ulrich would retain a trader who wasn't at the top of their field.

"Dad never said Johanne was doing poorly, just not as good as you."

Not long afterwards, Danielle called Layda and asked about her desire and availability to watch Monroe until Danielle could find a full-time caretaker on a permanent basis.

"I wouldn't want anyone else to take care of her," Layda said firmly. "But it's not me or Monroe I'm concerned about. It's you. Are you sure you want to do this to yourself when you should be relaxing before the wedding?"

"Really, Layda, my load is really light. You've done all the hard work." Danielle visualized the few wedding-related events that involved her: a lady's lunch and rehearsal dinner the weekend before the wedding. For the out of town guests, Layda had planned a boating excursion of Lake Zurich and tours of a few of the famous chocolate factories, but Danielle wasn't expected to attend.

Layda was unconvinced, but went along. "I don't want our beautiful bride-to-be tired is all. But if you say you can handle it, I'm sure you can."

Saturday, mid-morning, Danielle sent Lars an email affirming she was officially able to work full time; the rest was now up to him. Sunday, she was up at six, feeding Monroe when she heard a ping on her computer. An email from Lars in her inbox informed her the partners fully supported her return, and that all the clients except for one had elected to return under Danielle's management.

"Unreal," she said to herself, counting the hours since their conversation. Currency and gold would be traded in accordance with their account designation. The total amount under her management was 5.3 Billion dollars. Not bad for being out five months.

She put Monroe back to sleep and went to join Andre in bed, but he was already awake.

"Why aren't you asleep?" she asked him.

"We have a bike ride this morning and then a boat ride this evening."

Danielle slid under the covers. "Oh really? And who's going?"

"Us. My mother's coming over at ten." Danielle wrapped her leg around his, the grip of her inner thighs a subconscious effort to push down her nerves. "It will be fun and relaxed."

Danielle sighed out her tension and nodded. He thought she was hesitating about going on a boat with friends and leaving Monroe at home, when her mind was on the two of them—Monroe's parents—on a motorcycle. What if…she had wondered aloud to Layda one day. "All women go through it," Layda answered, referring to the worry of accidents happening. "I call it the new-motherhood fear. It goes away in time."

"Really?" Danielle queried. "When?"

"Right about the time you realize you are so busy taking care of the little one, you don't have time to worry!"

When Layda arrived, Danielle greeted her with kisses on both cheeks. "As casual as ever," Danielle teased. Today Layda wore black linen pants, flats, and a Yves St. Laurent pullover with three-quarter leaf sleeves, highlighting her perfectly French-manicured gel nails.

"Jeans and me have never gotten along," Layda replied with a smile.

Andre and Danielle headed to the garage, put on their helmets and mounted his sports bike. She leaned forward, placing her hands around his waist.

"Still nervous?" he asked, pulling the bike slowly out on to the street.

"I can't help it."

Once Andre had accelerated, he briefly patted her left leg before returning his hand to the bar. "We'll be fine. Trust me."

Andre drove along the Limmat River, then out of town, towards the mountains. He picked a roadside café for an early lunch before he turned around and headed back. The three-hour journey was short, scenic and non-eventful, just as Andre promised.

They arrived at the marina as the sun was starting its descent. Andre was helping her into the Stancraft cruiser when she saw Stephen and Lani walking down the ramp.

"You look gorgeous," Danielle told Lani. Her best friend wore a flowing, white skirt with flowers embroidered on the bottom, the matching top was billowy but flattering, the three-quarter length sleeves showing off Lani's taut arms. "If I didn't know better, I'd say you've been at the gym and not at the restaurant."

"She's a culinary Jedi," Stephen said, extending his hand to help Lani step into the boat. "It's one and the same." He shook Andre's hand and kissed Danielle's cheeks.

"It's true," Lani said happily. "I get a better bicep workout hefting food and cutting than I would from an hour of lifting weights."

"I can only dream," Danielle said.

"Of what?" Lani asked. "Standing on your feet all day or taking inventory?"

Danielle slapped her on the butt. "Working out! Hey guys," she said, waving to Andre's hockey friends. Lucas walked beside Christian with Max in the back.

"Hey mom," Max greeted her.

"A baby came out of you? Really?" Lucas asked.

Christian, usually the silent one of the bunch, kissed both of her cheeks. "You do look great."

"Guys, I was eight and a half months pregnant when you last saw me. What'd you expect after all this time?"

"Bosoms," muttered Lani, her comment setting Danielle laughing. She and Johanne were so alike. No wonder he missed her dancing. Max overheard and rolled his eyes. "What?" Lani said, turning to Max. "You could have some if you elected to date occasionally."

"And in a town full of blond amazons, no less," Danielle added, clucking her tongue with a shake of her head and opening the small fridge. "You show up on an evening cruise, in this boat with this food and alcohol alone?"

"I'm waiting for qua-li-ty," Max replied, accepting a beer.

"Since when?" Christian quipped. Danielle caught Andre's chuckle from behind her as he lifted the ropes.

"Yes, Max," Andre said. "Do tell me when did our perennial ladies' man turn commitment-ready?" Max took a seat beside Stephen, drink in hand.

"I said nothing about commitment. I just said I wanted better quality."

Echoes of the laughter bounced off the water like the conversation, touching on the life of single men in an expensive city filled with young professionals, many there to work, not raise a family.

"When marriage happens, the inevitable sets in," pronounced Max. "First a boat more expensive than most homes in the city, then soon enough, it's a home outside the city, then a long commute, late arrival from work, exhaustion, then getting fat."

"That sounds like Dante's seventh ring of hell, Max," Danielle remarked through laughter. "But we haven't moved outside the city yet, and not all men, or women, get big like cows in the field."

He eyed her. "It could happen."

Danielle giggled uncontrollably at the insinuation. "My dad always maintained bigness was a sign of happiness."

"Max will be content as long as he fits into his hockey uniform," interjected Lucas. Danielle's laughter subsided only when she saw a look pass between Lani and Stephen, and it wasn't one of humor.

Andre guided the boat out of the marina and along the shoreline, rounding the northwest bend. Stephen pointed to the waterpark, where a huge, rubber water slide was next to a trampoline half the size of a football field. "Just think of sending Monroe down that."

"I will, in about five years," Andre answered.

"And what if you have another one before then?" Max asked Danielle.

"Then Lani and Stephen will babysit so Andre and I can go."

Max turned to Lani, his eyes inquisitive. "What if you guys have kids yourself? Will you keep the restaurant?"

Lani crossed a leg, glancing at her husband, the way a woman does when she knows the answer will be different, depending on who gives it. "I can't see stepping away for a while. Having a friend with a baby I get to play with is enough for now."

Danielle leaned into Lani. "No more talk of babies, Max. I need to talk with my bridesmaid about wedding details."

"Thanks," muttered Lani, her smile of relief genuine.

The two began a decidedly female conversation in lower voices while the men discussed work, women and hockey. Danielle updated Lani on the monogrammed wine bottles and chocolate, then turned the conversation to her friend.

"Okay, so tell me all that I have missed in the last few months, because I'm feeling seriously out of the loop."

Lani raised an eyebrow in tandem with the drink to her lips. "Changes."

"That sounds ominous. Temporary or permanent?"

Lani took a sip of her wine. "Time will tell."

Danielle leaned back and glanced at the city skyline. They

were passing around the end of the lake, the Opera House already gone by, under a bridge and then out again, now in front of the streets where MRD had its lakeside offices.

"Well, I can tell you and Stephen aren't happy. You aren't touching. You avoid each other's eyes and you neatly side-stepped Max's question about kids. But, since I can tell you aren't going to divulge more, let me tell you what else is going on in my life. I went back to work."

"When?" Lani asked, her eyes round with shock.

Danielle grinned, rightly smug she'd kept the secret. "Two weeks ago. You and I are both now so busy it will guarantee we don't see one another again until the rehearsal dinner."

"So that's why Andre arranged this little excursion? I should have known. He practically threatened us with our lives if we didn't come."

"I'm sorry. It doesn't seem like it's doing you or Stephen much good." Seeing Lani's look of discomfort, she changed the subject. "Have you even taken a Saturday night off since Stars & Stripes opened?"

"Forget a Saturday. Any day." Danielle glanced at Andre, who was giving the wheel of the boat over to Stephen.

Lani turned her head away from Stephen and Andre, to the water, murmuring. "Are you worried about Lars?"

"Why would I be worried?"

"You once thought he was the father of your child," Lani said, with the 'you-have-lost-your-mind' tone of voice. "What if he can't keep himself away from you now that you're back at the office?"

Danielle smirked. "Sure, Lani," she said, her voice oozing sarcasm. "Having given birth to another man's baby is such an attraction. I think not."

"It could happen," Lani said, her eyes gleaming.

"I guess you haven't heard. He's engaged." Danielle had all the satisfaction of seeing her friend nearly choke on her drink.

"True story."

"That didn't take long."

"Nine months," Danielle informed her. "But I have no details on her or the engagement."

"Well, maybe he knew her before. I don't see a man like that moving fast with anyone. Or, hey!" she continued, perking up. "Maybe she just got divorced or broke up with whoever she was with and he struck like a snake!" Lani let out a burst of a laugh that bounced along the floating waves. "So," she started again, her voice low and mischievous. "How are you handling that?"

Danielle tilted her head. "I always said I wanted him to be as happy as I was, and I am."

"Really?"

"Really."

"Bullshit."

Danielle allowed a conspiratorial a giggle. "FYI. I'm marrying a man I love. But all that aside, Lars confirmed he's attending the wedding with a guest, so there's no avoiding it."

Lani whistled, then glanced down at her half-full glass with a look of longing. "Don't you remember the old days, where it was uncouth to bring dates to your former partner's wedding?"

Their laughter continued as the boat cruised along the waterfront. Danielle's mind did wander back to Lars and who he could possibly know well enough to marry and one—the only one—came to mind. Lars had told her about it. The woman and her husband had been clients of MRD. Lars had an affair with her, the relationship became public, they pulled their money out of the firm, and that spawned Lars' creation of the rule forbidding client-trader relationships.

Well, I'm not one to judge. An intelligent, handsome man wasn't going to remain alone forever.

Max requested one unscheduled stop at a local bar and then Lani another. The drinking increased for everyone but Andre and

Danielle, who watched their friends become louder, funnier, and more brutally honest. If body language were any indication of emotional state, Danielle would have guessed that Lani were a single woman in search of a good time as opposed to being married to the man of her dreams and part owner of the most successful restaurant in town.

The lights of the marina were in sight when the subject of one-night stands was raised. Max, who was highly intoxicated, was telling Lani she needed to have children so the world could have more beautiful women.

"That's what I keep suggesting," Stephen remarked with the grace of a husband used to men giving his wife attention. "Keep the gene strain alive."

"Well, if anything ever happens to Stephen," Max loudly slurred, "I've been fixed so I can't help in the department, but she can practice on me, right?" Christian nearly spit up his drink but Lucas laughed.

"What do you mean fixed?" asked Danielle, genuinely curious. "As in, fixed, fixed?"

Lucas put one leg up on the pad, raising a finger from his glass to point at Max. "He's been completely emasculated. A walking eunuch." The entire group laughed at Max's expense, who cared not in the slightest.

"There are a lot of good times out there waiting for me," agreed Max.

"What about you Lucas?" Danielle asked, wanting to redirect Max's eyes that were fixed on Lani like a cobra spying a mouse. "Do you see a family in your future?"

"Absolutely. I'd go for kids, natural or adoption. I'm an only child so I'd like a couple. I want them to have siblings."

"What about you, Christian?"

"Undecided." His one word response kept the group laughing.

In her peripheral vision, Danielle saw Lani patting Max's leg. "Don't worry. I'm sure there are plenty of girls out there who have no desire to have children."

The drinking and boisterous conversation continued until Andre slowed the boat into the marina. Stephen assisted in docking and tying it down before carefully guiding Lani out and stabilizing her on the boardwalk. The three men gave their thanks along with slightly slobbery kisses and left. Danielle removed the used bottles, placing them in a trash sack.

On the drive home, Danielle was contemplative.

"What do you think of Stephen and Lani?"

Andre took her left hand in his. "What light their relationship had when I first met them has dimmed significantly."

"Yeah," she said, her voice sad and quiet.

"Put yourself in his shoes," Andre began. "They have had the same goals since college—a dozen years. Suddenly they have eighteen months of success with a restaurant that we—you and I—funded. She goes from wanting kids to asking him to wait, and then changes it to not at all. That's a game-changer, even for the most patient, well-intentioned Swiss man."

Looking at Andre, she felt such a remarkable appreciation for their relationship. They both wanted all the commitment that went along with a marriage and family. "I love you," she said suddenly.

Andre smiled. "I'm so glad that hasn't changed, because pretty soon I'm going to be able to call you my wife."

Danielle couldn't wait.

CHAPTER 5

Sunday morning, Danielle took Andre and Monroe on a long overdue visit to the Asper Home for the elderly. Andre sat with the occupants, easily engaging in conversations about family and the city, holding Monroe as Danielle played the piano for the group. Danielle glanced over at her fiancé and daughter. Monroe had her tiny fingers wrapped around Andres' thumbs, her legs bouncing. Had anyone told her the maturing effect fatherhood could have on a man prior to her first-hand experience with Andre, she would have scoffed. But here he was with her, fully embracing the role of partner in all aspects of her life. Once, when she told Lani about Andre attending the evening events with the elderly, her friend had given her a look fit for an imbecile.

"I think he is very aware of the role he played," Lani said with a knowing glance. When Danielle and Andre had broken up, her father had suggested solace would be best found serving others. It was Layda who had suggested Danielle give the Asper Family Home a look. Danielle began making regular visits, bringing food and singing for the residents. It had carried her through the emotional ups and downs in her life, as well as the death of her father. For the months Andre was out of her life, it had provided solace when she had none. Now, he was here with her. It had come full circle.

Monday morning, Lars was at her door before she made her first trade. "Well?" he asked her. Danielle stifled a laugh.

"That's it? A single word to confirm I'm crazy enough to come back full-time and take the entirety of my clients?"

Lars kept his countenance even, but his eyes were alight. "I just wanted to double check."

"My only surprise was that it took you an entire eighteen hours to get it all according to your email. What happened to Swiss-style efficiency? I was thinking eight hours, max."

He smiled at her sarcasm. "Actually, it was closer to five. I stayed at the office that night until I got in touch with everyone." Danielle shook her head, smiling, but he shrugged, nonchalant. "I ran with the assumption that Andre would be on board and you'd figure out the babysitting part with Layda. Is that about it?"

"Unbelievable, but then again, not so much," Danielle remarked, unable to keep the laughter out of her voice.

Lars joined her, smiling broadly. His taught cheeks creased the corners of his eyes which were bright. "You have a very consistent personality, so I had very little to worry about."

"Oh, there is that," she said crisply, briefly looking up. "That's why you're there and I'm here. Someone has to be the all-knowing Jedi master and others the padawans."

Lars shook his head. "I come here trying to be serious and I get Star Wars."

"Not true. I can be serious. MRD has my full-time attention for three weeks."

"And was I right about Johanne?"

Danielle cocked her head, then got it. "Oh, about me not being able to exercise self-control as it relates to research and working off-hours? Of course, you were. Andre intends to play more hockey leaving me alone to research and trade, so we might actually pull this off."

"Good for you," Lars said genuinely.

"Good for the company," Danielle replied, pleased her voice was neutral and sincere.

Later that day she returned from lunch found an overflowing bouquet of flowers in a crystal vase. She opened the card.

I owe you, big time, Johanne.

He's going to owe me nothing if Dario doesn't take him back she thought to herself, as she placed the vase on the side credenza.

The day was quiet, the dominant sound in her office the tapping of her fingers on the keyboard and the dance music playing in the background. One client ignored protocol and called her directly. She tried to scold him but ended up laughing.

"I know my money is mice nuts in the grand scheme of things," said Max in his usual way. "But I'm glad the account is back under your watch."

By the end of the week, the only new development at home was Monroe started drooling profusely and Layda pointed out the little nubs on the bottom row of her gums.

"Nearly six months. It's early but not unheard of," Layda observed. "Andre's first two teeth came in at month five, then the second set two months later. At least that way, it was not drawn out and you go through the irritable, feverish stage quickly." The next day, after Danielle experienced a rather painful bite from Monroe, she told Layda she'd take her up on the offer to make pureed vegetables from her garden. Another milestone to be met; the nursing would be over which saddened her. Andre pointed out that she'd enjoy the freedom and sleep that came with weaning Monroe.

Saturday, Andre arranged a date night, enlisting the teenage daughter who lived next to his parents for babysitting duties. They timed it so Monroe was down for the night before leaving. First it was the jazz club where they listened to their friend Benny sing and play, then it was dancing. Johanne was at the club, but not with Dario.

"He found someone else in my absence," Johanne admitted, guilt written all over his face.

Danielle grabbed his hand. "I'll be back in a few songs," she told Andre. She led her friend up the steps to the platforms and cages hanging above the dance floor. She wasn't his partner or gender of preference, but she was his friend, and sometimes that was more meaningful than anything.

The following day was spent at the park on the lake. Monroe lay asleep on her blanket, shaded by the stroller as Danielle read a book. Andre read until he dozed off and Danielle closed her eyes as well, stretching her hands out overhead her belly flattening with the movement. She felt fingertips run across her bare stomach and hummed.

"I thought you were asleep," she said quietly.

"I was." Andre continued caressing her skin, down to her bikini line, across to her hips then up. "What are you thinking?"

"At that very moment, I was thinking how lucky we are to have this child, and how it would very likely be my last."

Andre's hand paused, then continued. "I listened to the doctor last week and didn't want to be rude, but I think he's wrong. Even getting pregnant was supposed to have been an impossibility and you did that, then carried to term. Monroe is healthy and above average for height. I bet you could have one more."

Danielle dropped her arms down, running one hand through his hair. She turned to him, away from the sunlight. "I'm quite happy with one and don't feel the need to aggressively try for another, at least not now."

"Now that's an interesting subject. The doctor had said that if we ever want another child, to start trying now because all the plumbing was clean." Danielle grimaced at the crass phrase. "I'd love for Monroe to have a sibling."

She gripped his hair, just enough to make him smile. "You cannot be suggesting this."

He laughed, kissing her palm. "No, I'm definitely not. Maybe in a year. If we are going to do it though, we should at least start thinking about it. Having kids close in age means they can play together."

"You have been giving this some thought," she observed, eyeing him carefully. "But to be a contrarian, spacing them further apart, like three years, means that one can be the older sibling and help out."

Andre added little bites to his kisses. "I'm happy to argue this point while we perfect our baby making skills later today."

CHAPTER 6

Although Danielle was now working fulltime, she made sure to reach out to Lani, calling her twice that week. Often, it was the voice mail that responded. When Lani did answer, the calls were short, with Lani talking in fragments. She'd ask about Monroe and the wedding, then give Danielle a snapshot of the restaurant and end with a promise to call later when she had more time. Had Danielle expected more of her bridesmaid, or been a good one herself when Lani was getting married, she'd have reason to be offended. But when Lani was preparing for her wedding to Stephen, Danielle had just moved back to Portland and her mother was dying. Instead of arranging a bachelorette party or going on bridal shopping excursions with Lani, she was concentrating on her new job and doctor's appointments. Lani had been a saint, moving around her own schedule to include Danielle.

Saturday morning, Danielle called Lani at home, knowing she'd be up. Lani answered on the second ring.

"I just want to be the friend you were to me before your wedding," Danielle said sincerely. "Can Monroe and myself stop by for lunch today?"

"As if you must ask, but I won't be able to sit and talk."

"I know. A glimpse of you is better than nothing. I want to see you at least a few times before the big day."

"Of course! See you later today."

Andre suggested Danielle get on the water for a few hours. He and Monroe would walk on the waterfront and watch.

The wind felt exhilarating through her hair, and she marveled at how strong and healthy she felt. Perhaps it was her age, or that she was in good shape when she became pregnant, but her body looked as though she'd never been pregnant or given birth. The only counter to that was her breasts, which were still large, but going down rapidly due to Monroe's enthusiasm for Layda's homemade baby food and the formula.

Not that it mattered in the thick wet suit, she thought.

When Danielle returned to the dock, her nose and cheeks felt hot. She touched both, wincing. Of all things, she'd neglected to put on sunblock today, mistakenly thinking the heat of early September wasn't as strong as August.

"You owe me, one," Giles said, meeting her at the pier.

"How's that?" she asked, wringing out her hair.

"I have a date for your wedding."

"What? You do not." Giles, one of Andre's oldest and best friends, had a penchant for water and boards, not relationships.

"No lie. Her, right there."

Danielle followed his hand that pointed to a woman waiting on tables at the restaurant next door. "Do you even know her?"

Giles lifted the board and gestured for her to proceed him. "Well enough to attend a fun event that's sure to have great food."

Danielle snickered. "Didn't being in the States teach you that inviting someone to a wedding is a big deal? It's like telling everyone you are getting married to that person yourself."

"As I'm not American, those archaic rules don't apply to me. I'm chill." His reply set her laughing again.

"You were there long enough to adopt the beach-ghetto slang. But I don't care who you bring if you have a good time." On her way out the door, she gave him a wave and texted Andre, meeting him not long after in the park. They took the metro over to Stars & Stripes, gratified to see a group of customers waiting to eat sitting on benches outside the restaurant.

"Your table is open and ready," Stephen said, showing them

to their seats and handing the menus to Andre. Danielle leaned against the high-backed booth, closest to the kitchen while Andre removed the carrier and placed the collapsed stroller around the corner.

"Go on," Andre told her, motioning his head to the kitchen. Danielle greeted the servers she recognized and caught Lani's attention.

"As promised," Danielle called. "Not interrupting or anything."

Lani raised her spatula. "Come try some." Danielle giggled as she accepted the spoon. It was dripping chocolate mousse, giving her the culinary equivalent of the first kiss on a honeymoon night.

"I can die now," Danielle complimented, licking her lips appreciatively.

"Don't die until after the lady's brunch next week," Lani suggested. "If you can stay for a half-hour afterwards, I'll have you try some new items and we can talk."

Danielle returned to the table and Andre touched his lip. "You missed a spot." Danielle wiped her mouth and smiled. "How is Lani doing?"

"At work, she seems fine. She did ask if I could hang out for a bit after the brunch next week and catch up. We'll see if she's in a revelatory mood."

"You're more worried about Stephen, aren't you?" he asked.

Danielle nodded. "Lani has a stubborn streak which is a strength and a detriment. On this one, the road they were once walking on was straight and narrow. But now it's like it became a Y, and the paths are diverging further apart."

That night Andre played hockey and Danielle decided to call David. Her former managing director at Russelz was flying over for the wedding, taking an extended two-week vacation with his wife, an event so out of character she couldn't wait to tease him. When she knew he'd be at the office, she called.

"I would have gotten married sooner if I'd known it was going to yield an in-person visit," she announced. "I'm surprised and flattered."

"And why would you be either?" he asked, his tone crotchety and affection filled, like the hard outer shell of a chocolate turtle hiding the gooey caramel inside.

"Because in all the time I've known you, you haven't missed a day of work. But, if you don't already have your entire trip planned, can I coerce you into spending a day or at least an evening with me and Andre here at the house or on the lake?"

"Just tell me the days and I'll work around it." He also asked for her suggestions for day trips during the first week of festivities. "I must say I'm intrigued to meet these two men of yours."

"Now that's funny," she said in her driest tone. "Only one counts now. The other one is engaged."

"You're kidding?" Danielle confirmed it was true. "Well, it will be good to meet Lars regardless of his romantic state."

Later that day, Danielle asked Layda to include David in the rehearsal dinner and the family-only events which she did without hesitation.

The following Friday, Danielle was rapidly punching the keyboard, getting in her last transactions for the week when a two-tap knock jolted her. She glanced up briefly. Whatever Lars was about to say was stopped when he saw her look.

"I'll come back when you are done," he said formally. "It's not urgent." Had it been less time-sensitive she would have stopped what she was doing, but instead, she gave a single nod. A refining firm in Latin America had posted unusually high earnings for the quarter, and while other traders were buying the stock, she was dumping them. The night before she'd read the refineries sources had held their inventory until the end of the quarter, artificially inflating the refinery's numbers.

Twenty minutes later, trading was done and she made her way

to his office, waiting until he buzzed her in. He was nearly at the sitting area and gestured for her to take the couch while he took the side chair.

"What's up?" she asked him.

"Your wedding."

She rested an elbow on the arm of the chair, determined to appear relaxed. "Yes, and you already confirmed you are coming, so that removes your ability to crash it," she said, pleased with her witty reply. "Though I like the notion of you crashing anything, particularly a party."

Lars twirled a pen in his hand. "I'll be coming through the main entrance if it's all the same." The notion of him sneaking in the side door set her laughing, and when he raised an eyebrow, she confessed her thought. "You've not lost your sense of humor during this time of pre-wedding jitters. That's good."

Danielle crossed a leg. "If one isn't happy before a wedding something is very wrong. But seriously, what's up? You're killing me."

"To get to the point, I'll be bringing someone." It was a fact she'd known for some time.

"Proving that it is possible for you to get a date. Must have been the cologne." Lars gave a half smile at her comment, appreciating the inside joke.

"Perhaps. Anyway, I only raise the topic because I wanted to be sure you weren't uncomfortable. I know we have both moved on, but still. We did have that one conversation."

The conversation, she though ruefully. It had been the same night they broke up. Danielle had mentioned she didn't relish the notion of him bringing a beautiful woman to a company event.

Danielle tilted her head in thought. "That applied only to company events, where I would presumably have been single and without a date. This is slightly different, so you are off the hook." The pen stopped twirling as Lars examined her as if to ascertain if she were telling the truth. She let out a little laugh. "Seriously, Lars. I'm getting married, for heaven's sakes. Who am I to deny you the enjoyment of having a beautiful companion by your side? In fact, bring two, one on each arm. It's the least you deserve." Lars' shoulders relaxed with her words. "I did hear that at least one of your female dates is a fiancé. Is that correct?" He raised an eyebrow. "And you weren't going to reveal that little fact?"

"I felt it was irrelevant."

"What? That we are both heading to the altar?" Danielle cocked her head back just enough to look at the ceiling before she made eye contact with him. "The only thing that slightly disturbed me was the speed at which you got over me."

"Not much different than the speed at which you overcame me."

Danielle paused. "Touché. So, the big question is if the other circumstances are the same. Is she pregnant?"

Lars' lower lip dropped slightly but he recovered it with a smile. "No. Not at all."

Danielle conveyed a sense of relief that wasn't entirely fabricated. Then she schooled her face into a serious look. "I do have one request to make of you, which you must enforce. It's an absolute requirement. Can you do that?" Lars slowly nodded his head, as if he wasn't sure he could make good on a commitment. "You may come to my wedding with your fiancé, but, above all else, you have to, *no*, you *must*, ensure that she does not outshine the bride. It's bad form."

Lars blinked in relief then chuckled. "It's a moot point. No one outshines the bride."

Danielle arrived home and played on the floor with Monroe until Andre walked through the front door. She wanted to keep him and her daughter all to herself for the entire weekend, one of her last before becoming a married woman.

"How does lunch at the restaurant tomorrow sound?" Andre

asked, an ice tea in his hand. "After you sailboard of course."

"I'll go on my board if you go on your bike," she replied, twirling a curl of Monroe's dark hair around her forefinger.

Andre pressed his lips against her forehead. "I love your sense of adventure," Andre remarked, "even when you make us separate for a few hours. And don't think I'm unaware of your scheming ways." Danielle giggled, knowing she'd been caught. She was still irrationally fearful of both of them being on the bike at the same time.

"Just be happy I support and encourage you."

The following day was clear and on the cooler side. Fall was indeed arriving, thankfully slower than it did the year before, but the winds had picked up dramatically, making for an exhilarating two hours on the water. Andre had taken Monroe for a walk in the park, the little girl in her stroller, and when she'd dried and changed, they traded off baby-duty. It was her turn to push the stroller, up and down the waterfront path, walking under the golden and amber colored trees.

"I'm hungry for some good American food," he said. Danielle was squeezing a lemon in her sparkling water and Andre was putting the stroller behind the back wall when a male chef approached, Stephen by his side.

"Meet Renaldo," Stephen began. "Renaldo, this is Danielle. Renaldo is our new sous chef."

The balding man with deep brown eyes gazed at her as though he were meeting the artist behind a masterpiece on the wall.

"It's my pleasure, Ms. Grant."

"Danielle, please," she corrected, and glanced at Stephen. "You think vacations are necessary?" Her comment, meant to be teasing, elicited a slight frown from her friend and business partner. "I'm glad you did it!" she quickly added, hoping he didn't misinterpret her comment as her being irritated that she wasn't consulted.

"We figured you had other, bigger things on your mind."

Danielle nudged Andre. "Just a little."

Stephen explained that after a long search, Renaldo was the perfect fit for the restaurant. "Even though he's not American, he knows a lot about the food."

"Good," said Andre. "Because Danielle will taste test every single dish." The man bowed as though he realized the seriousness of the situation, and Danielle hoped he would loosen up as time went on.

Danielle was nearly done with her marionberry cobbler when Lani emerged from the back. Her eyes were bright and her red lipstick lush. She didn't appear to be the overworked, stressed chef today, on a Saturday of all days, usually the busiest of the week.

"Well, what do you think of Renaldo?" Lani asked.

"I'm very proud of you while still being in shock. I mentioned to Stephen I thought this meant more vacation time for you both."

"No, it means I'm thinking that at some point," she paused to take a deep, noticeable, inhale as she glanced between Danielle and Andre, "we may want to expand. You, as two of the four partners, might want to noodle on that a bit." She exhaled, picked up a fried pickle and dipped it in ranch dressing. "You know, in all your free time between now and the wedding and honeymoon. I gotta go. Have to return to training Renaldo."

Danielle put her hand on Lani's forearm. "You drop a bomb like that and leave?"

Lani smiled wickedly. "Yes. But don't worry about Renaldo. He's all business. Even I'm a little intimidated by him. He studied at one of those hoity-toity French schools, then spent years in New York, so he's a good American chef, but he hasn't lost the aloof-part."

"I wasn't referring to Renaldo. I thought that if it weren't vacation you were after, it might be…?"

Lani pursed her lips. "No. Not in a million would it be *that*."

After Lani walked away, Danielle trained her eyes on Andre, who looked a little too calm. "Did you know about this?"

"Maybe," he said, taking a bite of his food. "But only about hiring another chef, not necessarily all the reasons behind it. After eighteen months, they were overdue for a back-up cook. No one wants a burned out chef."

"But the expansion part. Were you aware of that?"

"Nope. I swear."

"You never swear," she pointed out.

"When one is intelligent, one has no need to swear."

"Bullshit." They both erupted in laughter.

CHAPTER 7

The following Tuesday, Danielle joined Layda and her female relatives at Stars & Stripes for a women's celebratory luncheon.

"Whoa," Lani exclaimed, looking at Monroe. The little girl was in her stroller, gnawing on a rattle, looking adorable in her hand-sewn outfit.

"I know," agreed Danielle. "Layda has great style."

"That outfit is unreal, and these women are…" Lani didn't finish her sentence. Danielle put her hand under Lani's elbow. "They all looked like they stepped out of a Hermes catalog."

"You will impress them. Don't worry." Danielle whispered in her ear.

"I'm not," Lani replied, her ego intact. This was her domain.

Over four courses of food, the eight women asked about every detail of the flowers, food, gifts, music and any other bit of minutiae, each time comparing it to that of their own son or daughter who had gotten married. By the time the group disbanded ninety minutes later, Danielle understood what preparing a wedding was like for women who easily traveled between Geneva and Zurich, skied in the Alps and summered in the South of France.

Lani placed another tray of food on the table. "Try these, and don't give me any comments about fitting into your dress. You look great."

Danielle picked up a fork, inspecting the assortment of deserts. Peach pie was accompanied by chocolate mousse, pumpkin and strawberry-rhubarb pies. "Thank you. The dress mostly fits, except the bust. My boobs keep getting smaller."

"I can see why you'd get irritated about that."

Danielle inserted a fork into the peach pie. "Not that you've ever had that issue, ye of little sympathy." She took a bite. "This is amazing."

"I set aside jarred peaches. Are you all ready for this weekend? Isn't that when most people start coming in?"

"We have the rehearsal dinner Saturday night," Danielle said, dipping her spoon into the chocolate mousse and savoring the silky texture. "I'm sorry you can't make it, but I totally understand. Then Sunday is a boating tour of the lake for family and friends. Layda is giving people plenty of time to go sight-seeing. The afternoon tea is Thursday, and thanks in advance for coming. You hate tea."

Lani scowled. "Yes, sort of," she admitted. "But that's why Renaldo is here. I had to bite the bullet at some point, and this was a good motivator."

Danielle glanced at Stephen who was near the kitchen, his lean figure complimented by his olive colored suit, the slim legs only accentuating his height. "Is this going to continue after I get married?"

"What?"

"Don't play stupid." Danielle couldn't help herself from leaning forward, feeling like an accomplice planning a major crime. "The easiest way to avoid the whole topic of Stephen and babies is to be even busier than you are now, and the only way to do that is to open another restaurant. But you can't be serious."

Lani bit her lip, a guilty look written all over her face. "Well, maybe it was subconscious."

"But Lani, you *love* Stephen. Don't you think the excitement of having a restaurant will eventually fade, and you will get the maternal urge again?" She lowered her voice another notch. "Then you'll be looking for Stephen and he won't be there."

"Back-up. I do love Stephen, but our paths are diverging,

faster and more dramatically than either of us expected. And for what it's worth, this was already going on before you got engaged."

Danielle dutifully took another spoonful of mousse, dipping it into the homemade whipping cream. She tasted the vanilla in the whipping cream. "It's sweet enough but not overly so."

"At least when the earlier restaurant was failing, we joked about the misery of it all," Lani continued, her voice as fervent as her look was anxious. "Now, we are so busy, we don't laugh or joke. He's all business and so am I, but we're working towards different ends." Lani glanced to the door where Stephen stood talking to departing guests and Danielle followed her eyes. In Danielle's opinion, he'd become more refined and handsome in the decade following college.

"What about this tension between the two of you just being a phase?" Danielle suggested hopefully.

Lani shook her head. "I wish it were that. When Stephen talks about our future, it's because he's ready for a family and I'm not. It's like the present isn't enough. But it is for me. In fact, it's more than enough." She sighed. "I guess at the end of the day, I'm tired of feeling like what I want isn't good enough. Like *I'm* not enough."

Danielle sighed deeply. This was such depressing news she started in on the third dessert.

"Lani, is the real reason you brought Renaldo on board is because you are thinking he can work here, and you will move on to the new location, is that it? And along that train of thought, Stephen will want to remain here, and you'll hire someone else?"

Lani looked Danielle directly in the eye. "You know me too well."

Monroe started fussing, stopping Lani from talking further. "Don't worry about me right now," Lani said, collecting the plates.

"That's a ridiculous comment," Danielle scolded. "You're my best friend, and Stephen is a close second. I worry about you both.

On the second location thing, I can't even think about the financial implications until after my wedding, but I want to know one thing. Will you stay here or are you thinking of going back home?"

Lani's eyes got big. "Zurich is awesome. I'm not going anywhere, except back to the kitchen, which I have to do now."

As Danielle pushed the stroller home, she thought about the notion of how two people against all odds, real or imagined, could stay together. But the threads of the relationship had to be intertwined, not just tied at the ends for the sake of survival.

Danielle felt a rush of gratitude for Andre, and what they had. Granted, it had only been a year, but their relationship had no fraying threads or rough edges. Just a soft blanket of companionship, one which would be formalized in exactly eleven days.

Friday night, she and Andre lay side by side in the chaise lounge chairs, looking out beyond the lawn to the water. She watched the few boats on the lake, all covered with canopies protecting the passengers from the cool breeze. The temperature had dropped significantly. Cocktail dresses could still be worn but a light shawl or wrap would be necessary for the outdoor reception.

Andre took her hand. "Do you regret not having a real bridal shower?"

"Not at all. I have everything a woman needs and my lingerie drawer is full. The notion of my future mother-in-law or grandmother passing out risqué toys was never my thing. Do you regret not having a bachelor party?"

"I did all I wanted to do before I met you."

Danielle flipped his hand over, stroking the lines of his palm. "You know what I realized?" she said. "We have hardly taken any pictures of you with Monroe."

"Because you two are the best-looking."

"Promise me you'll get better about being in the photos?"

Andre's thumb stroked her skin. "I promise. Are you ready

for the rehearsal dinner tomorrow night?"

"I'm looking forward to seeing some of the people I met at the engagement party, and your mother has picked out some amazing desserts, which I'll get to sample at will, since your cousins from Geneva will be focusing on the beer."

Andre's wide smile matched how she felt. "We need to get some extra rest tonight."

"Then we better start early if we actually want rest."

They rose together, their fingers connected until they reached the bedroom. She didn't know if their intimacy was catalyzed by the impending marital state or sheer physical desire, and it didn't matter. She felt whole and complete.

CHAPTER 8

It was still dark outside when Danielle woke. She turned and saw Andre staring at her. "How about you get in a few hours of fun-time before the rehearsal dinner tonight?"

Danielle opened her eyes wider. "I have my final dressing," she reminded him.

"Then go directly to the water right afterward. I'll take Monroe to my mother because the Aunties have been complaining about not enough time with the baby. Dinner isn't until seven anyway."

"What are you going to do?"

"Hang out with Dad. Maybe work in the shop." Danielle shook her head.

"You have all winter to do that. Go up to the mountains one last time. It will be the final hurrah for both of us."

"I think I can manage that," he responded. She kissed his nose, then gave him a long, deep kiss on his lips. The touch of his morning beard tickled her skin and she gave him a little bite, then held off. They'd have plenty of one-on-one time during the honeymoon.

A few hours later, Danielle was just about to leave when she pulled her cell phone out of her pocket and took a picture of Andre and Monroe. He had one leg crossed over the other, foot on knee, Monroe nestled within an animal covered baby blanket, a gift from Glenda and her husband.

"I love you, so much," she said. Andre smiled, the happy, satisfied look of a man who returned her love in equal amounts.

"I love you, too. Have fun and use sunblock this time." She mockingly scowled, waving off the comment. She'd be sure to slather herself before leaving the shore.

At the fitting, Danielle turned this way and that in the front of the mirror, appreciating the elegant tea-length ivory dress. The seamstress came in, examining the fit. It was perfect save for her bust, which had decreased yet again. It was slight, but she and the seamstress agreed it should be modified. Danielle stood still as the woman inserted several pins in each side under her arms and ran her fingers along her waist and hips. The three-quarter arms hung just below the elbow where they should, the A-line over her legs smooth and clean. Danielle had elected to have embroidery for embellishment rather than layers of fabric and Layda had suggested adornments of pearls within the embroidered flowers.

The change would be made within the hour and the dress then delivered to Layda's home for safe keeping. Once again, Danielle was eternally grateful for Layda's proximity, planning and enthusiasm. The stylist, make-up artists and nail lady from the salon would all be coming to Layda's house. The morning of the wedding, she, Lani, Layda and her sisters were going to have an entire morning of beauty, an experience Danielle had never had.

When she arrived at the board shop, a woman stood at the front desk speaking to Karl, the only other employee Danielle knew by name, inquiring about lessons. Karl was politely explaining that the instructors did have a set schedule. Giles was helping another customer, but seeing her, he paused his conversation.

"Your timing is impeccable," he said, jerking his head to the front desk. It was their signal he had a customer who would like sailboarding instruction.

"Happy to," she gamely replied. "Sixty minutes." Danielle quickly found herself explaining the board to a thirty-one-year-old woman from Milan, then demonstrating technique and soon thereafter was in the water, holding the board to assist with her student's balance. When the hour was up, she led a very tired, but pleased student back to the marina.

Without going in, Danielle turned her board around and headed back to the center of the lake. The wind had picked up nicely, as it usually did in the late afternoons, and she knew just where the best spots for hitting the highest waves were likely to be. By the time she sailed back into the marina, her legs burned with effort as she simultaneously pushed against the board and pulled back on the sail to gain the maximum amount of speed towards her destination.

Danielle was half-way down the wooden boardwalk when Karl came towards her, his hands outstretched to take the board.

"I got it, Karl," she said with a smile. Seeing his expression, it faded. "Really, it's okay."

"No, I'm sorry, I'll take it," he said firmly. "Giles asked me to relay the message that you should go straight home."

She cocked her head. "My home? Is everything okay? Scratch that. I'll ask Giles what's up."

Danielle went directly to the changing room and found her phone. There were no texts or phone messages from Andre or anyone else. Feeling a little uneasy but not unduly worried, she stripped off her wet suit, gave herself a quick towel-dry and went to the car. Five minutes later she was calling Andre, but it went to voice mail. She started dialing Layda, but realized she'd be home in minutes and hung up.

Monroe. It had to be Monroe. Something had happened. That's why Andre wasn't answering.

She pressed her foot on the gas pedal, going as fast as she dared down the street, taking the left up the hill harder than she'd ever done. The edge of the wheel rim cut in to the pavement, and she gunned it.

Nearing her block, she scanned the street. No ambulances or fire trucks. It was absent of police cars or any automobiles she recognized. The white, wood gate was open, and she drove through it, seeing Layda's car and next to it, Georgy's. Danielle's heart rate slowed. Andre's Mustang was parked in its usual space. If something had happened to Monroe, he would have taken her to the hospital.

Must be something to do with the rehearsal dinner this evening.

The nerve-induced tension that had been building within Danielle continued to fade as she walked to the side door. She heard Layda and Georgy talking and caught a glimpse of Monroe's head resting in the crook of Layda's arm. Layda's back was towards her and although she heard Georgy talking, Danielle couldn't see him.

Relief washed through her legs. Her baby was okay. Andre was here with his parents. Whatever urgency Giles had conveyed to Karl was obviously misconstrued.

Danielle walked inside, calling out her hellos. Layda turned and Danielle stopped, stunned at the raw grief radiating from the older woman.

"Danielle…" her future mother-in-law choked, her chest heaving, and she wavered.

Danielle rushed to her side, holding her steady. "Here," she offered, slipping her hands under Layda's.

"No, Danielle," Georgy said. "You shouldn't." His voice was rough, as though he too, was having trouble talking.

"Why? Layda, here, let me take her." Layda kept her head down, moving side to side, as though swinging Monroe in a cradle.

"Georgy…" she started, looking at her husband for help.

Words failed Danielle and cohesive thoughts she might have formed dissipated at Georgy's expression of utter devastation.

"Danielle, its Andre. There's been an accident…" As he spoke, excruciating pain ripped through her chest and head. "Bus…sudden impact…didn't make it…" A flash of bright lights passed through the blackness that started overtake her.

Not again, she told herself, then she lost consciousness.

CHAPTER 9

The room was quiet when she opened her eyes.

"Danielle. Danielle, honey." It was Lani. Danielle felt her best friend's warm hands holding hers. A strange, disjointed notion of Lani not at the restaurant came to mind. She never left work. Hated leaving it. She was here, only because…

A sob tore through Danielle's throat. A dry, muffled choking that turned into full, chest-wrenching sobs. She felt Lani's hand on her shoulder and she turned over, in a fetal position. She couldn't handle this, not after losing her father, then saying goodbye to Lars, and now her daughter's father….

Lani continued stroking her back, telling her she was here. Stephen was here. They would take care of her. She'd make it through. They were her family.

The word family penetrated her fractured mind. Then another flash, a memory, came bright and clear. Andre, holding Monroe, and her taking the picture, saying he loved her. His last words.

Danielle continued sobbing. Her little girl would never remember her father. Not know his laugh or kindness, his handsome face, his funny comments. Her pillow was wet with grief, an ache that spread through her body, down to her feet and to up to her skull.

"Monroe," she whispered.

"Layda has her. You had enough bottles and Layda's homemade food. She's sleeping now."

Lani continued to stroke Danielle until her cries died down again and she felt a dull throbbing in her head. Though she could barely utter the words, she asked what had happened.

"He was riding his motorcycle," Lani said softly. "On his way out of town. He passed a car on a straightaway, before a corner, so he was legal. He tried to move back into his lane, but apparently, a bus behind him moved just enough to catch his tire, pushing him into the oncoming traffic. It was…instant."

That fearless, wonderful, aggressive man, who had so much passion it couldn't be contained even on the roadways.

"My father told him to be careful," she mumbled.

"What, sweetheart? I didn't hear you."

Danielle pressed her eyes shut tightly, shaking her head. He must have thought he could make it. He would never have done anything to jeopardize the family he'd fought so hard for. But then, chance doesn't recognize a person's good intention.

"Here. You could probably use this." She felt Lani tenderly taking her hand, and one by one, opening the fingers and within them, placing a handkerchief.

"Thanks," Danielle said, her words barely audible. "The restaurant…"

"Don't worry about it. Renaldo is doing fine and Ivan has taken over for Stephen. I'm going to make you some tea. Or would you like hot chocolate?" Danielle couldn't bring herself to speak. "Well, I'll bring both and you can decide."

Danielle's eyes remained closed, barely hearing the door shutting.

I want to die. But the desire was both wrong and impossible. *I have to live for Monroe.*

Her sobs returned, the pain behind her eyes now so intense she wondered if it were a migraine or the first stages of a brain aneurysm. She finally gave into sleep and faded in an out of an agony-induced awareness.

Danielle woke with a start, her nightmare manifesting a sharp pain in her stomach and she staggered to the bathroom. Her headache was far worse than before, now combined with nausea. She had told him to ride his bike. He was going to spend time with his father, working in the shop. *She'd encouraged him to go!*

Closing the door, she vomited violently.

A soft knock proceeded Lani's voice. "Danielle, are you sick? Do you need the doctor?"

"No." Danielle struggled to get to her feet. "If you could just get me some ice I'll be out in a bit." Andre's parents needed as much comfort and love as she did.

Danielle was leaning against the counter when Lani returned with the ice, a banana, raw almonds and aspirin.

"I know you don't feel like it, but eat at least a few bites of banana then some almonds. You're going to get sick and dehydrated if you don't alkalize your body. The almonds are protein so choke them down. After that, the aspirin."

Lani's detached, clinical tone cut through the haze in Danielle's mind and she followed directions. After a few minutes, she focused, sitting down in the side chair, taking in the room and her friend, for the first time.

"What's happened since I passed out?" she asked, her voice fractured and defeated.

"Georgy went to the hospital and met Giles there. He had to…" Lani stopped, watching her carefully. Danielle knew what Lani was going to say. "It was good that Giles was there. Layda said it was excruciating for Georgy."

Danielle nodded. "Are you sure the accident wasn't Andre's fault? Are you telling me the truth?"

"Yes," Lani affirmed fervently, gripping her arm, forcing Danielle to look at her. "The driver behind him said that he saw the bus swipe Andre when he tried to swerve back into his lane. He had no room to maneuver. The impact and speed caused him to flip. Layda said Georgy pressed the officers and first responders until it nearly caused a scene. They all said the same thing. He had no chance."

Danielle closed her eyes. When her mother died, she knew it was coming. It had been the same with her father. The time had given her the ability to say her goodbyes and get mentally prepared. But with an abrupt death, there was no closure, like a sentence without the period.

"Did you…were you able to speak with him before you left?" Lani asked quietly.

Danielle nodded. "He was holding Monroe, I told him I loved him. He told me he loved me too. I took a picture."

Lani bit her lip, the strength she'd been displaying weakening. She put her arms around Danielle and they cried together.

"I'm so sorry," Lani whispered. "I don't know why you have had so much heartache in your life. It's just not fair."

Danielle pressed her eyes tight. "Lani, it's all my fault. I suggested he go. He was going to be with his dad while I went sailboarding but I suggested he go for a ride. It's because of me…" she broke off, unable to say more. Through the roaring noise in her ears, she heard Lani say over and over she wasn't to blame. That Andre might have gone on his own once he was at his father's house and Andre had been riding since he was young.

"He did what he wanted, Danielle. Look at me," Lani demanded, taking Danielle firmly by the shoulders. "You did not cause a bus to hit him or choose what road he took. It was fate, that's what it was. Not you."

Lani's stridency cut through Danielle's haze of regret long enough for her to get it together. She wasn't alone. Others were grieving too.

"I need to go see Layda and Georgy," Danielle said. Lani rubbed her back and kissed her hair, the act so comforting Danielle started crying again.

"Are you sure you can do this?" Lani asked. "You don't have to come downstairs. They will understand."

"I want another twenty-four hours to grieve Lani, but you

heard them. It's better to do it now, rather than wait. It's not fair to the others."

"I don't care about the others, I care about you." Danielle hugged her friend with the last bit of emotion she had left, then pulled back, resolved.

"I don't know what I'd do without you." Then Danielle inhaled deeply and closed her eyes one last time. When she opened them again, she exhaled. She had to be strong for her daughter, for Andre's parents, and even for those at the office like Johanne who were relying on her to help keep the business rolling. Her father's main belief was that the pain of the past was used to create a better, more fulfilling future. She had to figure out how to keep her inner light on for the sake of those around her.

A few minutes later, Danielle stepped through the doorway from her bedroom. It was symbolic. She was doing it alone as a single mother. She was living the nightmare she'd imagined months ago, not long after learning she was pregnant. It seemed that this life was foreordained for her.

CHAPTER 10

Danielle heard Georgy and Layda speaking as they walked down the staircase and she gripped Lani's hand, stopping her.

"They will arrive in a little over three hours," Georgy was saying quietly.

"It's supposed to be a rehearsal dinner, not—not this." Layda replied, her voice thin and fervent.

"Layda, there is no good time to deliver the news. We can't expect everyone to leave town and then turn right around and fly right back for the funeral."

"I don't want to talk about the funeral!" Layda's voice escalated with the words, the high-pitch emphasis followed by a surprised sound from Monroe. "I'm sorry, honey," she said, her voice returning to its soothing tone until Monroe quieted down.

"Layda, all our family is here. We must do this now." Danielle heard a sob from Andre's mother.

"Look at me," Georgy said, his tone gentler than it had been. "We tell our family tonight, all at once. We share the grief with them." Danielle didn't hear Layda respond, only Georgy's words. "They will all help us. Your sisters can—" Georgy's voice broke. He coughed, clearing it. "Your sisters can help with the details, and taking care of Monroe. Danielle's going to need it. We need to be there for her, because no one else will be."

Danielle released Lani's hand, walked down the stairs and went straight to Layda. They held one another, the bind tighter when she felt Georgy's arms around her shoulders. When they released, she wiped her eyes.

"I heard you," she began softly. "And I agree with you. It's going to be a shock, but we will do this together." She took another deep inhalation, collecting her thoughts. "Also, I can manage this." Georgy stared at her hard, as though assessing her mental state. "Georgy, I've handled two funerals for my parents. Lani, I'd like you to join us please." Danielle asked Layda to get her planner, and as a group, they sat at the kitchen table.

One by one, Layda went through each event on the list to determine what to cancel and what to keep. They agreed to insist people maintaining their schedule of boating excursions and day trips. While the guests would be suitably impacted by Andre's death, many had spent a great deal of money and taken time off to come into town. Danielle pointed most knew Andre well, but some, like David, did not. He'd only met him at her father's funeral. It would all be positioned as a celebration of Andre. And, as her father said, one's life shouldn't stop when another's did.

There was only one event Danielle could not—would not—attend. It was the viewing to be held for family and friends, replacing the scheduled afternoon tea on Thursday.

"I'm sorry," Danielle said. "I want my last image of him holding Monroe on his lap, saying he loved me..." she put her hand over her eyes, leaning forward. She felt a gentle hand on her back, not knowing who it belonged to. They waited until she was ready to continue.

In place of the wedding and reception would be the funeral and luncheon. The room, food and officiator were already booked. "Benny can play jazz tunes Andre loved so much during the luncheon," Danielle said, feeling a stab across her chest. She knew Benny would appreciate being involved. She also suggested they hand out the gifts she and Andre had chosen. The funny, little things they'd spent hours selecting meant more now than she ever imagined.

Lani spoke tentatively. "May I suggest note cards? In the US, for weddings and funerals, guests write a special memory of the loved one. All the memories that he would have shared with his daughter, the others can share for her."

Layda bit her lip so hard it bled. "I think it's a lovely idea."

Lani seemed to gather strength at the response. "Also," she said with a bit more confidence. "I agree with having the dinner tonight, but disagree on telling the people what happened to Andre in person. It's going to come as a serious shock and some of the women might break down. Why don't you let me call them now? I'm the bride's best friend and can provide the necessary information without these people asking too many questions." Layda and Georgy nodded again. "Layda, let me also handle the caterers and the on-site details for the funeral and reception, okay? Monroe will want to be with her grandma or Danielle, not me."

Danielle squeezed Lani's leg under the table. Lani was stepping up when she was most needed, the restaurant and her tenuous relationship with Stephen be damned.

"Now, to the funeral itself..." Georgy started.

Danielle lightly placed a hand on his arm. "I think Lani should start calling the list of people before the dinner tonight." Layda removed the list from her folder, giving it to Lani, who excused herself to the other room.

Danielle began. "We need to create the funeral announcements, the arrangements with the home..."

"Danielle, you really shouldn't be doing this," Georgy said, his voice full from compassion.

"No one should be doing it," she said, feeling as empty has her voice sounded. But the truth was she knew the details far better than either Georgy or Layda ever would.

Georgy took notes as she itemized each activity. As they went through the list, Danielle was on autopilot, her response for grief. Her eyes stung, the tears replaced by a dry, barren sensation, that of the dessert. Her father always said the best counterbalance to heartbreak is service. Danielle forced herself to look at the entire week as serving others who would come expecting celebration and instead receive heartbreak. She would hug them. Feed them. Love them.

When they reached the end of the list, Danielle paused. "The worst will be when everyone has left. Then it will be quiet. I'm just so thankful we will have each other."

Georgy wiped his eyes and gripped Layda's free hand. "You are right, my dear girl."

Lani entered the room just as the three had finished creating the funeral program: who was going to speak, in what order and the music selection. Georgy and Layda asked Danielle's opinion on the gravesite, and she gave none, other than suggest he be with his family.

"And words on the tombstone?" At this, Danielle put her hand to her eyes, closing them briefly.

"I'm not exactly sure of the wording, but I think it should include the words loving son, father and partner." Georgy pulled his lips inward, and Danielle took that as an agreement.

Not long after, he and Layda left to prepare their home for the guests, and Lani followed, leaving Danielle alone with her daughter.

The acts of feeding, bathing and holding Monroe were accomplished with as much affection and love as she could manage. She fought the tears with smiles and hummed when her cracking voice made singing impossible.

Thirty minutes before she was to leave for the dinner, Danielle changed Monroe into the outfit Layda had purchased for the rehearsal dinner, a pink ensemble with embroidered flowers on the lace hem of the skirt and sleeves, a matching hat and slip on shoes. Monroe's eyes gleamed bright, her plump cheeks full as she fumbled with the toy on the bed while Danielle sat down and put her head in her hands. She'd wept so much over the last six hours she wasn't sure more tears could come. Her chest ached with a hollowed out feeling, like the hard shell of her chest was all that was left. When she rose, her arm went out to the wall to steady herself. She wasn't hungry, but she knew food was a requirement, not a desire. She'd eat later, if she could.

Danielle finished her hair and stood in front of her closet. The cocktail dress still had its tags on it and would be returned at some point. She pulled a pair of dark slacks from the closet and an olive colored turtleneck sweater. Chills that had nothing to do with the weather were now constant, and she knew it was a feeling that wasn't going to go away any time soon.

CHAPTER 11

Hundreds of lights lit up the trees on Georgy's property, just as they had been that spring evening when Layda and Georgy hosted her engagement party. Danielle recognized Stephen's car, comforted that he and Lani would be among the other family members. She recalled the guest list of aunts and uncles, cousins and Andre's nearest friends. The expressions and thoughts, feelings and words that Max and the guys must have had flashed through her mind. Only David was absent, having sent her a text hours before that his plane had been delayed in Germany and they would be arriving the following day. She hadn't communicated the death in text. The news could wait.

Danielle unlocked the straps for Monroe, keeping her in the car seat. She caught a gulp of air in her throat, brought on by the recollection of the day before, sitting with Andre and his parents, laughing about her going back to work.

The gravel crunched under her feet, reminding her of another time she'd spent with Andre in this very parking lot, when he'd arranged for her to deliver food and he'd greeted her by opening the door. It was then that he'd admitted his interest in her was far more than physical.

The foyer was quiet when she entered. The wrought-iron staircase was draped in matching ropes of flowers and twine, the look of orchestrated elegance likely to be found throughout the house. A huge bouquet of flowers on the marble-topped credenza had been ordered for the rehearsal dinner, the symbol of what was to be now representing a life that was.

He is looking down on me now, wanting me to be happy, to comfort others. To help Max and Lucas and Christian and Giles, who would be as devastated as she felt.

Maybe worse. I have Monroe. They have nothing.

Danielle walked around the corner, catching Stephen's eye. Instead of rushing to hold her, he waited, as though he knew imparting his sympathies were going to bring more emotions to the surface.

"It's okay, Stephen," she said quietly. She placed the car seat on the counter, away from the edge and felt Stephen's arms close around her.

"It's not okay, and I'm so sorry." She only nodded, the tears she expected to come absent. He released her, holding her arms, scanning her face in a brotherly fashion. "I know you don't drink, but can I get you tea with something in it?"

"Thanks, but no. Is anyone else here?"

"It's just me. Lani's with Layda going over some details."

"I'm glad she's here. Is the restaurant going to be alright without you two being onsite?"

"I could scold you for asking the question, but will save that for later. Ivan is more than capable. He also asked me to give you his love and prayers. Renaldo had a week of getting his feet wet and is now running the show for a few days. It will be fine. Lani said to also tell you Giles won't be coming tonight."

Danielle glanced around, regretting she'd arrived early. As family and friends walked through the door, she wanted to be standing by Andre, shaking hands, not by herself, giving and receiving hugs of condolences.

"I don't think I can do this," Danielle admitted, scared about keeping it together.

Stephen gave a squeeze. "Why don't you hold Monroe as people arrive? That way you won't be in a position of having to embrace everyone."

Danielle's eyes blurred, and she gulped. "Stephen," she said, looking at him, her voice breaking. "You're like the brother I never had. Thank you." She barely got out the last words because her throat closed.

Danielle rested Monroe's head on her shoulder, grateful babies could sleep through almost anything.

She made her way to the back deck, beholding the scene before her. The trellis above the courtyard was a vision of white flowers, the contrast against the orange sun breathtaking. She tried to refrain from creating metaphors about the light of one's life going down leaving only dark and cold behind, but she couldn't help it. Every point she focused upon had a negative connotation.

"Hi sweetheart," Layda said, coming from her left. "Georgy would like to speak with you for a moment privately. He's in the study."

Danielle made her way to the wood-paneled office. Georgy was at his desk, the high-backed leather facing her. The click of the door shutting alerted him to her presence, and he turned to her. She went to the window, swaying back and forth as she watched the water on the lake pick up.

It was getting dark out, the cloud cover turning the water grey. *Lifeless*, was how it looked. The whitecaps were picking up, smaller on the outside, but large crests in the center, crashing down as they rolled to the far side.

"Danielle." She turned. His face was puffy, his eyes red. "Come."

Danielle took the seat nearest the fireplace, the orange, red glows of the embers warm and soothing. She felt Monroe's small chest moving in and out, her light snore unchanged as she positioned herself. Danielle could have stayed in this room all night, free of the obligation to see others.

Georgy sat in the arm chair adjacent to her, his look serious and apologetic. "I feel protective of you and my granddaughter, and took the initiative to call Lars. He needed to be aware of the situation so they could make internal arrangements." Danielle nodded blankly. Concerns for her employment had not once entered her mind. "I hope you don't mind, but I was very clear. You are the priority, and Monroe. Not my money. Not his company or other clients."

"Thank you." Danielle absently stroked Monroe's back. She hadn't thought about life *after*. After Andre's death and the life of a single, working mother.

"I'll need to get a full-time babysitter," she said, her voice monotone.

"You can't be serious."

"When I've gone through loss before, my father always encouraged me to focus on things that build me up. Being at home, every day, is not going to do that."

Georgy exhaled a chest full of air, one filled with concern. Danielle knew Georgy had a multi-international conglomerate to run, and she guessed that on the Monday following the funeral, he would be back in the office, doing what he knew how to do best, not sitting at home. They weren't all that different.

"Do you think Layda will wish to continue watching Monroe?"

"My dear girl, losing a son is hard enough, but losing contact with her granddaughter would be devastating. Please, don't change a thing, at least if it's reasonable."

Danielle glanced past him and out to the water. "Of course. But Georgy," she paused, looking back at him. "I can't guarantee I won't change other things."

"May I ask what you are considering? Moving cities?"

"No, absolutely not. I was thinking of the house. I could barely function today by myself in the home, where every item is a reminder of Andre." Andre had wanted to put her name on the title when they became engaged but she insisted they wait until after they were married. She wanted the joy of making it official all at once. They could legally eject her from the home, but the thought hadn't occurred to her until he brought it up.

"We would never ask you to leave or expect you to do so. No more future plans for now," Georgy encouraged. "Focus on Monroe and getting through the next week."

Sounds of the doorbell penetrated the silence, followed by muffled voices. The guests were arriving. Georgy stood, holding out his hand for her. She closed her fingers around his. She bit her lower lip so hard it hurt.

"Georgy, I encouraged him to go out riding. He…he loved it, as much as I loved the water. I—"

His grip tightened and she stopped talking. "No, Danielle. I won't let you take on this guilt. He has ridden bikes since he was a boy. I taught him. If anyone should be blamed, it would be me." Danielle shook her head.

"I could have stopped him, suggested anything else," she broke off, muffling her cry so Monroe wouldn't wake. Gently, but firmly, Georgy separated his hand from hers and placed it against her cheek, wiping her eyes.

"No, my dear girl. He loved life, and his bikes. Layda and I are grateful you weren't on that bike with him. Focus on that. Promise me." Danielle gulped back more tears, disagreeing with his words but not willing to argue.

Danielle made an effort to inhale and nod, as though she accepted his challenge. They walked down the hallway and into the dining room, where Lani eventually found her, holding a glass of water in one hand, slices of oranges and almonds in the other.

"Eat," Lani said, her command infused with caring.

"Thanks. You're being all that a bridesmaid should be."

"Screw being a bridesmaid," Lani muttered in a fair imitation of normalcy. "This is what a friend does." Lani handed her the food which Danielle nibbled on along with a few sips of water.

"How did the calls go?"

"A lot of silences and oh-my-God's. Some swearing. Most everyone asked about you and Monroe first, then I spoke of having the dinner tonight and the purpose of it all."

"Was anyone upset at the notion?"

"No, or at least they didn't say so. I think it's so surreal and such a shock, people just went with it." Danielle understood the feeling.

"What about Max and the guys?"

Lani raised her eyes and inhaled, her shoulders rising. "Max swore a lot. He seems really angry."

"At what? The accident or Andre?"

"I don't know. I still don't speak Swiss-German that well. He pulled it together to ask about you, the same as Lucas and Christian. I already told you Giles isn't coming tonight. He had it the worst, meeting Georgy at the hospital. He got really emotional then ended the conversation." Danielle's heart endured another round of pounding at the thought of him identifying the body with Georgy. Giles had known Andre since elementary school.

"I hear footsteps," Lani said, her voice low. Danielle felt for her Lani's hand and held it.

"Don't leave me, okay?"

"Right by your side, all night long."

CHAPTER 12

Over dinner in the large formal dining room, those present tried their best to honor Lani's suggestion and share happy memories of Andre. Lucas and Christian in particular, made a concerted effort to cite examples of Andre's abilities, sense of humor, love of the outdoors and passion. In contrast to his usual demeanor of the table lead, Max was subdued. He ate little and drank frequently, his eyes often on herself and Monroe.

One of Layda's sisters told a story about Andre as a child, swimming in Lake Geneva and his ability to jump off the dock on a slalom ski. "Ever the athlete," she added.

"Like how he played," said Lucas. "Hard and fast."

"Let's not forget boating," said Stephen. The talk naturally went to Andre's passion for motorcycle riding. An uneasy silence subdued the conversation.

Danielle knew what needed to be said could only come from her.

"Andre loved his motorcycles as did I. We spent hours on his bikes, going out of the city, feeling free." Aware of the many eyes riveted on her, she felt like a hypocrite, because since Monroe's birth, she hadn't wanted him on his bike, especially with her. "So please, I'm asking he be remembered as someone who lived life to its fullest, because that's what I'm going to do."

"Well, I appreciate that," Max said, his face showing not a single sign of gratitude. "But I'm beyond angry. He had a kid and the most amazing woman in the world who was going to be his wife. Why he had to go out and risk his life riding a bike..." he trailed off, shaking his head. Danielle spoke to him like it was just the two of them at the table.

"Max, he encouraged me to get on the sailboard while he took his last ride as a single man."

Max took a drink and moved his chair back. The room remained quiet as he walked around to Danielle. "I'm sorry Danielle. I love you and Monroe but I need to go." Before she could respond, he gave her a kiss on the cheek and left. Lucas and Christian followed him with their eyes but stayed in their chairs. After the front door opened and shut, Georgy spoke, his low voice filling the room.

"We each deal with grief in our own way. Anger is a second emotion to hurt, and that's strong right now. Please, if you feel both or either emotion, know that we love you and are here for you. Let us be here for each other. That's why Layda, Danielle and I wanted to be together. Those of us here in this room will need to support one another and those attending the funeral."

Heads nodded. Danielle figured the stiff upper lip resolve she saw had a basis in European values and traditions, where an ability to carry on regardless of circumstances was foundational.

Layda then spoke. "To add to my husband's words, as a mother, I don't want Andre's death clouded in rumor or mystery. You are welcome to share the details of what happened with others."

After a pause, Christian, the ever-quiet one, raised his glass. "There was no mystery about how much he loved Danielle, so let's raise our glass to her. She and Monroe are the ones who we all will adore in Andre's absence."

"I've never heard you say so much in a single sentence in my life." Danielle remarked.

"I was waiting for the right time." Her smile informed Christian he'd chosen wisely.

That night, Danielle changed into her warmest set of pajamas, brushed her teeth and went into the master bedroom, paused, then turned around. The notion of sleeping in that big empty bed gave her a queasy feeling.

As she walked back into the hallway, a sheen of light caught her attention. It was the small, digital camera on their dresser. They'd just had the conversation about taking more pictures with him and Monroe. Now he was gone, along with the opportunity.

Danielle made her way into the guest bedroom. There, under the covers, she bit her fingers and sobbed.

CHAPTER 13

That night was the hardest she'd ever known. A headache, bad dreams and Monroe being off schedule combined to ensure she slept fitfully. Sunday morning, still in her pajamas as she fed Monroe, she was sure she resembled a character out of the zombie apocalypse.

Just yesterday, he was here with me. We were a family.

Heavy doses of heartache hit her in waves every time she thought of Andre and what was happening the day he died. At eight am Monroe was on his lap. The next hour she'd been trying on her wedding dress. At eleven, Andre was riding his bike and she was sailboarding. Then twelve, when she saw Karl's face and he told her to call home.

Then now…he's been gone twenty-four hours.

Dammit! She'd forgotten to call David. He would be at his hotel and since he had no idea of what had happened, he was probably getting ready to go out for the afternoon on the boat, an event which had been cancelled. She put Monroe on her tummy on the floor then called his hotel.

"David Russelzs," he answered, every bit the dispassionate business traveler.

"Hi David, how are you?"

"I'm well, and you? Shouldn't you be getting a massage or something?"

"Yes, probably so if the circumstances were different."

"Are you intimating you called it off? There were easier ways to get me over here than to concoct a wedding."

"David, Andre was killed while riding his motorcycle yesterday morning." She heard a sharp inhale, then a more calibrated exhale.

"My Lord, Danielle. I don't know what to say." Danielle spared him the trouble. She shared the facts about the accident just as Layda had suggested. She also related the family's decision to continue to hold the various scheduled events.

"You think it's realistic for people to enjoy themselves knowing what you are going through?"

"Maybe not, but the last thing a person who has lost someone wants is for others to be in pain as well. We've asked people to forgo black at the funeral. My father advocated one's life should be celebrated not mourned, and black is mourning. It's also why we are keeping the excursions and sightseeing and are basically insisting people use them."

"That's a pretty tall order."

"I know it is." Although she was physically exhausted and emotionally hollow, her thinking was clear. "It will give me comfort to know that you are taking an overdue vacation, seeing the Alps, eating all this amazing food Andre and I spent weeks picking out. If you can't do it for yourself, do it for me."

David reluctantly promised. "I admire your courage and strength in the face of unrelenting odds."

"David, there is heartache around us, every day. Bad relationships, unsatisfying jobs. I want you and Jolene to leave here filled with wonderful memories." She paused, stopping her voice from breaking as she thought of her father's sage words of wisdom to choose love over life.

Her former boss emitted a wintery laugh at her stern tone. "You have my word. But I won't hold you to seeing me other than at the funeral. Let's play that by ear." Danielle thanked him, much relieved. "One more thing, Danielle. You will make it through this, and at some point, I know you will find happiness again."

Happiness of the kind she had with Andre, or even Lars? She doubted it.

Not long after, Danielle began receiving emails and calls from her former co-workers at Russelzs. The conversations were short, each one full of warmth. Her emotional reservoir had been drained, yet each word of love and caring was like a drop of rain behind the dam, eventually filling it up. By the time she finished responding to the emails, it was the early afternoon.

I must get out of here.

Danielle bundled up Monroe in a hat, coat and a light blanket, along with enough food for a long stroll. She tucked the leopard print chenille blanket around her daughter, staring into those little hazel brown eyes. Andre had remarked that Danielle's brown eyes and his blue had created a lovely mix. He was right. Monroe's eyes were exquisite.

"It's time to get outside," she whispered.

Her walk was in the opposite direction from Layda's home. Down the hill, along Seefeltstrasse, beside the marina, continuing past the waterpark towards downtown. The wide, long concrete path under the trees that were now glorious shades of reds. In forty minutes, she was walking past the Opera house, then taking Quaibrukke, pausing to watch the geese floating on the Limmat River. Once she was on the other side, she turned back, the miles under her feet therapeutic.

Her thoughts followed no order or pattern. Much of the time, she simply observed others, wondering about the man in a suit rushing into his car, a briefcase in hand, backing out with a brief glance. A young woman, maybe nineteen, dressed in yoga attire, riding a bike, her curly hair poking out from under a cap. Each had lives, with joy, sadness, triumph. Had they suffered job loss or divorce, a new relationship or a death? If they looked at her, they would assume a married woman with a child, not a care in the world in the middle of the day.

She periodically fed Monroe who had been content to ride and sleep. Now she was restless to get out of her confines and Danielle couldn't handle a multi-hour walk back. She hailed a cab, returning home as tired as if she'd run a marathon, mentally and physically. She bathed Monroe and played on the floor for an hour before feeding her again and putting her asleep. She looked at the time. Six p.m.

I'd normally be doing research, she thought. *Normally.* There was no normal now. She robotically checked her email again, this time finding it full of messages from those at her own workplace. Lars must have waited until the end of the day to inform the others. She was glad of it. One part of her thought it would be cathartic to respond to the queries and sympathy notes, while the other part wanted nothing more than to ignore it all.

Because I don't want to deal with reality.

Danielle shut the computer lid and wandered into the bedroom, a sick feeling hitting her belly that didn't abate until she went into the kitchen. She poured herself a cup of hot water with lemon and sat in the living room.

The emptiness hit her as forcefully as the quiet. She rose and went back into the kitchen. It slowly dawned on her that she felt most comfortable there, probably because it was her domain, where'd she'd spent the most time alone. All the other rooms in the modestly sized home had been full of Andre. He'd chosen the home before they had gotten back together, picked out the furniture, the art. Every detail in every room was his, except for Monroe's room and the kitchen.

Andre. She could try all she wanted to avoid thinking about him but it was impossible. The hours kept ticking by, and she counted each one, as though the hand was going to go in reverse, and her life would be turned back in time. There was only one activity she could do to keep herself occupied. She positioned her laptop in front of her and opened the lid.

CHAPTER 14

The ring of her cell phone caused Danielle to jump. She stared at the phone number. She waited approximately two more rings until she picked up.

"Hello, Danielle."

"Hi, Lars."

"Danielle, I'm so sorry."

She lifted her free hand from the keyboard and placed it on her lap. "Thanks."

"Danielle, I've never been more serious and more concerned for another person. I can't imagine what you are going through. Georgy doesn't know how you are keeping it together."

"At present, I'm working."

"You are not," he replied, his voice controlled.

Danielle silently nodded her head. "I would only say this to you and David. Through all my losses, both parents, you, and now Andre, work has been there. It's the only thing that keeps me sane."

"I can understand that, although I'm not sure I should be included in the category of loss."

"You were a great loss in my life, as you well know. And just like this—unexpected and difficult." Danielle spoke as though it wasn't her going through the experience, but someone else. "It's like it's not real Lars."

"I don't believe it will for some time. And then it will be months more before things return to normal." Danielle thought she heard a regretful inhale. "On that note, I called first as your friend, to check on you, but I am also calling as your boss. Under normal circumstances, I would never be so callous as to bring up work, and certainly not this soon, but your situation is unique, and we need to make arrangements here to cover for you. Can I revert to being your managing director for a moment?"

"Yes, of course," she said, sitting up a little taller.

"Georgy said you mentioned coming back to work. I can't allow it."

"Ever?"

"No, of course not. But you need to take some time to care for yourself and Monroe."

Danielle glanced at the open screens on her laptop. "I was going to be gone next week anyway."

"In a week you will barely begin to go through what's called decompression from the stressful trauma of the event."

"Lars, I need to be productive."

"Exactly. Be productive by investing in your daughter. If you need a break from that, you have Lani and Stephen. Others in your sphere who can be there for you."

"There are no others, Lars. Work is the one thing that can distract me from the silence of this place." She completely understood where he was coming from, but the image of being in this house for hours alone was inciting an internal riot of desperation.

"Danielle, if you were in my position, what would you do? Would you take the risk of putting your top trader with billions under her management back in the hot seat immediately or would you wait for a period?"

She felt rolled over, like dirt being crushed by a paver. "I'd wait."

"Danielle, you need to trust me. We don't know what will happen. You may decide to stop working for several years, until Monroe reaches kindergarten and is in school full time."

"I doubt it."

"Doubt is subjective," he pointed out, his voice full of compassion but unbending. "Georgy hasn't been subtle about the potential of you leaving MRD and working for him. I'd be disappointed of course, but--"

"That is not even a consideration," she broke in. "I'm sorry for interrupting, but I have no desire to leave. The last thing I want is to emerge from this situation to a new company, people and culture. If that were the case, I might as well leave this country entirely."

"You'd do that?" he asked, sounding startled.

"Never, but it makes the point. I'd leave the country before leaving MRD."

"Point well taken. Now to the time we want you to take off, we propose four months. Anything less is fraught with risk for you and the company."

They still wanted her, even after her absence from pregnancy, and then with just a few weeks back at the office, this. She closed her laptop with finality.

"What will my clients do? How will they react?"

"If history is any guide, even if all your clients walked, I'm confident you'd have a full book again in several months. What I want is for you to take care of yourself. If I might make a suggestion? Get out. Travel. Go someplace where it's warm, a beach perhaps. It's going to be freezing here in the next month. A change of scenery might sound slightly offensive and hard, but it will do you good."

"Why? Changing surroundings won't change my life."

"Because I know you trust me, and I've haven't been wrong yet."

The pain in Danielle's heart was lessened by the comfort she felt at his words. "I don't know where to go or what to do."

"Leave that to me. I'll send you an email with suggestions that you can take or leave."

Danielle fiddled with her pajama pants. "The one forward direction I had was going back to the office, and now that's gone too."

"Not gone," he corrected. "Just delayed."

"Lars?"

"Yes?"

"I appreciate you being here, for me. It has to be strange for you, with your…situation and all, so thanks."

"Danielle, I'm here for you, irrespective of what is going on in my life. Now get your rest. Monroe is going to need all her mother can give her."

Danielle rose, her legs feeling heavy and tired as she walked to Monroe's room, finding her sound asleep. She then went into the bathroom and ran a hot bath. Her feet were now feeling the effects of her long walk, and her body craved the break the steam would provide.

Danielle slunk in the bath, the heat touching the bottom of her ears before she turned off the water. She felt for the scrub brush and proceeded to vigorously rub the soles of her feet. The physical sensation was calming, the muscles gradually relaxing the more aggressively she moved the brush. Maybe it was a metaphor for how she needed to be. Wear herself out physically so she could escape emotionally.

CHAPTER 15

Sunday night, Lani called. Danielle told her of the discussion with Lars about taking four months off.

"Four months is a really long time. On a normal day, you can't sit still for two hours."

"Lars also suggested I take an extended trip to a place where beaches and sun are plentiful."

"Can you even get your head around that now?"

"No."

Monday morning, Danielle waited until Monroe's morning nap before she called her assistant, Glenda. After listening to the other woman's words of condolences, she apologized.

"What could you possibly apologize for?" Glenda asked.

"I'm sorry this is so up and down for you financially."

Glenda said words in her native language Danielle didn't understand. "Do I want to know what you just said?"

"The American equivalent of you're crazy, but with a bit of affection." Danielle thanked her and hung up, trying not to dwell on what else Glenda had told her. Several of her clients had left, tired of the back and forth to Johanne, who had once again taken over the majority of her accounts.

Danielle returned a call from Giles, who apologized for not attending the dinner.

"I'm sorry," he began. "I can't deal."

"You know Andre wouldn't want you to be so miserable."

"We don't know what he would say, Danielle. He never had a friend die on him. For all we know, he might want us to spend a month crying over him.”

The crazy statement almost got her to smile. “No, Max has that kind of ego, not Andre.”

Giles grunted in the affirmative. “I heard he got up and left the mourning dinner. Idiot. He shouldn’t have shown up if he couldn’t stay. That’s why I didn’t bother.”

“Are you going to bother attending the funeral?” Her words carried a bite.

“I’m not sure. I don’t agree we must mourn in public to show our emotions for a person. It’s like appearing in public is the only way to prove we cared. It’s crap.”

His words struck her. She had no right to judge his manner of grieving. “You’re right, Giles. Everyone has a right to privacy. Well, I’ll see you at some point.” She didn’t add next season, because she wasn’t sure if or when she’d want to sailboard again on a lake where she had so memories with Andre.

“Danielle,” he interjected. “I’m sorry I’m being an ass. I can’t handle death. Not this one, not like this.”

“I know Giles. You and me both.”

Two hours later, her doorbell rang. She opened it and came face to face with a large bouquet of yellow lilies and white roses. She thanked the delivery man who told her he’d be right back with another. She’d put the vase down in the living room and returned to the door to accept the two additional bouquets.

“Pretty,” Danielle cooed to Monroe whose eyes followed the movement. She sat down and opened the card.

I really am sorry for how I’ve been. I love you like a sister. Giles.

She mentally thanked him. It was as much as he could do and it was enough. The second arrangement was much larger, from MRD. The porcelain vase looked hand crafted and she noticed 24 karat gold around the trim at the base. Sure enough, the card identified it as Lenox porcelain, and it was filled to the brim with roses, lilies and blue delphiniums. The note was equally formal.

From the entire staff at MRD, our deepest sympathy during this time.

She lifted the card out of the third arrangement, this one of blue hydrangeas and white roses. It was from Lani's parents.

We love you as our own. We are praying for you and Monroe. Love Ryan and Pilar.

The rest of the day was peppered with calls from Layda. In the third call, Layda requested pictures of their family.

"We don't have any," Danielle with regret. "The day before his…Andre and I joked about how he was always the photographer. I only have one, the last image I took of the two of them. It was that morning."

Layda sniffled and finally spoke. "Please send that, along with the ones I've seen of your earlier trips, when you were dating." Danielle promised she'd send as many as she had.

It took her an hour to comb through the images they'd taken during their time together, starting with their first motorcycle rides. Images from the Lichtenstein Castle when he'd told her they were made for one another; she the unabashed American and he the reserved Swiss man, a perfect balance of personalities.

Danielle turned on the television. The news was on but the sound was off, the right amount of distraction without noise. She heated up soup for herself and warmed the homemade pureed vegetables from Layda for Monroe, who was content to be held and fed.

Lani called after she'd gone to bed. "I'm sorry, did I wake you up?"

"No, I was just laying here."

"Do you want me to come over and stay with you tonight, or any night this week? I'm worried about you being alone."

"If I could make it through last night, I can do the rest of them."

"Oh, Danielle, I'm so sorry. I didn't think you'd want anyone there last night. I thought you'd go right to sleep."

"That's exactly what I did. But I'll be fine tonight."

"Are you sure? Renaldo is finishing things up here. Do you have food? I bet you haven't eaten in forty-eight hours." Danielle admitted that much was true. "Then I'm coming over and bringing enough for the week."

"Thanks, but I'm not really interested in food."

"Too bad, I'm coming anyway."

"No, really Lani, I'm serious. I'm in bed and I don't want to get out of it for any reason, even to see my best friend and eat some food. Besides, Layda, has stocked us up for days."

"Okay for tonight, but Tuesday I'm going to drop by. It's as much for me to know that I'm looking after you like Andre would want me to do."

Tuesday Danielle simply went through the motions. Lani and Stephen came by but Danielle didn't allow them to stay. "You guys have a business to run and that's where you should be, not here, watching me." With no research to distract her, she turned on the television, the background noise her only company. For dinner, she warmed up a small portion of meatloaf and potatoes, feeding a bit of the mashed potatoes to Monroe until she turned her head, the clear signal of being done. A bath for her daughter, then bed.

Wednesday, her doorbell rang at 8:30. This time, the delivery man stood in front of her and soon her kitchen counters were covered with symbols of sympathy.

The smell of lilies was still with her when she left the living room and saw a glimpse of herself in the mirror. One thing she didn't want to do was become a woman without the ability to get out of bed and take care of herself and her daughter. Her father always said the way one looks is the way one acts. Looking presentable was a good start.

An hour later, she was dressed, her hair dry and combed and her make-up minimal, but at least it was on. She was going to make sure her daughter saw her with a smile.

At three in the afternoon, a final delivery was made: a long metallic silver box and an exquisite arrangement, so large it nearly overwhelmed the table where she placed it. When he'd gone, she sat on the couch. Her hands automatically reached for the long box.

"God grant me the serenity to accept the things I cannot change, courage to change the things I can and the wisdom to know the difference."

We liked this saying and think it works. Your forever dancing partners, Johanne and Dario.

Did this bring them back together? She wondered. If so, it would be one good thing to come from the travesty.

She lifted the lid, and gazed at the metal wind chime with the quote engraved on the metal disk at the bottom. She held it up, testing the sound. She was instantly brought back to the time when she and Andre had learned they couldn't be together and had ridden out of the city, towards the mountains. There, under the aspen trees, they'd held one another, the breeze through the leaves sounding like these chimes.

She replaced the chimes in the box, then gazed at the arrangement on the table. It was predominantly pastels, with gladiolas, bells of Ireland, button poms, daisies and other flowers she didn't recognize. The card itself was linen, a monogrammed L was on the front, the border a deep ocean blue.

You will make it through this, for Monroe and for yourself. You have many people who care about you and love you. Myself included. Lars.

Danielle read and re-read the card until she felt the words seared in her mind. Then without warning, she burst into tears. Her heart felt ripped open all over again.

CHAPTER 16

Saturday, Danielle arrived at the Baur Au Lac hotel an hour before the funeral was to start. She pulled up to the valet parking and immediately saw the large, oval arrangement announcing the special event for the Metterlen Family. The most exquisite hotel in Zurich was decorated as was to be expected for the wedding of one of the city's most prominent families.

Danielle lifted Monroe from her car seat and walked inside. She glanced around the cavernous banquet room and saw the place card holders and mementos for guests already laid out. The hours they'd spent poking fun at the little things that were supposed to represent them and what they loved now seemed so important.

How had I thought they were silly, or Andre believing it was a waste of time? The guests would be taking home a little bit of Andre's personality with each bottle and packet of candy, the silver spoons lasting a lifetime.

She stopped when she saw the board. It had been changed to the Metterlen Funeral, instead of the Metterlen Wedding. Danielle took a deep breath and exhaled slowly. There was no avoiding it, she told herself dispassionately.

Monroe squirmed in her arms and Danielle instantly regretted not bringing in the stroller. She turned around and went back out to the valet, had the car ordered and retrieved the stroller from the back.

"I can help you with that."

The familiar voice caused her heart to fill with happiness. She turned and saw Giles. He lifted the stroller from the trunk, but let her unfold it and place Monroe inside before he gave her a hug.

"Thanks for coming."

He nodded and stepped back. "I agreed to speak and a call-in video would have been rude."

Danielle smiled, grateful his humor hadn't left him. "I'm taking it your date wasn't interested in a funeral?"

"I disinvited her," he said without remorse. "If I'm going to cry I don't want an audience."

Out of her peripheral vision, Danielle noticed a familiar, four door metallic grey car pull up. She focused on adjusting Monroe's cap and finished just as the driver emerged. The man stood, handed the keys to the valet and walked to her.

"Hello, Danielle."

"Hi, Lars." He closed the distance quickly, kissing either cheek befitting acquaintances. She then turned. "Do you know Giles? One of Andre's close friends."

"Yes, you own the board shop down by the marina." Giles acknowledged the relationship, shaking Lars' hand.

"Can we follow you in?" Lars asked. Danielle nodded, walking slightly ahead of the two men. She was grateful Lars did not bring his fiancé. Not that it would have been inappropriate or hurtful, but it was nice he chose to be sensitive to her feelings.

Ushers were on either side of doors within the main room, handing out programs. In the front and to the right were three tables of items honoring Andre: his awards from primary and secondary school, trophies and photos, a timeline of highlights from his life. The last table included photos of herself and Monroe, along with the wedding announcement that had been framed. Danielle experienced a surreal feeling of both loss and acceptance merging together like cars on a freeway.

Lani came to her side, giving Lars a hug and kiss on either side of his cheeks. Danielle introduced her to Giles.

"I'm so glad to finally meet you," Lani said to Giles, calling

Stephen over. "Sailboarding is her passion." Lars left them, approaching Georgy to shake his hand. Layda gave him kisses on either cheek, her hand lingering on his arm as they spoke in low tones.

Danielle turned her attention to the guests who were now arriving en masse, most wearing bright colors. "They listened to you," she murmured to Lani.

"And you took the advice as well," Lani responded, giving her a side glance. Danielle had chosen a two-piece sky-grey St. John knit ensemble, the knee length outfit form fitting yet conservative.

David and his wife walked through the door, giving Danielle the opportunity to introduce the couple to Georgy and Layda. They'd seen one another at her father's funeral but hadn't spoken.

"She's been an amazing addition to our lives," Georgy told David. A smile on David's face made him look years younger.

Ulrich, his wife and daughter came through the line, then Glenda and her husband. Johanne was accompanied by Dario, both striking in grey suits with slim-fit legs.

"Thank you for coming," she said quietly to Dario as she embraced him. "It means the world to him."

"This was less about him and more about you," he responded. She squeezed him harder. "Okay, maybe a little about him."

Danielle drew back. "I love the chimes. Thank you both."

As noontime neared, Georgy suggested they take their seats. Danielle found his hand, following him to the front row as Lani offered to take Monroe during the funeral, pushing the stroller down the hall.

When the music began, Danielle took in the scene before her. The extravagant wedding bouquets had been adjusted. Instead of vertical arrangements with flowers springing from the top and draping over the sides, roses and lilies covered the oval formations, the appearance pretty but subdued. The platform for the ceremony had been eliminated and in its place was a single, waist high podium typically used by speakers at conferences. Soon a man in a dark suit approached Georgy, shook his hand, then went to the podium. Danielle concentrated on his eyes, watching as they darted inquisitively around the room, before nodding. She heard doors shutting, and the man bowed to say a prayer. It was time.

—

CHAPTER 17

The next hour felt like a dream. One of Andre's hockey-playing cousins from Geneva gave the eulogy. He recounted Andre's youth, his drive and insistence on winning at everything he touched, not just hockey. Danielle heard of his love for learning but his overriding desire for practical application and his adoration for working with his father in his business. She then listened to a summary of Andre meeting herself, the first love of his life, and about the birth of Monroe, the second love of his life.

Giles rose and spoke about another side of Andre. The one of his youth, where two boys saw life as an adventure, whatever the course and wherever the journey.

"He said he fell for Danielle the moment he saw her in the restaurant, but I believe it happened when he saw her in the wetsuit," Giles said, catching Danielle off guard. "But then, anyone who sees Danielle in a wetsuit would do the same thing." The audience laughed, leaving Danielle grateful for Giles' ability to move beyond his pain so that he was here when it mattered most.

A special musical piece was played by their friend Benny, a soulful tune Danielle had never heard before. He too, had watched their journey, just as a handful of others in the room had done. The pastor then took his position, thanking the group for coming.

"The family has made a special request of those in attendance. The ushers are passing out cards for each of you to write a special moment, interaction or memory of Andre. These special moments will be kept and shared with little Monroe as she ages, to help give her a perspective on her father that she won't have experienced herself. You may drop them off in the white boxes outside the doors anytime between now and after the end of the reception, which will be held in the adjacent hall."

He gave a closing prayer and invited the family to be dismissed first.

Lani met her at the door alone. "Stephen is strolling Monroe around the grounds. She's not very happy right now."

Danielle excused herself from Georgy and Layda and located Stephen outside. The manicured hedges were cut with precision, the hues of reds, oranges and yellows of the fall reminding her of the Maples and tri-colored beach trees in the Northwest.

"You make a pretty good uncle," Danielle observed as she approached. Stephen's content smile was exactly what she needed at that point.

"I was better a few minutes ago," he answered, moving the stroller back and forth. Monroe held a chew toy in her hands, the little rings clanging softly but Danielle saw the signs of irritation. Her clangs were increasing in impact and she was emitting sounds that were invariably a prelude to crying.

"It's her, not you, trust me. I'd been hoping that you and Lani would be her godparents, in case something happened to me." She waited for his reaction, hoping to gain a little insight on the status of marriage.

Stephen's normally steady expression changed to one of affection. "I'm flattered by the idea. Just not capable of saying yes, for the reasons you saw on the boat and probably talked about afterward."

"Nothing has changed?" Danielle whispered.

"Yes, but for the worse."

"Hi, you two," greeted Lani from behind her. "People are starting to take their seats in the dining room. Everything ok?"

Danielle focused on Monroe, unnecessarily adjusting her blanket. "Monroe needs some food." She excused herself to the ladies' room, not wanting to remove the containers full of baby food and potentially spill. With any luck, she'd eat and fall asleep. When Danielle emerged from the bathroom, she saw Max who stood in front of the table of momentos.

He spoke first. "I'm sorry I left the other day and was late today. Are we still friends?"

"We will always be friends." They walked into the ballroom together and she left him to find a seat while she approached Lars.

"Lars," she called. "I have someone who wants to meet you." The two of them walked to David and his wife, Jolene and she introduced the three.

"Finally, after all these months," David said to Lars, taking his hand.

"It's my pleasure," Lars said with respect to his overseas peer. Danielle recalled all that her former boss knew of her new life here, her romantic involvements and how Lars was integral throughout it all.

"I took the liberty of placing the three of you at the same table." Jolene, a fair-skinned woman of Asian descent, gave a shy nod. "Jolene, Lars has a home in St. Moritz and is a wealth of information about all the best out of the way places only locals can find. Lars, Jolene and David are spending the next two weeks vacationing in the area, and I knew you'd have some ideas." Jolene perked up significantly and Lars took the hint. He smoothly continued the conversation about restaurants as he walked with the couple to their table.

Danielle found Layda already seated at the round table with Georgy, her sisters and their spouses. At first, Danielle tried to listen, but Monroe was fussy at being stuck in her stroller and showed no signs of falling asleep. She was soon tapping and banging her small toys, then squirming. Danielle repressed frustration. During the very time she would have most appreciated a perfectly behaved six-month-old, she was getting the 'I'm-going-to-have-a-meltdown-child.'

"I'll be back," Danielle said to Layda. Lani caught her eye and Danielle gave her a subtle shake of her head no. It was her turn to be the mom, not Lani's. She felt the compassionate looks from those at the table and sensed the stares from other diners as she exited.

Leaving was a blessing. Her mental stamina for making small talk with cousins, distant relatives and acquaintances was starting to fade.

Monroe settled down the moment Danielle began walking. It was now cooler, but Danielle went outside, under the veranda, keeping near the heat lamps that gushed warmth from above. Along the perimeter of the hotel she strolled, admiring the fall flowers and night sky, the view from the hotel remarkable.

Danielle eventually returned inside and found a plush chair nearest the patio. She sat down, grateful Monroe was now content to sit on her lap, half-bouncing.

"May I join you?"

"Lars, of course." He was one of the few people she could handle right now.

Danielle's attention was on keeping Monroe upright and her little chubby legs wobbled as she moved side-to-side, lifting one leg then another randomly.

"I've never seen Monroe before today you know. You never brought her into work to show her off."

"I didn't think that was done here."

"There's always a first time."

"True enough. And I guess I am master of the first times at MRD."

"That you are."

Danielle smiled at Monroe, lifting her arms high then down, whispering "soo-big," just as her mother had done with her. She felt Lars staring at her and glanced his way.

"Would you like to hold her?"

Lars shook his head. "Some other time. I'm just enjoying seeing you happy with your daughter."

Danielle laid Monroe on her back, playing with her feet as Monroe tried to reach up. "Jacqueline sent me a note about returning on the fifteenth. Are you still sure I have to be away from the office that long?"

His lips turned down, clearly dismayed she brought up work. "Given what I'm seeing between you and that little girl on your lap, do I even need to respond to that question?"

"It doesn't hurt to try."

"If I was wrong, you'd say so."

She sighed. "And since that never happens, I likely won't ever have the chance."

Not even a hint of a smile played at Lars' lips. It struck her he was in a charcoal-black suit with a dark blue shirt and gold tie, a combination she'd never seen. "Thank you for the flowers. They are lovely."

Lars silently accepted her comment. Giving a gorgeous bouquet because of a death was bittersweet. "Did you have a chance to read the email I sent you?" he asked.

Danielle's shoulders raised and lowered. It was his list of favorite places to visit. She'd glanced through it, unwillingly resigned to being out of town or otherwise occupied for four months.

"Well?" he gently pressed. "Will you do it?"

"Possibly," she hedged. She wasn't used to being on the end of a disappointed look from Lars. "I might take the routes you provided or I might just put Monroe in the car and see how far we get. I did promise Lani to return for Thanksgiving then be here with Layda and Georgy for Christmas. Lani agrees with your idea to go someplace warm, but I haven't checked out the hotel recommendations you sent me. Maybe later."

Danielle shifted her focus to the door, feeling a growing sense of dread. The luncheon was winding down. Soon, the mourners would depart, the emptiness creating a new void that couldn't be filled with another event. David would leave for Italy with his wife, Lani and Stephen would go back to their normal routine, and her life would commence, without a job or a husband.

"I'm not doing this to make it worse for you," Lars said quietly. "I think it's for the best."

"You aren't making it worse, Lars. In fact, I do think leaving town for a while is a good idea, since going home and being alone is awful, if you want to know the truth. You suggesting travel is like the dreaded but appreciated personal trainer who makes their client pick up a fifty-pound medicine ball."

"I'm a personal trainer now. A nice visual." The image of Lars, the self-styled master-of-the-universe, in a gym working for an hourly rate was so absurd it caused the corner of her lip to curl up.

"I'm sure this wasn't in your master plan during this period in your life. It's not fair to you or your fiancé. I'm so sorry."

"Danielle, we've had this discussion," he said, his voice a notch lower, his eyes firmly set on hers. "No more worrying from you. No more scolding from me." She nodded reluctantly. "Danielle, you promised."

Her chest ached. "I never break my promises," she said quietly.

"I'm counting on it."

CHAPTER 18

Danielle returned to the dining area and found many of the guests had left. She spent half an hour with David and his wife Jolene, the time therapeutic and comforting. David asked about her plans for the next few months and the year beyond. She admitted she had weeks of time to fill.

"Why don't you try going to Austria in November?" Jolene suggested gently. "Salzburg is always full of festivals celebrating Mozart, and you being a student of music would adore them, especially the church and cathedral where he played as a youth."

"I think you should consider what Lars suggested and go someplace warm," David added, taking a sip of his black espresso.

"Have you two been conspiring?" She envisioned the men as two pillars, one younger, the other older, standing on either side of her, ushering her through times of darkness.

"To the degree you will listen, sure."

Jolene excused herself to use the ladies room and David placed his hand on the table, curling his fingers in thought.

"Now tell me, Danielle, you've endured more heartache in a year than most do in two decades. How are you really doing?"

Danielle didn't have an easy answer to the question. "How am I coming across?"

"Actually, quite together. You look pale and thinner than I've ever seen you, but not unhealthy. A normal person would crack, and a part of me thinks you are normal, that any moment I'll see the break, but it's not evident."

Danielle cocked her head. "I'm not sure if you are

complimenting me for keeping it together or insulting me for being a robot."

"Neither. I'm not one given to outward expressions of emotion, but I'm also not a believer of holding things in. It's bad for the body and hell for the soul. You need to let it out."

"Trust me. I have. But after a while crying is exhausting, then enduring numbness and denial is equally draining. Besides, I think children can sense moods. I know Monroe definitely can."

"See? You're talking completely coherently."

"Did you expect me to become stupid while grieving?"

His eyebrows and dark look scolded her. "Depressed, yes. Stupid, no." Her mentor rubbed his cheek, the way elderly statesmen do just before proffering wisdom. "Have you thought about not working at all for the foreseeable future?"

"A forced hiatus is bad enough David. Never have I thought about stopping work permanently. Do you think I should? And please give me the unfiltered version."

"Financially, it's a non-issue. Intellectually, I believe you would suffer. You're too driven to retire. Emotionally, I can't say. You have a daughter and your priorities might change over the next year or so."

Eventually, it was time to close the room and Danielle said her goodbyes, expressing her pleasure that David and his wife were going to keep their vacation as planned. In the foyer, she met up with Layda and Georgy who had been waiting for her.

Layda touched her arm. "You will call and let me know when I can watch Monroe?"

Danielle kissed her. "Of course, but for the next two weeks, why don't you take a break yourself? After all this, you need a rest as much as me." Layda nodded, her face drawn and tired. Georgy gave her a great hug and kiss and called for the cars.

In her rearview mirror, Danielle watched the hotel fade from view. When it disappeared from site, a door shut within her. Fate had given her two chances at love and both had ended badly. She was sure it would be many years before she'd have another opportunity, and for now, that was just fine.

CHAPTER 19

First one week passed, then another and finally a month as she roamed the countryside with Monroe as her backseat companion. She called Layda and Georgy once a week, limiting her communication to quick updates that she was safe. Every few days she spoke with Lani, the decline of her relationship with Stephen mixed with an increasing desire to work in a different environment, one without her husband. Danielle could see the inevitable conclusion, even if Lani couldn't. Her friend was talking herself out of her marriage.

A good counterbalance to Lani was speaking with Johanne. He invariably proved to be an irreverent source of information, a combination of gossip and fact slanted with his post-modern take on life.

The afternoon she crossed over the German-Austrian border, Danielle was speaking with him about Dario. From the noise in the background, she guessed he was on the metro.

"On my way to Dario's," he confirmed.

"You've moved back in?"

"No. I'm collecting the rest of my things. We got back together around the time of the funeral, but it didn't last."

"I'm so sorry."

"Don't be. I've chosen to earn a living at this company which treats and pays me very well. By virtue of that, and the stress that he says I'm emitting even on the dance floor, he can't take it anymore."

"Emitting even on the dance floor?" she repeated, incredulous.

"Yes. He says I'm positively sweating tension."

A burst of laughter escaped Danielle's lips. "I'm sorry twice over. I know I've done this to you."

"No, Andre did it," he bounced back without a pause. "You may redirect any hate to him because you are in a no-fault zone."

Danielle's conflicting emotions of truth, sadness and pragmatism erupted into a belly laugh. It was nice to have one person in her circle who could be real, respectful and humorous at the same time. It had been five weeks since the funeral, and the humor felt strange but welcome.

"You do you realize by saying that, you have just purchased a ticket on the express train to hell?"

"Given how Lars is breathing down my neck, I'm already on it."

"Sorry again," she said lamely.

"It's not like he will let you come back and don't think I haven't tried every argument and maneuver possible."

"Maybe Lars will be so focused on his engagement that he will lay off a bit."

"Perhaps that's why he's all over me. He's still a frustrated bachelor, or this situation is causing him to lose his relationship just like the rest of us."

Danielle doubted it. "Lars doesn't strike me as a person to let his personal life interfere with his work."

"That's the point. He's never *had* a personal life. This is all new to him."

Danielle smiled. Some things were best kept as secrets. Danielle used her sisterly soothing tone. "The bright side, if there is one, is that the holidays will soon be here."

"Yes, and then the New Year. Are you really coming back? Mid-January is what we've been told." Danielle confirmed he'd heard correctly. "It can't come soon enough."

As she drove, Danielle talked out loud for her daughter's

benefit, pointing out the fields of wilting sunflowers. If she wasn't talking, she had on classical music, not dance. Come to think of it, since Andre died, she'd rarely listened to anything other than ambient or classical.

It's because the music has no words or strong beats, nothing to remind me of him.

That night as Danielle turned down the bed at the boutique hotel, she thought of her emotional evolution. The once gut-wrenching pain she felt had dissipated to episodic moments of loss. It wasn't enough to bring her to tears, but she'd feel dark for a period of time.

Yet, even that was evolving. Thanks to, or because of Monroe, she didn't allow herself to be morose for long. A memory or thought brought pain, but like a breeze going through a screen door, it passed around her and moved on, only a little chill of the experience remaining.

Danielle placed the blanket on Monroe, who promptly flipped over, something she was doing with regularity. In bed, Danielle opened her computer and reviewed her itinerary for the week. Museums, castles and everything in between. Filling her time didn't mean wasting it.

In early November, she returned to Zurich. The home was dusty and cold, one easily taken care of with a dust cloth and the other with warmer temperature settings. Her absence had frayed the tenuous bind she had with the home. She called Layda for a visit and learned she and Georgy were preparing to leave for a month to the south of Spain.

"Georgy and I have heard your own voice sounding a little brighter every time you called and felt we should try the same approach." Layda asked to see Monroe the following day, suggesting a few hours for herself would do her good. Danielle took Monroe over at noon, planning to visit Giles and stop by the restaurant.

As Danielle walked through the parking lot to the marina, the chilly breeze slipped through her upturned collar, making her wish she'd worn a hat. She was surprised the snow hadn't started falling yet but knew it would arrive soon. The marina was quiet, the slip where Andre docked his boat was empty like all the others. They'd been moved to storage and wouldn't come out again until April or May. The boat, like all of Andre's belongings, would go back to his parents unless they decided to give it to Monroe or place it in a trust. Andre had left no will, or direction of any sort, although Danielle supposed Monroe would have some rights to Andres' things. At present, she had no inclination or desire to even bring up the question to Georgy or Layda. What she had earned in her own right was more than enough to take care of herself and her daughter. Material things meant zero in the grand scheme of her life or her daughter's.

Danielle glanced around the quiet shop. "Giles?" she called. She walked through the floor area and into the waxing room. He was folding an unruly piece of sail. "What happened to your help?"

"Long gone," he said, thanking her as she assisted him in sliding the end into a protective canvas cover. He gave her an inquisitive glance. "You need some color."

"You're one to talk. When was the last time you were on the water?"

"End of October. Been getting ready to go snowboarding in the States."

"Nice." Danielle watched him for a few moments. "Will you be back for Thanksgiving dinner at Stars and Stripes? It would be nice to see you there."

"Only if you'll be working."

"No promises, but if I'm not working, I'll be eating and keeping everyone company. You ought to come. I can assure you we'll flip the music over at midnight."

"Sure. If I'm in town, I'll be there." It was as though part of his spirit was snuffed out—the fun, adopted California part which she loved and reminded her of home. Yet she was all too aware that people had to go through stages of loss and grief and recovery, and no number of trite platitudes, no matter how well intentioned, were going to speed the process along.

Her next stop was Stars & Stripes where she went directly to the bar. She greeted Paul who gave her an overly kind look and a menu. She didn't want to sit at the booth she had shared with Andre. She was reading the appetizer list of crab cakes with aioli sauce and potato skins when someone sat down beside her.

"Hi, Danielle."

"Hey Max," she said with subdued surprise, leaning into the hug he offered. "How are you?"

"Hungry."

"The usual, Max?" Paul asked.

"Do you have this menu memorized too?" she quipped.

"Yep," he said, "Lani says you have been traveling. How has it been?"

"It was an escape." He nodded and she glanced at the menu. "What's your favorite?"

"I've recently been going for the onion rings in anticipation of working it off this season. You could stand to gain a few pounds. Join me?" She nodded, and asked Paul for an order of crab cakes. "Have you seen Lani yet?"

"No, I just got here."

Max took a drink and raised it her direction. "Here's to you being back. She seems to be doing well," Max said, motioning his head to the kitchen. "It's quite a job running this place and making all the food."

"It is," Danielle agreed. "Constantly changing menus and retaining a husband aren't easy to handle."

"Right."

Ivan, the lead waiter came over the moment he saw her.

"Bella!" She stood, nearly crushed in Ivan's embrace. "The place hasn't been the same without you." He wanted to catch up but the tables were filled and a line was starting at the door. "Promise to come in more and say hello when you can." Max was consumed with his phone so she pulled out her own device, checking the news in German.

"Can you read that, or are you looking at pictures?" Max asked her.

"Reading. Eighteen months has done me good."

"Impressive. Lani said she still can't read the papers."

"I didn't know that. Maybe if we could all convince her to spend less time here she'd have the chance to learn."

"That's what I tell her." Danielle glanced at him. They were on the same page.

The appetizers arrived and Max ate a few bites of his order, finished his drink, put a twenty on the counter then stood. "Gotta run. Glad you are holding up."

Danielle pushed aside what was left of her meal. Lani still hadn't come out, so she went to the kitchen, greeting Renaldo. Seeing her, he waved but kept working.

"Is Lani around?" she asked one of the servers.

"Haven't seen her." Danielle checked the restroom, then the kitchen again and out behind the restaurant. Oh, well. She'd send her a text and catch her next time.

Back at Layda's, she had Monroe in her arms as she waved to Georgy from the doorway of his office. He was on a call, putting it on hold to give her a hug, kiss and welcome, then returning to his conversation. She wished Layda safe travels and left with her daughter.

Returning home, she flipped the pages on her visual snapshots of the day. Georgy in his office doing work. Max eating at the counter of the restaurant. Giles at his shop, preparing to close and leave for the winter. Life did go on after the death of a loved one, and it was the little things that cemented the fact. She didn't believe in walking around as if in sack cloth and ashes, but the normalcy of living didn't feel right either.

Danielle called Stephen and made her request. Could the restaurant spare food for a group tonight? Knowing it was for the elderly home, Stephen told her he'd have Renaldo prepare plenty of food and it would be delivered so she wouldn't have to stop by on her way.

Monroe allowed herself to be held by the myriad of grandparents in the room as Danielle played the piano. A stately gentleman asked her if she would sing, his quiet request carrying a hint of hope.

Danielle's voice was rough, but the old man didn't seem to notice or mind. He smiled pleasantly, as though thinking of another time and another place.

Later that night, after she put Monroe down for bed, Danielle searched the listings for available properties. There wasn't a lot on the market, and she recalled her first date with Andre when he expressed such surprise at the penthouse MRD had found for her. What had he said? So many properties never made it to listing status, or at least that was what she inferred.

Maybe that's how Zurich operated. Homes passed among owners, or the agents, the pocket listings keeping the home away from the public. Only one person would know about such a thing other than Georgy, a man with whom she didn't want to discuss this particular topic, at least not now.

Seven-twenty. Would he be alone? Should she call him at the office? No, his mobile phone.

"Hello," Lars greeted, his tone smooth.

"Hi Lars. Am I interrupting anything?"

"No," he answered, although Danielle thought she heard footsteps which meant he was walking. Probably away from his bedroom or wherever his fiancé was located. She thought she should feel guilty but didn't. He'd told her to call, she was doing that. Nothing more, nothing less.

"I won't be long," she said. "I just wanted to ask you something, gain a bit of insight if I can. All as friends and confidential, okay?"

"Of course. What can I help you with?"

Danielle began, a little unsure of herself. "It's about real estate and trying to find a place to live. Do you happen to know, or would you be willing to put me in touch with, someone who is aware of properties that aren't formally listed? I'm having a hard time finding places for sale, or even to rent, and I don't want an apartment or condo. I'd actually like a home, even if it's really small, with a yard."

"The answer to your question is yes, I know of several professionals who can help you, and I even know of a few places myself—homes of friends. But can I back up a bit? Is something wrong with your place now? You aren't..." and then he paused. "Is everything okay with you and the family?"

"This home is great, and only a couple of blocks away from Georgy and Layda, but it's Andre's not mine. The paperwork was going to be changed after we married."

"Ahh, I see. But you aren't being forced to leave."

"No. It's me. I can't be here anymore. Every time I come home I want to turn around and leave."

"That could be called avoidance."

"Lars, until you have to come back into a place you shared with an individual who is now dead, it doesn't matter what you call it. It sucks, is depressing and makes me feel stuck in a place in the dark, not light."

A longer pause followed her words. "I've never heard you use the word suck before."

"It doesn't count as a swear word in America just in case you are wondering."

"It doesn't matter to me if it is or not, it's rather funny, even though your secondary comment isn't. How soon do you want to start looking?"

"Immediately. I'd like to have the move done before I return to work." Lars committed to getting back to her within a day or two.

"One last thing, for the professionals or friends I'll be contacting, will you be around during the holidays—to go on showings?"

"I was planning on leaving tomorrow for Italy then Prague, following your suggested itinerary, then returning for Thanksgiving."

"Given that, I'll send you a couple of homes I know of that are available right now." He also suggested clumping home tours together on Thursdays or Fridays if not the weekends. "It will allow you to enjoy the tourist destinations during the week when it's less crowded."

"Lars, I've not told Georgy about this, so please don't mention it to him or Layda."

"Danielle, I told you this was confidential, and I meant it. Everything between us is, and unless you tell me otherwise, will remain so."

Danielle thanked him, eternally grateful that some things between them had never changed.

CHAPTER 20

The following afternoon, Danielle received a text from Lars.

Check your email

She read the contents, gratified. In less than twenty-four hours, Lars had learned four of his friends had available properties, and he had forwarded the name of a property specialist who knew of another half dozen. The prices varied dramatically. At the bottom of the page, Lars provided a bullet point list of restaurants to try in Hungary and Prague. She smiled. She tended to share his taste in food.

She printed the list, writing Lars a quick thank you note, then checked on Monroe before she began placing calls. The first was to the property specialist, who effusively told her he would begin researching homes befitting of her taste and price range. She gave him her schedule, he sent over the agreement for representation and after signing it, packed for her next trip. Layda called with a few names to be considered for potential babysitters while she was gone, giving her personal endorsement to a woman named Emma.

"If you are recommending her, do I really need to talk to anyone else?" Danielle asked, a little tease in her voice.

"She would be my preference," Layda said, her tone apologetic, as though she were over stepping her mother-in-law bounds.

"Layda, if you trust her, then so shall I, assuming we get along."

"If you can get along with me and make me love you, she's a piece of cake."

Danielle called the woman, Emma Kluge, and thought the conversation professional yet comfortable. They set an appointment for the week after Danielle returned, just before Thanksgiving.

The drive down to Milan was breathtaking, the Swiss Alps covered in a thin layer of snow, the roads clear and easy to drive. Over the top and into Italy she went, down the twisty-turvy road full of potholes and lined with slate-roofed homes that seemed carved into the mountainside. She had no idea how rocky the Italian mountains were in comparison to the Swiss side, now appreciating why Lars had preferred rock climbing in the Italian Alps over those hills in his home country.

Through Lake Cuomo, then Lugano and on down, another two hours until she reached Milan. Her GPS made driving in the city of four million easy. The following day Danielle took Monroe to the Duomo Cathedral and spent over two hours taking pictures, admiring the mausoleums of the cardinals, in awe of the multi-story pipe organs throughout the main worship area and the massive outer doors.

She ate across the square, at another restaurant recommended by Lars, where the hot chocolate was more like dark pudding with a dollop of whipping cream. The sky was clear and the air cold, but she felt warm and Monroe issued no complaints, so Danielle went to the Galleria Vittorio Emmanuelle, walking underneath the stone archways and into the celebrated shopping area. She purchased gelato and a watch at the Mercedes store, the rubber and ceramic timepiece accented in rose gold both understated but durable.

She felt it on her wrist, comfortable and heavy. The impulse buy reminded her of what Andre loved: things that were sporty and luxurious. This was both.

For three days she toured the city, getting her fill of museums and tourist stops before heading through Austria then up to Prague. She spent hours at Karlstejn Castle, grateful she was placed in a group of Australians, forcing the guide to give the tour in English. Outside, a man with a massive mastiff dog sat waiting for his wife, unhappy the castle didn't allow inside his beast of a four-legged animal whom the owner had named Saffron.

"You should make time to see Czesky Krumlov," he told her as she touched the dog's head that seemed twice the size of hers. "It's truly one of the most amazing castles in the Republic." Danielle took him at his word, looked it up on her map, adjusted her route and arrived the following day.

The town of Czesky sat below the multi-story castle, and through the light snow, she walked up and down the narrow, cobblestone streets. It took a full day to take in the town and the castle, going through the now paved entrance once used by royalty, through the labyrinth of rooms and terraces, stopping to take pictures of the town through the portholes seven stories up.

Danielle spent a solid week in Prague itself. Before she left, she took Monroe to another restaurant on Lars' list near the famous Astronomical Clock Tower. Thoughts of him came in and out as she immersed herself in the sites he'd suggested, ones that included the Dali and Warhol Exhibit at the Czech National Gallery in the Kinsky Palace.

Danielle continued her journey down through Hungary, thinking the Hungarian countryside was breathtaking. She discovered she and her daughter both loved goulash, and that packing her daughter in and out of two castles taxed her legs and shoulders. From one end of the country to the other, Danielle continued ticking off those places recommended by Lars, eating and driving, the latter part of the week significantly louder because Monroe cut another tooth and suffered from a mild fever.

When she arrived back in Zurich, the snow was two inches thick on lawns, but the sidewalks and roads were completely clear. She adored the efficiency of this town.

Danielle waited as the garage door lifted. Zurich felt like home, but this structure did not. She sent Lani a text, knowing she'd be at work. Moments later, she received a call.

"Hey! Are you free?" asked Lani.

"I'm unpacking and getting Monroe ready for a bath, if that's what you mean by free."

"Great. I'm coming over. I'll bring food." Before Danielle could say no, Lani had hung up.

At least she sounds happy. It wasn't long before the doorbell rang and Danielle yelled that the door was unlocked. Her hands were elbow-depth in the bath water, sudsing Monroe's hair. Lani gave her a hug from behind.

"She's your little mini me," Lani told her, sitting on the toilet. Danielle glanced at her, then did a double take.

"What happened to you? Half your hair is gone."

"I wanted a change."

Danielle dried and wrapped Monroe in a yellow Big Bird towel with a hoodie. "Yes, but to cut off six inches and go shoulder length as winter is starting? You're going to freeze."

"I'm not going to freeze, but I am feeling rather liberated. Can I take her?" Danielle held Monroe forward to Lani. Her little girl was reticent but allowed herself to be held, as long as she kept her eyes on Danielle. Lani followed Danielle into the bedroom, and after Danielle had put on her diapers, asked if she could put on Monroe's one piece pajamas.

"Are you practicing for something you haven't told me

about?" queried Danielle.

"Hardly. I'm using the skills inherent to the female sex." When Lani finally handed Monroe off, Danielle was sitting in the rocking chair. She put a lush blanket around Monroe, slipping a bottle into her mouth. The little one eagerly began sucking, and it wasn't long before she closed her eyes.

"I give. What in the world is going on?"

"Well, now that you've asked, I've decided to reinvest the money I've saved to open a second location of Stars & Stripes, but if you are violently opposed to the idea, a new restaurant entirely, with a different name, menu, the works."

Danielle sighed. The writing had been on the wall for some time. She just thought it would take longer to get to the end. Not today. "You are really sure about this?"

"Totally," Lani said, her voice rising with strength.

"Let me put Monroe to bed." Danielle closed the door to Monroe's bedroom and started the gas fireplace before sitting on the couch.

"You aren't excited, that I can already tell," Lani said, her voice perturbed in the tone a teenage girl uses when she doesn't get her way.

"I'm sad about the notion of you leaving the restaurant and Stephen as well," she answered, feeling glum. "In the back of my mind I was praying that the notion of another restaurant was more of a fleeting idea to get away from the subject of children."

Lani grimaced. "After what I told you the afternoon of the lady's brunch?"

Danielle was unapologetic. "Is it wrong of me to want you and Stephen to make things work?"

"No, it's just not super realistic."

"Okay, give me the details. One chef, two locations. How

does that work?"

"One chef, one location. Renaldo has been doing great in the back," Lani said confidently. "Ivan has mastered the hiring and management of the wait staff. Stephen is the overall manager who makes everything work."

"But he is only one person."

"This is where it gets interesting," Lani said, taking a deep breath. "Max wants to be involved."

"Max?" Danielle knew his annual salary and net worth, neither which she could reveal to Lani, but she didn't think it was plausible a man who earning over three million a year as a consultant was going to change vocations so he could sit people down at the restaurant. "How?"

"Investor and manager. First, he'd like to buy out Andre's portion of Stars & Stripes, because it's a known money-maker. Then he'd like to participate at some level in the second location."

Danielle's mind blanked and then she fought back a surge of possessiveness. Andre's best friend coming in and taking his portion?

A nice, long breath. That's what this situation needs. No, it needs her father's sage words of wisdom. *Don't kill the dream, let reality kill the dream.*

"I'm assuming you and Max have talked this through? How much would he put in, or rather, what percentage of ownership would you both have?"

Lani shrugged. "I'd have the majority, but we haven't worked out the details. And this assumes you invest in the second location as well."

"What about Stephen?"

"I've not asked him."

Danielle tilted her head forward. "He's one fourth share in

Stars and Stripes and a co-founder. You can't start a new venture using the same name and not ask him to invest or participate."

"Why not?"

"Because it's rude and in some cases, the paperwork may state that founders have the first right of refusal."

"Does ours?" Lani shot back.

Danielle was irritated at her friend's question and approach. "No, but the letter of law doesn't change the spirit, Lani."

Lani's attitude was more than disturbing. To push Stephen aside so abruptly after all they'd been through, and then expecting Max or herself to come in and invest in another Stars and Stripes when the existing one was working just fine? Ridiculous. "I thought I heard something from Monroe's room," Danielle lied. "I'll be right back."

When Danielle returned to living room, she'd calmed down. "Back to the restaurant, Lani," she started, her composure friendly and informative. "When Andre and I put in our quarter of a million, it made us equal financial partners, and you and Stephen shared the other fifty percent. If you are thinking of using some of that money, you will have to rework the paperwork with Stephen to separate out the ownership first."

"Oh, wow. I didn't think of that."

"I don't know how long it will take but that might bring up other issues."

Lani was gnawing on a finger. "Yeah. No kidding. Okay, thanks. I think I need to go now." Lani gave her a quick kiss to the cheek and left. Danielle felt like she'd avoided several potential landmines, but had the uncomfortable feeling it was only a temporary reprieve.

Not long after, Danielle glanced once more at her watch. *The second time in a month.* Would he be alone or bothered by her call?

Finally, she determined it didn't matter. Monroe was more important than Lars' romantic life.

Lars picked up on the second ring. "Are you back in town?" he asked pleasantly.

"Yes, I have been for a few days. Can you talk?"

"Of course. Do you need more advice?" His voice had a lilt, as though he both expected a call and was glad to be the recipient. This time, she didn't hear any background noise. He might be alone.

"Indeed, but before that, thanks for the suggestions on travel. I went to all the places on your list save one, and that was because the wait was too long. I'll tell you about it later when I have a bit more time."

"No rush. I'm at home now with my laptop on my knees."

"It's Monroe," Danielle began. "Specifically, who will take care of her should something happen to me. This whole time I'd been planning on Lani and Stephen as the godparents, but it has just become crystal clear their situation isn't stable enough for me to assign them that role in any official way." Lars listened quietly as she summarized the situation. Because Danielle wasn't a Swiss citizen nor had she been married to a Swiss at the time of birth, Monroe didn't have Swiss citizenship, and although she was related to Georgy and Layda through Andre, in the event of Danielle's demise, Monroe would go to Danielle's closest living relative in the United States, a first cousin.

"I could put paperwork in place for her to stay with Georgy and Layda," Danielle said, "but my concern is that they're older, and honestly, I'm not sure it's what I want."

"And you anticipate Lani and Stephen will be separating?"

"Yes."

"I think what you're getting to is that you don't have any

person who you trust with Monroe."

"That's it. So, I'm calling you, because—well," she hesitated. "I thought you'd have objective council on the best course of action."

"I'm flattered you thought to call, but I don't have a perfect solution for you."

"I was afraid you'd say that."

"To be blunt, Lani is not the ideal choice. A woman lacking the motherly instinct or desire is not the person you want watching a child who's not even her own, and that's in addition to her already working one, and potentially two, full-time jobs. Stephen might not be bad but he's male and is working as well. Transferring Monroe to a stranger in the States guarantees nothing and Georgy and Layda are elderly. Shared custody, perhaps? One primary and the other is a visitation arrangement?"

Danielle ran through the scenario. "With her grandparents as the primary care giver?"

"No. What about me?"

"What about you?"

"Georgy and Layda can have shared guardianship with me as the primary guardian. Besides yourself, I'm the only one who has loved that little girl with every fiber of my soul and is of your generation."

"But..." she got out before words failed her. "It's..." Crazy? Impossible? "I could be wrong but last I knew you were running a business and about to get married. I think I'd rather have her aging grandparents raise her than a strange woman neither of us know."

"Both are non-issues. If you were to die an early death, I'd resign my position. To the other item of having a fiancé, yes, I'm still engaged, but not married. There is a difference."

"Semantics. I could put you on the paperwork today, die

tomorrow and then where'd we be? Actually, I can't even believe I'm having this conversation, it's insane."

"Is it, Danielle?" His tone of voice, one so familiar and close to her treasure trove of happy memories, gave her pause enough to listen. "Love doesn't fade, it just goes underground. You, who knows me better than anyone alive, must believe I'm capable of showering that little girl with all the love and attention she'd require. You and I think the same, have the same value system and drive for life along with the ethics and morals required to be good parents. At one point, we thought that's exactly what we'd be together—good parents. Tell me this: if you'd been married to Andre and were on the edge of death, would you have any doubt Andre would do a fine job as a man?"

"No," she answered firmly.

"Exactly. And if you and I were married, and the exact same situation occurred, would you have confidence I could raise a little girl?"

"Of course."

"There is no difference now, other than not having a blood tie. Sometimes, Danielle, when it comes to having and raising children, what's in the heart and mind is more important than DNA." His words rang true, but at the moment, she couldn't begin to wrap her head around the implications of doing such a thing.

"If you are concerned about what Georgy would think, I don't believe he'd be morally opposed to it." Probably not, thought Danielle. He respected and admired Lars.

"This…is…very different than the conversation I thought I was going to have."

"Not surprised. During the last two months, I've given thought to many scenarios that I'd never previously considered and it makes a person reevaluate their life and priorities."

"And you'd really quit?" Lars hmm-mmm'd a confirmation. "What about your fiancé?"

"I told you, it would be a non-issue. I'd bring the one and most important female into my life and forget the other one."

"That easily."

"Yes. That easily and immediately."

"And if you were already married?"

"Unless I got married the day of your demise, you would already know that, don't you think?"

"Oh, right," she answered, a little embarrassed.

Danielle took a mental pause. What he was suggested was so logical and crazy she needed to think about it later, not now. "Speaking of dates, I never got my invitation to your wedding. Was that intentional? I did invite you to mine after all."

"You didn't miss it. It's not been sent."

"Okay, so on the remote chance I actually chose you be a guardian to Monroe, or co-guardian, how long do I have to get my proverbial house in order regarding paperwork?"

"I'm not entirely sure about that. The holidays have provided a few unexpected scenarios for both of us to work through." *Unexpected scenarios?* Who even uses such words to describe a relationship?

"Well, that was suitably vague," she remarked dryly.

Lars laughed. "You'll be kept in the loop. Don't worry."

She wasn't going to. She had other things on her mind.

It was strange then, that later that night she was in the tub when she thought of his words. Unexpected scenarios that had come up during the holidays. Unexpected, like the death of your former lover's fiancé?

She couldn't allow her mind to go there. She *shouldn't* allow her mind to go there.

CHAPTER 21

Danielle chose to put her will and the custodial concern to the bottom of her to-do list for the next eight weeks. It wasn't the smartest thing, she knew, but she had a babysitter to hire and potential homes to review, all the while making it through the holidays with her in-laws who were technically not in-laws at all.

"They will be grandma and grandpa to you," Danielle said out loud to Monroe, hefting up her little girl. The moment Danielle did so, an urp of food emerged from Monroe's mouth, going straight down Danielle's cleavage. "Very sexy," she commented to her obliviously happy daughter.

Danielle gently lowered Monroe to the floor so the goo wouldn't spill out. She then rinsed out her top, took a quick shower and dressed. An hour later, Emma Kluge came over for an introductory visit.

A stout woman with blond hair greeted Danielle with the warmth of Kris Kringle's wife, her puffy nose and red cheeks either a testament to the cold or a bit too much blush. Danielle welcomed her inside, finding her demeanor as easy and comfortable as Layda had predicted. The woman was immediately on her knees with Monroe, talking to her as an adult, just as Danielle and Andre had done.

"I see no sense in talking down to people just because they are small," Emma explained in her moderately thick accent. "And do you mind if I speak in both English and Swiss German to Monroe?

Layda said you are already quite proficient as well."

"That would be lovely. It was what we were starting to do with her."

They spent a half an hour discussing care-taking philosophies to make sure they agreed. Emma suggested Danielle take her through the house, but Danielle told her it could wait until early January.

"Emma, I know Layda referred you to me and that the two of you are close, but I need to bring up one thing that is very important to me. Vital, in fact, to our relationship. It's confidentiality."

Emma grew very serious, reminding Danielle of the very trait revered in this culture. Secrecy. *Discretion.*

"You have my word that nothing which transpires in this home will be shared outside it," she said very formally.

"Thank you," Danielle replied, graciously. "Of course, you are welcome to tell any story about Monroe where she is reflected in a good light," she said, winking to let Emma know that she wasn't without a sense of humor.

They agreed on her wages and schedule, with Emma offering up an extra weekend or two a month as necessary.

"I've done that for my nieces and nephews on occasion." She explained that her husband, a pilot, had long stints overseas, leaving her alone for two weeks at a time. "I'd really rather be busy with a lovely child than be at home watching cooking shows." Danielle appreciated the offer and flexibility in her schedule. She also agreed with Emma's suggestion to have a few afternoons together, with Emma visiting while Danielle was at home. "That way you can correct me if I'm doing something not in line with your style. And then perhaps you can be gone for a half a day once or twice, then a few full days before I come on board full time."

Danielle felt Emma's entry in to her life was a gift from heaven.

Layda called her the day after returning from Spain, inviting her and Monroe over for dinner the following night. Danielle offered to bring a salad or dessert, and Layda took her up on both.

"I'll eat the greens and Georgy your sweets so we'll both be happy."

By then, Emma had been to the house three times. During each visit, Danielle increased the hours away from home until she built up to a full day. Danielle thought Monroe seemed happy and unaffected.

For dinner with Andre's parents, Danielle chose cashmere bottoms and an oversized matching top, both a deep ocean blue and comfortable. She dressed Monroe in a leopard print set of pants and sweater she'd purchased in Prague, the coordinated hat fashionably drooped to the side. Over this, she placed Monroe inside a one-piece shearling body suit, another gift from Johanne. He'd proactively stated he had no one else to spend his money so it might as well be her daughter.

She arrived at five and was greeted by Georgy with a big hug. "Hello dear."

"You took off another five pounds with that," she teased, eliciting a good-natured scowl as he gave her a fatherly inspection.

"We're going to work on getting you back up to a healthy weight."

"I've been trying hard," Danielle said a bit defensively. Her appetite was still low, but she wasn't worried about it. She never felt faint or tired, so her body must be getting what it required. "I need to go get the food I brought, including a pie, which I'll eat plenty of tonight, thank you very much."

Layda had her apron on and stood behind the expansive

counter, removing the foil on some type of casserole. Danielle placed the salad and pumpkin pie on the counter. For a couple worth as much as the Metterlen's, she had initially found it odd that they had so few helpers around the house. Andre told her his mother liked the domain of her kitchen without interference and Georgy valued his privacy. The few housekeepers they had moved almost ghostlike between rooms and stayed out of the kitchen.

Layda wiped her hands. "Georgy, show Danielle our surprise." Georgy still had Monroe in his arms as he gestured for Danielle to follow him to the sun room. On the floor was a fully assembled walker, the outer rim round and filled with assorted bars and handles that bounced, pulled and bent in all directions.

"The rollers are multi-directional," Georgy pointed out proudly. It was the highest tech mobile walker she'd ever seen. Georgy had sounded so much like Andre that she envisioned him standing before her, explaining it with the same inflections and pride. Gratitude and love hit her heart hard, the emotional punch something she'd refused to feel for many weeks.

Refused or didn't feel at all?

"Here, let's try this out," she said with determination. She gently set Monroe inside the walker, knowing it was a little big. She tucked Monroe's small blanket behind her back, providing her a bit more support and gave the roller a slight nudge. "Go!" Danielle encouraged. It wasn't long before Monroe had her feet on the ground, standing up and then down. Soon after, she was pushing forward, the walker moving in this direction then that.

"She may not want to ever leave," Danielle observed.

"Yes, she will. We bought another one for your home."

They aided Monroe down the hallway and back into the kitchen. "She's very proud of her new toy," Danielle told Layda, thanking her as well.

Over a dinner of meat stew and homemade rye bread, they talked about their trips and the upcoming holiday season. Danielle had been prepping for this part of the conversation and shared her experience about meeting with and hiring Emma. She reiterated Layda wasn't being displaced but preserved as a fun-loving grandma.

"I want you to be excited about seeing Monroe and not see it as a job, which I'm afraid it would become very soon."

Layda nodded in understanding and what Danielle interpreted as a bit of relief, glancing at Georgy.

"And to that end we have another surprise to show you after dessert," Georgy said mysteriously.

Danielle made short work of her pie, including the heaping load of whipped cream, and was then led upstairs. She'd never been to the second floor of the large home, and it felt like it was a hotel with hallways stretching down and around corners at either side. Near the end of one of the wings, Georgy paused at a door that had a pink M on the front.

Danielle was quiet as Layda opened the door. "We created this for Monroe, for when she's here." She invited Danielle to step inside the large room. It was a nursery completely outfitted with a crib, twin bed with canopy, rocking chair, changing table and a bookcase filled with books, all in an off-white elegant color with hand-painted fairies in a mystical wonderland. It looked like a set replicated from a movie.

"And this is for you," Layda said quietly, opening a connecting bathroom that led to another room, this one for a female adult. It was larger, with a dresser, wardrobe and sitting area, along with a leather-topped desk. The bed was a king size piece of artwork, little pieces of different wood embedded in the headboard to create a mosaic.

Georgy came to her side. "We thought that sometimes you may not want to be at home alone, or as time goes on, you may want to go out at nights or on trips by yourself. Monroe can stay here with us, and you can come and go as you please, no strings attached and no judgments. We love you as our daughter."

At that, Danielle closed her eyes, felt arms around her, and sobbed.

CHAPTER 22

Thanksgiving afternoon, as Danielle picked out the overnight items for herself and Monroe, she couldn't stop thinking of Andre.

Ten weeks now. Two months and two weeks. I never thought I'd make it this far.

And yet…the days *had* gotten easier. Her routine, if she could call it that, was now her new normal. Monroe woke, ate, scooted around, doing all the things a child her age does without the sobbing and mood swings of a child who truly knew about the loss of her father.

At David's recommendation, Danielle read several books on the stages of grief. Her conclusion was that her experience was different from "the norm." She'd felt shock, but there was no denial. She certainly didn't blame Andre or feel anger towards him. Lani had initially pressed her about that, sure Danielle would be angry he went riding on his bike at all. Danielle told her it simply wasn't there. Andre was cautious, loved her and wouldn't have knowingly put himself in danger. His death had happened, it was tragic, and she acknowledged some days were better than others, often recalling a line her father had said after her mother died. "The void left by the death of a loved one is acknowledged and respected, but never filled. One doesn't even need to try."

If she had one nagging emotion, it was guilt. She still felt partially responsible for his death because she suggested he ride his bike that day. Lani knew she harbored this feeling like a dead weight at the bottom of the ocean and counseled Danielle to stay away from the 'guilt zone,' as she thought of it.

As Danielle stopped at a light, her thoughts drifted from the past to the future and finding a new home. One that she could make hers without feeling the sadness associated with Andre in every room.

"One with you, little girl," Danielle said out loud, looking at Monroe in the rearview mirror.

Ten minutes later, Monroe was in Layda's arms. "You look very nice," Layda told her.

"Thank you. Make-up works wonders on dark circles. I'm not sure how long I'm going to stay tonight though," she continued. "It depends on the load and number of wait staff."

"As long as you want and need to," Layda said affectionately. Danielle gave her a kiss and left.

The parking at Stars & Stripes was so difficult she went back home, parked and took the metro downtown. All the while, she wondered if it were possible she was already moving towards the last stage of grief, the "meaningful life," part where she could engage in "normal activities" like work, hobbies and relationships.

My life does have meaning. And I'm guiding it like the captain of a boat, not wandering rudderless. If she had one lingering fear, it was that she had passed through the phases too quickly, and somehow, that meant she wasn't as attached to Andre as she should have been.

As attached as eight months of living together allowed, she thought.

At the restaurant, Danielle went through the back door near the kitchen. Renaldo was manning the main preparation area with Lani overseeing the grill and ovens.

"Impressive," Danielle whispered in Lani's ear, causing her to jump.

"Dog!" Lani hissed, her smile broad as she kissed Danielle on the cheek. "Ivan told me you weren't working tonight."

"I haven't worked since before the baby was born, but I remembered last year and…well, if you need me, I'm here. Otherwise I'm going to sit at the bar."

Lani gave her an inquisitive look. "Did you have a chance to read my email this morning? And? What do you think?"

"That you're crazy, but I love you."

Lani winked. "Normal for me then. Go eat some of my marvelous food and relax. We can talk later."

Danielle was happy to delay the conversation Lani wanted to have, one that included more details on Max and her plans for Stephen, the restaurant, and her need for more money. She rounded the corner and instantly knew avoidance was not to be had.

"Happy Thanksgiving gentleman," she said, touching Max on the shoulder as she walked by, taking the only available seat, which was in between him and Lars.

"And to you," said Max.

"Have you been coming here a lot too?" she asked Lars, "or did I just catch you on the busiest night of the year?"

"More so recently," he answered, the response making her want to ask additional questions. Instead, she casually peered at his plate. It was a small dish appetizer of salmon with chives and asparagus, the clump of crab legs in the center drenched in hollandaise sauce.

"That looks amazing."

"It is. Have some. I intend on having dessert." Lars glanced at her face and frowned slightly. "And some extra hollandaise if you'd like."

Danielle lowered one of her eyes in a half-frown. "Don't you start on me, too."

"Monroe needs a healthy mother, not just one who looks good."

Danielle flipped open a menu, appreciative of the flattering comment. "Max, what have you been up to? I understand you are seriously considering entering the restaurant business."

"If you'll have me."

She scoffed. "I'm the least of your concerns. A chef, management and money are much higher on the list." Paul put a plate in front of Max who thanked him.

"How hard can it be?" he asked. "A great menu, good location, funding enough to make it through to the profitable stage."

Danielle continued looking at the menu, her smile placid. If it was that simple, everyone would be doing it.

"Well, I suppose you have only one option," she said, placing the menu on the counter. "Learn all you can from Stephen and ensure Renaldo is highly trained before you take Lani away, because if you are the cause of this restaurant going down, no amount of running will save you from my wrath."

Max looked momentarily stunned with her declaration and she felt Lars' eyes on hers. "I'm a pretty good businessman," Max said, somewhat defensively. "I definitely won't screw this up."

"Good, because I've got five hundred grand in Stars & Stripes which I don't want lost."

"Five hundred? I thought it was only two-fifty." That gave her pause. Lani had told him the amount, which broke the agreement's confidentiality plus it was uncool.

"Andre and I went in half and half, but his portion is now Monroe's. As the trustee for her portion, it's still five hundred."

"Would you be interested in selling it?" Danielle didn't know whether to smack him, which was her initial feeling, or laugh at the absurdity of his uncouth question.

"Ever the enterprising investor," Danielle said, laughing away the comment. "The good news is we have all night to talk about it, but first, I'm hungry." She turned to Lars. "What's with the scalloped potatoes. That's supposed to be saved for New Year's Eve."

"Or Easter," he smoothly answered, as though he'd not heard her conversation with Max. "But in New York, anything goes."

"You spent time in New York?" Max asked Lars, leaning around Danielle. She motioned for Paul and ordered the traditional turkey dinner as the two men engaged in a discussion about Lars' stint in the US.

Lars asked for a small plate, depositing a third of his appetizers on it, pushing it in front her.

"Boss' orders," he said, his voice a moderate imitation of the tone he used at the office.

"I think he means it," Max said, tilting his chin up as he took a drink.

"How's the client transition going?" she asked Lars. "I understand a few left. I'm sorry."

Her comment elicited a frown, though his eyes were still bright. "According to my calendar, it's not the middle of January yet."

She rolled her eyes with exaggeration. "And I can't even ask about work?" she grumped, making him chuckle. "Fine. Your outfit. The tie. Has it come back on permanently? What happened?"

"I have a lot of meetings that required something more than a button-down shirt."

"You mean the clients left and you are trying to get them back with your ties?" She laughed and he grinned.

"You aren't that far off," he said. "I'm of the belief that informality breeds complacency. With clients leaving, that's not a trait I want much of at the office."

"I see," was what she said, but she wondered if he guessed she'd be here tonight and wore a tie because they both knew of her affinity for the look.

No. That was not on his mind. She was sure.

"I'm sorry about the clients, Lars."

"We will survive something as minor as a few clients defecting. You won't if your weight loss continues. Well? Do you do it yourself or shall Max and I force feed you?" Lars had said the last words loudly enough for Max to lean forward.

"I'll take her arms, you shovel and we'll get Paul to pour drinks down her mouth."

Danielle glanced at all three men, who were at least half-serious and muttered. "Fine, okay," she said, shoveling an overfull helping of salmon on her fork.

"And no more business," interjected Max. "Can we talk turkey please, as in, why is this meal such a big deal to Americans?" Danielle's mouth was full and her eyes were wide as she tried to keep her food in while she laughed.

"Allow me," Lars said with a bit of gallantry. Danielle ate as he gave an accurate historical account of pilgrims, Indians, starvation and the first dinner the two had shared, thereby saving the European immigrants and cementing a relationship between the two cultures, at least for a time. When Lars got to the subject of the actual food, like the cornbread stuffing, Danielle rejoined the conversation, which devolved into the types of bread stuffing and myriad ways to cook a turkey.

"This is a lot of detail for a dead bird," Max quipped.

Danielle observed Max with interest. He seemed to have a watchful eye on every aspect of the room, as if he were mentally calculating all that had to be managed. Perhaps he was more serious than she'd originally given him credit, and she shouldn't be so resistant to the notion of Lani branching out.

The meal was done and dessert ordered when Max wiped his mouth.

"I'm going to go in the back for a bit to check out the kitchen," he said. "Paul, you can give my seat away if someone else wants it. It's nice to see you doing so well, Danielle." He kissed her cheek, shook Lars' hand and went to the back of the restaurant.

Lars turned to her. "I didn't mean to overhear the conversation with Max but it couldn't be helped. One observation: you aren't very good at hiding your thoughts, regardless of the words coming out of your mouth."

Danielle glanced sideways at him and spoke in a quiet tone. "I'm not sure of the timing, but at some point after Andre's death, Lani said Max approached herself and Stephen about being involved and it has all evolved into Lani wanting a second location."

Lars slowed his cutting to precise, measured slices of meat. "Max could be a decent investment partner. Perhaps Andre's death has shifted his priorities."

They were silent for a few more moments as Paul set homemade pecan pie with vanilla bean ice cream.

"Something else on your mind?" Lars asked. Danielle glanced around, keeping her eye out for both Stephen and Max.

"Since you heard what I said, I was right wasn't I? It's Monroe's now, no one else's."

"Correct. I suppose it could be argued that the investment could revert to Georgy and Layda, but I think they'd push it back to Monroe in to a trust, with you as the executor and guardian until she is of age. All the profits since his death should be going in to that trust as well. Of course, you could sell that portion for a profit, put that in a safe place, earn interest or invest in something else you support. It would spread your risk and leave you less dependent on a restaurant that appears to be going through some serious professional changes."

Danielle went quiet, touching his arm lightly, the expression of utter appreciation. "You are invaluable to me, do you know that?"

"Yes," he replied, matching her gaze. "I'm an objective sounding board, like an attorney without the premium."

"No, you're more like my priest. A free, confidential outlet."

This elicited a mild chuckle. "First I was a personal trainer and now I'm a priest. A dubious path forward. I will echo Max's comments. You do seem to be doing well."

"I've had some help along the way, first with you and your helpful advice and most recently, Layda and Georgy." Danielle told him about the rooms they created. Danielle had never heard Lars utter the word 'wow,' but if his expression could have manifested itself in a verbal word, that would have been it. "They wanted Monroe to be comfortable when they watched her, and for me, in case I wanted company or if I wanted to be gone overnight."

Lars gazed at her inquisitively. "Will you actually do that?"

"Tonight was supposed to be my first night staying there, but with Max gone and you probably leaving soon, I think I'll go back early."

Lars pointed his fork to the clock. "I'll tell you what. I'll keep you company until the Christmas music comes on." When Danielle started to interject, he stopped her with a look. "I've known Layda a long time. I bet she'd love to have Monroe to herself as long as possible." She considered his statement for a moment.

"I'll make you a deal," she started. "I'll stay if you promise to catch me up to speed on what's really happening at the office, within the bounds of propriety of course." It was a safe and interesting subject that they both shared. "Can you do that?"

"Deal." Was it his tone or look or smile, she would later wonder to herself, that gave a lift to her mood, like a bird taking its first flight of the morning? The combination of the senses, she would determine, all communicated he was where he wanted to be, with the person he wanted to be with.

And that person was her.

At one twenty in the morning, Danielle quietly unlocked the back door and made her way through the massive home. Upstairs, she checked on Monroe, who was on her back, both arms splayed out over her head, her mouth slightly open. Danielle pulled the blanket up to her chest and went to the bathroom. Her eyes were red, her lipstick faded and her cheeks sallow. Perhaps it was time to start taking some vitamins or getting more sleep.

Some color won't hurt, she thought, thinking of her final trip before starting work. It would take fifteen hours to fly direct to Hawaii for three weeks with Monroe. Strange how her life was evolving. Not what she imagined, but then, nothing in her life had turned out as she'd planned. Nothing, except her career. She wondered if that would change as well.

CHAPTER 23

"Welcome," greeted the young woman dressed in white slacks and a short sleeve button-down shirt as she placed a lei around Danielle's neck. "Please watch your step." The woman held Danielle's arm as she descended into the small boat. It was more of a ferry, attached to tracks below the water's surface. Monroe squirmed on her lap. She was overtired from the flight, unable to sleep and upset from her ears popping on the take-off and landing. Then just when she was dozing off, it was time to exit from the plane. The cab ride over was exhausting, and by the time she reached the hotel room, all Danielle wanted to do was take a nap.

She fed Monroe, drew the curtains, put Monroe in her portable crib and starting dozing before her daughter had stopped crying. Eventually the wailing ceased, and two blissful hours later, Danielle woke. Quietly, she slid open the door to the balcony and sat down in the chaise lounge, closing her eyes, listening to the sounds of the waves on the shore.

The Waikoloa Hilton on the island of Kona was one more recommendation from Lars. He'd said it was a diversified and fun resort, with areas for adults, children and families. The far end of the resort was for adults only, the protected cabanas guaranteeing privacy. Nearer the main buildings was the family area with rock slides into shallow pools and multi-level decks affording unobstructed views of the inlet where one could watch the wild turtles swim into the naturally protected bay. In was in the center of the resort, just past the outdoor Japanese restaurant surrounded by a moat stocked with enormous Koi fish.

Danielle picked up the resort map and had just figured out her plan when Monroe stirred. She slathered herself and Monroe with sunblock, placed the hats, books and food in her bag, attached it to the stroller and headed out to the pool. She stopped by the dolphin training area but Monroe was too young to appreciate the jumping creatures. Then she saw the beach where turtles swam just below the surface and watched as adults and children picked leaves and fed the tame animals. Ordering French fries and a burger to go, she finally made it to the main pool area, thinking it was even better than what Lars had described. Overhead were wood and rope paths reminiscent of Robinson Crusoe, the pools below appearing to be carved out of sheer rock with sandy beaches on the sides for wading and playing.

For three days, Danielle spent her time in the same area, moving herself and Monroe between the wading pool, hot tub, café and sandy beach. When Monroe fussed, Danielle put her in the stroller, laid the back down and walked her until she fell asleep before returning to their spot. Several times, Monroe closed her eyes on her own while on Danielle's lap. During those precious moments, she too fell asleep, absorbing the heat, lulled into relaxation by the ambient noise of the ocean.

The fourth day, Danielle was a third of the way into her book when a voice spoke above her.

"Is this seat taken?" She looked up to see a man in his early forties with his hand on the chair beside her.

"No, not at all." Drink in hand, he sat down, stretching out his long, tan legs. She continued to look at the page in her book, not reading the words.

A suntanned hand swept part of his wet, dark hair back from

his face and he smiled. "Been here long?" he asked.

"A few days." She strategically used her right hand to move back a piece of hair behind her left ear. He'd see it and leave.

The man's eyes went to the ring and...he didn't blink. *Of course.* It was on the wrong finger, doing her no good.

"Where are you from?"

"Zurich, at present."

"As in, Switzerland?" Danielle nodded, her thin smile feeling stretched. "What took you there? Work? Romance?"

"That would be a long way to go for romance," she laughed. "It was work."

"Tell me about it. Do you like it? What are the people like?"

Danielle felt like she was in the cross-hairs of the real world. A nice-looking man who was working hard to start up...something. She'd never felt so overtly un-chatty in her life but wasn't the kind of person to just get up and walk away.

"Yes, I like the work very much and the people are wonderful."

"I'm Justin."

"Hi, Justin," she said, smiling once, glad her glasses were still on. "Danielle."

"Not much into talking, are you?"

Danielle smiled apologetically. "I'm sorry. I've just been through a really hard time." She watched Justin's facial expression, his glance at the stroller then down to the fourth finger on her left hand.

"Divorce?" he asked, the question filled with a combination of understanding and pragmatism.

"No," she answered. "Death." His head tilted slightly, as though he hadn't heard her, but then he absorbed what she'd said.

Now he's wondering what to do with that information.

"I'm divorced. Two kids, a boy and a girl, nine and twelve. They are with their mother up at the Four Seasons, twenty minutes away or so. We swap the kids during the day, then every other night have a family dinner together." Danielle imagined the Four Seasons being very quiet, no waterslides or turtles.

"I bet you have more fun here."

His freckled lips drew up in a grin. "Better believe it." Justin began listing his favorite things to do with his children but she wasn't even listening. She observed Monroe, feeling a rush of loss moving up, through her chest like a stream that has reversed course due to an earthquake. At one point, he stopped and turned his upper body to her.

"Philly is a long way from here," he told her, misinterpreting her silence. "I don't even know your last name." Danielle forced her back straight and he noticed. "I can see how well that came across. You're not ready, are you?"

She grimaced. "My fiancé was killed seven days before we were to be married. That little girl is our daughter." Justin's look of shock was accompanied with compassion, and she continued. For the first time, she spoke of the incident from the day he was killed to the present. When she expected tears, none came, and it was oddly objective, like a conversation you have with the stranger sitting next to you on a plane.

"That's unreal," he observed, his comment blessedly lacking emotion. Here, with a stranger, she had the objectivity of a person who was untouched by her reality, and it was freeing.

"There's more," she said. This time, she told Justin about Lars without using his name. "The irony was that both of us were engaged to be married, and now only one will be going through with it."

"And you are planning to go back to work with this man, he'll get married and you'll just go on as a single woman," Justin summarized. "May I make a suggestion?" he asked, dropping his legs over either side of the chaise, turning his back to the sun. "If you don't want the men hitting on you, move the ring on your right hand to your left." The comment wasn't what she had been expecting.

Danielle stretched out the fingers on her right hand, the diamonds of the eternity band glittering in the sun. "You think?"

"Given all that you told me, I think that's where the ring belonged in the first place. Don't you?"

CHAPTER 24

When she'd been in Hawaii five days, Danielle sent Lars a text.

The place is great. You were right. Again. Thanks

Danielle and Justin had a few other conversations until he left, mostly about him, his ex-wife and his children. Their interactions lacked a romantic vibe, and she got the feeling he liked the companionship of a woman without the pressure of a climactic ending. One afternoon, her sixth day there, and his last, they got into the deterioration of his marriage and how it all ended.

"I'm not into shopping and parties," he said rather flippantly. "She likes both."

"What would she say about you?"

He smirked. "That I work too much and that I'm into my own things."

"Are you?"

"Yeah. I like scuba diving and road biking. Both solitary and intense."

Danielle fiddled with the pages of her magazine. "I have a question, if you don't mind. If she would have compromised on some of her issues that were a big deal to you, even a little, would you have still gone through with the divorce?"

Justin whistled, squinting in the sunlight, then finally made eye contact. "No. Absolutely not. I loved her more than any other woman. Still do, but to be fair and honest, I wasn't willing to bend on my issues. Not on the things that bugged her the most."

"Do you regret it?"

"If anyone but you asked me, I'd say yeah, for the kids. But with a relative stranger, I will say that's a lie. I regret it for me. I should have been less stubborn. Maybe that would have gotten her to ease up. Which person should have gone first is anyone's guess. And now, we are two years beyond it, and things are working out pretty well. We had a really rough first year or two during the 'transition,'" he put it in air quotes. "The kids' grades dropped, my son got quiet then needy and finally angry. But," he said, taking another drink, "we got out of one another's way enough to make it work so we could still do family things, like this. We don't have to sleep in the same room to get what we both want, and the kids aren't jerked around."

"It sounds good," she said absently, the notion of having any time at all with a husband and children making her envious, an emotion she hadn't felt since Andre's death.

"It's the best of the worst," he continued, not noticing her silence. "She didn't want to change and neither did I."

Change is hard, she thought. Few of us do it willingly.

One evening after she'd put Monroe in her portable crib, she turned out the lights then went on the veranda with her laptop. Her real estate agent had forwarded four properties that looked promising, but only one near Georgy and Layda, and it was the most expensive of the group. Other, larger homes outside the city were available at a much lower price. She thought back to Max's words on the boat: getting married, moving to the suburbs, commuting back and forth. She wanted another viewpoint.

She looked at her watch. It was seven-thirty in the morning Zurich time. She debated if it was better to call Lars at the office or wait until after work.

A voice whispered in her ear. *He'll pick up for me no matter what time it is.*

On the second ring, Lars answered. "Greetings from Zurich."

"And from Kona, one of your better recommendations."

"Since I imagine you by the pool, sunglasses on and a big blue hat, drinking some non-alcoholic concoction, this must be important."

"I just need…well, more advice."

"I'm ready," he said with alacrity. "What's the subject this time?"

"*This time*," she said with a smile, "it's about homes." Danielle related all she'd learned with the specific intent of understanding commuting times, traffic, bad weather and anything else she might have missed.

"What about schools?"

"What schools? What do you mean?"

"Schools for Monroe. In two years or so, she will actually be attending one, so unless you intend on homeschooling so that's an important factor in your decision."

"I haven't even thought about it," she admitted.

"It's not a big of concern if you are going to rent, because you have the flexibility to move in a few years. But I'm assuming you don't want to move again in two years."

"No, not at all." Danielle focused on the waves washing to shore as she listened to Lars talk about what he knew, sharing all his knowledge was through his friends with children.

"The home you are in presently is centrally located to many of the best schools in town."

"What about outside of town? I could commute in."

"Yes, but why would you want to?"

"I grew up outside town and liked being able to ride bikes and be free. It was fun for me."

"By bike riding, you mean riding motorcycles?"

"Yes, I told you about riding dirt bikes."

"I do," his words stiff. "Outside of town is fine," he started again, "but it will require you to drive in, find a place to park, then take the metro to wherever it is you want to go. Alternatively, you will need to drop Monroe off at her school, then park, then take the metro. Regardless, you will probably add another forty-five minutes or so to your commute each way."

"Are you okay?" Danielle asked, stopping him. "Your voice changed."

"The notion of you on a motorcycle doesn't make me happy, for obvious reasons, even though it's not my life or my decision."

What an idiot I am. "Lars, I have no intention of getting on a motorcycle in the near future or teaching Monroe to ride. Continue, back to the house topic. Given the commute, what would you do?"

"Stay put."

"Really?"

"You have no incentive to leave."

"But Lars, I can't stay there. Everything I touch and look at is hard, it's the ever present reminder of what I don't have."

"I see the point, but it's not logical."

Danielle felt irritated she was having to justify why she wanted to leave the home she'd shared with Andre. Of all people, she would have expected Lars to be on board.

"Not to be rude, but you don't know what this is like. I mean, it was never even my home to begin with. All I brought with me to this house were my clothes and holiday items."

"You didn't decorate it?"

"No, Andre had it all done months before I moved in. I never had the need or chance to acquire anything with personal meaning."

A pause preceded his words. "That does change the equation. It's no wonder you aren't attached to it. Let's go through the homes you like best then."

Danielle looked at her watch. "How about another time? I know you've got the staff meeting coming up."

"I've already sent a note to Ulrich," he said, his tone crisp. "He'll handle it. Now tell me those addresses."

Danielle gave him the information and heard the tapping of keys. One by one, Lars listed the pros and cons of the neighborhood and location relative to the schools first, then the commute and neighborhood. He also brought up the direction each home faced, since none were likely to be air-conditioned. In the end, three made the list, one didn't.

"If these don't work, let me know as soon as you can. Homes are always coming up on the market, and those in my network are always changing things around."

"Lars," she said cautiously. "It's Christmas, and I expect you will be going to your place in the mountains over the holiday. Even though I no longer have a romantic life, you do, and I want you to know that I'm sensitive to it, in the most appropriate, caring type of way."

"I appreciate that, but you don't need to worry. That weekend I will be ice climbing. It's a relatively solitary activity."

"No family or anything on Christmas? That sounds…" lonely, she thought, but changed her words, "slightly scary." She remembered the time when he entered the office with a bandage over his eyebrow. "Can't you find a hobby that doesn't require you dangling from a rope a hundred feet up?"

"This particular one is indoors on a man-made ice wall. Still dangling but it's a controlled environment."

Danielle had never heard of such a thing. "Still, there is no way

I'm going to call you while you are skiing or at your chalet. I'll just hold off until I see you in the office."

"Danielle, at the moment, I enjoy our periodic interactions, and the outreach you make to me. Furthermore, at some point, I too, may need insight." She felt a heat under her skin, and it was the kind of warmth she'd not experienced for a very long time.

"You?" she teased, thinking of him in his expansive corner office, a smile on his face, his dark, wavy hair with a curl flipped over just above his forehead.

"Even me. So, let me handle the decision to take your calls, and in the meantime, I'm not going to break my promise to pick up the phone."

"Fair enough," Danielle said, placing her palm to her cheek to cool it down. He was going to be alone for Christmas, at his chalet outside St. Moritz. It was romantic, beautiful, and not her reality at all. It probably never would be again, no matter how good a friend Lars was to her. "I promise to call if I need more advice."

"You do that. Have a Merry Christmas."

"You too."

After the phone call ended, Danielle sat staring at the ocean for a very long time.

At the moment...the phrase lingered in her mind. If she were honest with herself, she wished *at that moment* he wasn't engaged, and that she was with him, at his home in Zermatt, playing the black grand piano he'd engraved with her initials, drinking a cup of decadent hot chocolate. Monroe would be in one of the bedrooms, sleeping, or in town with her grandparents.

Ridiculous. He was no longer a part of her journey and letting her fanciful imagination run riot wasn't going to help. *He was and is my friend. My dear, handsome, engaged friend.*

CHAPTER 25

"Merry Christmas!" Layda exclaimed, clapping her hands lightly. Wearing a satin plaid print skirt with a black angora sweater, the thin, red velvet scarf draping around her neck, she was the epitome of class, elegant but not ostentatious. Georgy sat in a deep brown leather chair, nearly identical to the color of his fuzzy, mohair sweater. His eyes were brighter than Danielle had seen in months, the tan of his recent trip to Spain still present.

Monroe clapped her hands in response, her four-tooth smile wide and bright. She'd been sitting up but immediately dropped to the floor and raced over to Grandma, who scooped Monroe up, smothering her with kisses.

The great living room was filled with Layda's collection of nativity scenes purchased from around the world. One made from coke bottle caps she'd found in Africa, another made in the fourteenth century from Sweden. One from the West Indies featuring a black baby Jesus and wise men. In the corner stood a fourteen foot Christmas tree, the largest Danielle had ever seen.

Danielle walked over to the credenza picking up a hand-carved wooden baby Jesus. "It must have taken you years to find these ornaments."

"We've lived a lot of years," Georgy pointed out.

Layda gave him a pleasant reprimand of a look. "Instead of buying a shirt or trinket when we travel, we picked up a new ornament. Andre would select each one so carefully and choose just the right spot on the tree." Layda's mouth stayed in a happy smile as she spoke of Andre. "If you don't mind, we'd like to continue this tradition with Monroe."

"That would be lovely," Danielle said, a spike of sadness moved up her throat and rested on her tongue, where she held it. "We didn't have any traditions started, and I don't have many ornaments. This can give us both."

A moment followed, the three adults all focusing intently on the little hands and drooling mouth in front of them. It was Georgy who spoke first.

"Tell us about your latest trip. How was it?" Danielle took a quick breath and described the island, the resort and the turtles in detail.

"Had you been there before?" asked Layda.

"No, I'd never been to any of the Hawaiian Islands at all. Lars, in his great effort to keep me away from the office, suggested it."

Layda led them into the kitchen where Danielle fed Monroe, then held her as she fell asleep in her arms, not waking as Layda put her in her crib.

The three of them sat down to enjoy a meal together.

"Now, tell me Danielle," Georgy began as he dished a large spoon full of potatoes au gratin on his plate. "Have you come to any conclusions regarding next year?"

"Well, my favorite father-in-law," she began with a sly look. "I do have a few things to share."

Georgy guffawed. "Favorite father-in-law. I like that."

"Yes, because I have had so many, and you need to know that you are first in line."

"Technically, I'm only Monroe's grandfather."

"Yeah, well, I've never been much to worry about paperwork, have I?" Georgy laughed, but she could tell her words had touched him. A look to Layda confirmed her guess. "And you, are forever going to be my mother-in-law."

"Sweetheart, you really don't have to do that. It wouldn't be right if…. you know, you get married in the future."

Danielle scowled. "My future is going to include you as my in-laws, no matter what happens. And trust me, after what I've been through, I'm not going to involve myself with a man who won't accept you as part of my family."

"Now that we have that settled," Georgy pronounced. "You may proceed."

"I've found several homes, not far from here that I can afford and are perfectly situated for Monroe's schools." Layda was quiet and Georgy looked as though the information didn't surprise him. "Did you know I've been looking?"

"Many people knew Andre and are familiar with your name."

"I'm sorry," she said quietly, feeling as though she'd been dishonest.

It was Layda who responded. "You have a right to privacy. We are not here to tell you how to run your life, but to simply enjoy being in it."

"Continue. Tell us more," Georgy said, between bites. "I want to offer my opinion even if you don't ask."

Danielle laughed heartily, releasing the anxiety she felt at the subject. Layda was a source of neighborhood gossip, identifying which of the prominent families lived close by, or if certain streets were known to have one or more rental properties that attracted transients or out of town renters. Georgy helpfully suggested testing the satellite and internet, since many of the homes along certain ridges were known to receive terrible internet connection.

"And work?" Georgy asked. "You are positive you don't want to come work with me as my personal advisor and for our family network? You could legitimately make millions of dollars a year in fees, all the while bringing us that much more."

Danielle was flattered he continued to bring up a potential role with her in his business and found it humorous he continued to ignore her refusals. "Georgy, you know I'd require a broker who would sponsor me and that takes months to set up."

"I could find a firm who would sponsor you, as long as you split fees, but I guarantee you'd be taking home a larger percentage than you are now."

She tried another tack. "Georgy, even if I had a broker and was prepared to take on the responsibility of managing your family's money, I couldn't drop MRD, not after all the considerations the firm has given me."

Georgy slowed his chewing, speaking only after he'd taken a drink. The last point was the most meaningful to his family, and it was not lost on him. "I respect that."

"There is one thing I have to mention, if you don't mind," Layda began.

"Please, Layda. There is nothing I'm uncomfortable with you asking."

"Well, the ring you have on your left finger. It used to be on your right hand. Does that mean something?" Danielle was appalled at her lapse in judgment. She'd gotten so used to wearing it on her left hand for three weeks in Hawaii, it had become a part of her.

"I'm so sorry," she said, looking down, feeling its presence required an explanation. "During my trip in Hawaii, a man started making conversation. Since I wasn't interested in him, he suggested I put it on my left hand to ward off romantic possibilities." She lifted it up. "To American men, having a ring on the fourth finger of your left hand is like kryptonite to Superman."

Danielle started to remove it but Layda put up her hand. "Leave it," she said. "I have no problem with it on that hand. It makes perfect sense to me."

"You're sure?" Layda nodded, and Georgy looked positively elated. Not long after, they said their goodnights.

Christmas Eve, at my in-law's home. And the ring Lars gave me on my left hand. Where it should be, Justin said.

Danielle lay on her side, watching the snow fall. It was early still, not even ten pm. She'd been planning on raising two other topics with Georgy and Layda, both involving Andre. Ultimately, she decided against it, not wanting to offend or insult either one of them. At the same time, she needed objective, impartial feedback. On each topic, Lani couldn't be either. That left only one person.

No. Not tonight. The day after Christmas will be soon enough. *But then again, he said let him worry about his ability to take my call.*

Ten thirty. Hmm. She delayed, instead, phoning Lani. Danielle answered Lani's questions about her trip, making small talk when her mind was on Lars.

"What's the latest with Max and investing?"

"Max would invest up to fifty percent in the new business, exactly what Andre did."

"Two-hundred and fifty thousand? That's wonderful." Danielle feigned enthusiasm.

"Plus, he wants to get it done before the New Year."

"But where does that leave you with Stephen? Did you have the conversation about adjusting the contract?"

"Yeah. That didn't go so great, but we are still working on it. There is a problem though." Only one? thought Danielle. "It's not liquid. You and Andre put in actual cash. Our fifty percent is on paper. It's worth something only if we sell it."

Danielle was stymied. "Who do you sell it to?"

145

"You?"

"Me?"

"Sure. You have the money and could then be in partnership with Stephen, while I could get my money out and move on."

Danielle had a surreal moment, like she was a cameraman filming a reality television show; the words and scenes were pre-scripted to heighten the drama and maximize the shock factor.

"Lani, with a potential move, hiring a babysitter and going back to work, taking money from what is now my only savings account for me and Monroe and putting it into a new investment is nowhere on my radar. No investing is, actually."

"Not even for a friend?" Danielle literally moved the phone from her ear and stared at it.

"Lani, let me repeat. Single mother. Daughter. No investments. In fact, I have a bit of a mess on my hands because Andre didn't leave a will, I have other things to figure out that take priority. I hope you understand," she added.

"Well, think on it," Lani said, as though she'd heard not a word Danielle had said.

Once the line went dead, Danielle typed out a text.

Are you free? Lars responded within a few seconds.

Yes, need to talk?

Of course - want to wait until tomorrow? don't want to disturb

Not disturbing call when u r ready

With a much lighter conscience, she phoned him. "Merry Christmas," she said.

"Why are you semi-whispering?" Lars asked with his own mock-whisper.

"I'm here at Georgy's. Did you have a nice day?"

"It was uneventful."

"Ice climbing should be."

"Actually, I delayed it until New Year's Weekend. I had work items that needed my undivided attention, so I've been here in my apartment running spreadsheets."

A little burst of laughter escaped Danielle's mouth before she clamped it shut. "Now that is seriously sad. Are you at least in your chaise lounge with your fur covering you and your feet?"

"Close. I'm on the couch in the living room, wearing lounge wear and slippers." Danielle felt a wave of interest. "I'm ready to help you out with your next set of items."

Danielle groaned. "I'll preface this by saying I hope at some point I can add some value to your life by giving you insight or advice that's meaningful."

"I'm sure your time will come."

Danielle told Lars of Lani's desire to get rid of her portion of Stars & Stripes.

"I mentioned this before at the restaurant, but you, or Lani, for that matter, could put your investment on the open market. Open it up to the highest bidder." Danielle knew that non-public stocks were traded all the time, but had no knowledge of how it worked in the food industry. "It's no different," Lars explained. "A third party holds the paper, they promote and sell it and you get your money. Very clean and easy, no emotional ties."

"And no one can get offended."

"Exactly. Let's say you want to sell Andre's portion, to set aside the money for Monroe when she's older. You told me the original paperwork for Andre stipulated the investor is silent, with no vote or say. Those terms will carry over to the new buyer. Now, in Lani's case, that's different. She, like you and Stephen, are all equal and active investors." Danielle could deal with that. She and Stephen would have the majority vote as long as they were aligned.

"I love it, but have no idea how to go about it. Also, I don't want everyone knowing it's up for sale."

At that, Lars, did chuckle. "This is Switzerland…" he began, and Danielle cut him off.

"Don't even say it. I already know." *Discretion*, like everything else. "Are you volunteering to help me out?"

"Of course. Forward me the paperwork. I'll contact the agency and give you the right contact to share with Lani if she wants to pursue that route."

"Okay," Danielle said, much relieved. "The last thing is a little strange," she hedged, sitting up in bed. "I have a wedding ring that has never been worn. My first thought was to offer it back to Layda and Georgy, but with all you have said about Monroe, I'm thinking of giving it to her."

"I agree with that, because it represents her father and mother, which is very special. Perhaps you raise the topic with Layda and make sure it's not a family heirloom, but I can see her wanting it for Monroe even if that is the case."

Danielle breathed out a sigh. "I hope a semblance of my functioning brain returns before I come back to work. After all you've counseled me on recently, I'm feeling a tad insecure."

"As if that word even exists in your vocabulary."

"You'd be surprised Mr. Egle. Now do you have anything I can help you with?"

"Yes, actually. How does one disinvite a person to an event?"

"That's a little vague. Can you be more specific?"

"I have a female who I invited to my rock climbing event for New Year's and I actually don't think I want her there."

"Are you talking about your fiancé?"

"Yes."

"Does she make you nervous or something?"

"Actually, rock climbing is a very concentrated sport.

148

Distractions aren't great."

"I thought a person is *supposed* to be distracted by their fiancé." She heard him clear his throat.

"One of the reasons I enjoy climbing is because it's a freeing experience; just me and the rock."

"But hasn't she come to one before now?"

"No. It being New Year's, she's wanting to make a party of it afterward." Danielle tried to ignore the little voice in her head that suggested he might be having second thoughts for reasons that had nothing to do with his fiancé or the concentration he required, and that bringing this up was his way of testing the waters with her.

"Are you opposed to the party or her being present at the party?"

"Both?" he replied, his answer a question.

Easy, she coached herself.

"How about you avoid the issue entirely by saying you aren't sure when you'll be climbing and don't want her to freeze."

"She'll be bundled up in fur, waiting in the lodge for me as she drinks expensive wine."

"Can you get sick at the last minute?"

"She'll want to take care of me."

Danielle snorted. "Then you have no choice but to resort to extreme lying, which I'm not sure I'd advocate as the starting basis for a marriage. Sans dishonesty, the only alternative left is you are totally honest with her. Tell her that's just the way you operate. She may be happy to stay home or spend time with her girlfriends."

"Why are you laughing?" he asked.

"Because despite all your relationships this is like a first date for you. And I never imagined you with a clingy-needy type of woman."

"She hasn't been all these years, but people can change."

All these years? Was the woman his past love, the one who had been married? "That begets the natural question of what would cause her to change from being non-clingy to clingy?"

"Perhaps she's feeling insecure. I don't know."

"Well, I'm sure it will be fine," Danielle said, feigning nonchalance.

"Doubtful."

Danielle wished him a safe and Happy New Year, committing to send him the restaurant investor paperwork shortly. She kept her emotions in check by doing just that. There was only one reason why a woman felt insecure about her fiancé, and Danielle tried not to dwell on that possibility and failed. Touching her face, she felt the smile, large and bright.

CHAPTER 26

Danielle met Lani and Stephen at the restaurant the following Monday before nine. Monroe was with Layda and Danielle had an hour to spare. More than enough time to talk about their future partnership, or rather, the disintegration thereof.

The heavy snow fall had slowed traffic making the steep roads from Layda's home down into the city more dangerous than she'd ever encountered. Inside, she shook her coat off, hanging it on the metal prong alongside the red and black leather booths.

"Anyone here?" she called out. The sounds of doors opening and shutting several times resonated through the room and Stephen came out from the back. He wore jeans, boots and a black turtleneck shirt.

"Who are you and where did you come from?" she asked, scoping him from top to bottom. He gave her a peck to the cheek and sat down. She eyed him with wonder. "You look great, it's just so…un-you."

"We are entering a new phase of life," he said vaguely. Danielle thought of Lars, when he changed his look, and her wondering about the influence of another woman. Could it be…? No. Never. Not with Stephen. Even though Lani had already checked out, Danielle couldn't imagine Stephen doing the same. He was too…committed.

"Whatever it is, it's sexy and I like it. How was Christmas?"

"Busy. Lucas and Christian came in quite a bit. Lars was here a few times, always eating at the bar and by himself. Max is pacing around, wanting to get started."

"Not here," Danielle muttered under her breath. Stephen gave a firm, crisp nod. They were as one on the subject.

"You seem to be doing well."

She smiled. "A tan always helps. Stephen," she said, abruptly serious. "I don't know what I thought this would be like, the months after, but it's not this."

"By 'this', you mean normal?"

"Yeah. The first week after Andre's death was crushing. Then it was weeks where I walked around in a functional daze. It's coming up on four months now, and sometimes it feels like it was yesterday. Other times, it seems like years ago or that it never happened at all."

"You didn't have the most normal courtship, on, then off, then on. Maybe what you are going through isn't as weird as you think." Danielle had run the math many times. She and Andre had only lived together about eight months. "Not to sound Swiss and overly detached, but how much can you be emotionally invested in a person you were with barely a year if you count the initial getting-to-know you-dating period?"

She didn't have a good answer that wouldn't come out as callous.

"You know the strangest part? In the beginning, I felt guilty when I didn't think about him all the time. Now, I don't think about him a lot, and when I do, I don't feel anything."

"And that troubles you?"

She nodded. "Very much so. Like I didn't love him as fully and deeply as I did—which I know I did."

"You always said he wouldn't want you to be sad and depressed."

"I know. Instead it feels..." she trailed off.

"Like you are already transitioning?"

"Exactly. Is that wrong? Does that make me a bad person?"

"Danielle, before when you and Andre broke up, you were tortured about it for several months. What was harder on your heart? Loving him and not having him, or the finality you have now?"

"Then," she said somberly, "without question." The uncertainty associated with wanting someone and not being able to be with them was far worse than a death. At least death was immediate and final, allowing for the semblance of closure.

"Thank you," she said sincerely. The subject had been increasingly weighing on her, the constant conflict of letting go and holding on fighting a fierce battle that made finding peace difficult. "Do I dare ask about you and Lani?"

Stephen shrugged. "Nothing I can say that you haven't already guessed. I'm not the one going through a success-driven crisis of life. I'm the person on the other end of the rope, who's been hanging on for dear life."

"I'm so sorry, Stephen."

"I've been coping in my own way, for better or worse."

There was nothing else she could say without completely encroaching on their personal life.

"I'll go get her," she volunteered.

Danielle rounded the corner, hearing Lani talking to someone on her phone. Danielle touched her shoulder and Lani jumped, placing her hand to her heart, rolling her eyes then lightly smacking Danielle's arm with her free hand.

"Yeah, talk later. Bye." Lani placed her cell phone in her pocket and opened the fridge. "You hungry?"

"No, not really." Lani removed a plate of food.

"Salmon spread. It's good anytime and I'm starved." Lani retrieved two bagels that she sliced in half, then added a tablespoon of capers and a huge dollop of salmon spread. "Grab two glasses will you, and the orange juice? Stephen might want some, or you." Danielle thought it obtuse to be eating during a conversation of such a heavy nature, but then Lani hadn't been sensitive to Stephen's feelings since the boat. Why she expected her to be now…it was unrealistic, and she set her mind accordingly.

At the table, Danielle accepted a half a bagel, but only got in a few bites as she answered the myriad of questions Lani had about Danielle's recent trip and her potential move. When Danielle described the bedrooms Andre's parents had decorated for Monroe and herself, Stephen whistled.

"They are amazing cool," he complimented. Danielle agreed, shifting subjects. She wanted to get this over with.

"On to the work topic," she began. "I have made a decision regarding Monroe's portion of the business." She used her matter-of-fact voice to identify the process for putting the investment up for sale. "Max is welcome to bid of course, and for that matter, you or Stephen could do the same. The system doesn't discriminate."

Lani scrunched her mouth. "Oh, well, I guess that's good."

Danielle held firm. "The three of us, as remaining owners, won't have to deal with a partner in the traditional sense. That person will be silent, because that's how Andre's paperwork was drawn up." Danielle then related they could each sell their portions. "I might be the only one left with an investment in this place!" she said, her humor forced.

"No," said Stephen. "I'm not selling, to anyone." He stared at Lani. "You will be left to do that."

Lani returned his look in equal portions. "Well then, I'll go to the next thing I want to bring up. Us all investing in a new restaurant. A second location of Stars & Stripes." Danielle had been afraid of this, but remained quiet. "Renaldo is doing great and he is confident he can handle being the lead chef here. Max would fill in Stephen's role and he'd hire and manage the operations. It's sure to be another winner. Danielle, I'd really like you to invest, even though you said you aren't interested." She looked at Stephen. "Stephen declined."

"Lani," Danielle began reasonably. "What about extending the take-out to a catering business you could oversee? That way, you'll be in the kitchen with Renaldo, controlling the menu and leveraging existing customers. We, the original investors, could go into catering, special events, home delivery, even packaging foods, all the while making money with the restaurant. Even if you two— change your situation," she said diplomatically.

Lani frowned. "My heart is really set on a second location."

"But why? We have reputation, profits and security. Why not ride this train for a few years?"

"Because the restaurant is fine, but *we*, me and Lani, are no longer working," Stephen interjected, his words leaden. Danielle's eyes moved between her friends. They were sitting apart, one with his arms folded, the other with her legs crossed, hands gripped. It was over between them.

"Wow, okay," she said, attempting to give each neutral, caring looks.

"I will reiterate I'm not investing in another restaurant," said Stephen coolly. "Max knows nothing about restaurants. Let him invest his own money."

"And you, Lani?"

"Max is a good customer and was one of Andre's best friends. Now..." Lani inhaled, lifting her chin up, focusing on the ceiling. "I'm going to open a new restaurant. I think I'll go through that agency and put my share of Stars & Stripes on the market to the highest bidder."

"Wouldn't it be wise to wait another year?" Danielle suggested. "Save up more money?"

Lani shook her head. "I don't want to be here anymore, in any capacity."

"But, Lani, even if you and Stephen aren't together, we can still be in business together."

"This phase of my life is finished. I need to do what you are doing. Make a clean start with the New Year. New restaurant, new apartment, new life."

Danielle was disheartened. "After all the three of us have been through, I'm sorry to see it dissolve so quickly and in this way."

"It's what it is Danielle," Stephen said, sounding detached and pragmatic, the perfect specimen of an emotionless Swiss man, all the things that she knew Stephen was not. "As Lani said, it's over. Let's get this done."

There was nothing more to say. It had taken less than ten minutes to witness a dozen years end right in front of her.

CHAPTER 27

On her way home, she called Lars, updating him on the situation. "That's a shame, but not unexpected. You have some homes to see this afternoon, don't you?"

"Are you clairvoyant or are you having me followed around town?" She was only half-kidding.

"Neither," he answered with a laugh. "I was the one who referred my real estate friend, remember? Tell me how it goes. I'm curious."

"Why? Taking bets on which one I'll like?"

"Maybe."

Two and a half hours later, Danielle had found it. *My new home.*

The outside was built of concrete and steel, the inside light wood, brushed metals and lots of windows, both modern and yet airy, a fortress with almost zero maintenance. It was large for a home in Zurich but small compared to the one she'd share with Andre. It had two bedrooms and a den which she intended to use as an office. It was rectangular shaped, with the master bedroom, office, kitchen and living room facing the water. A small deck off the sitting area led to fenced in lawn, another rarity for a home in the city.

It's also happy, she thought on the drive home. Happiness being defined by the cream-colored French maple floors and fur wood on the ceilings, the grains warming up the clean lines. The architect had used tan, brown and earthen tones for the rock fireplace in the living room, applying the same treatment on the outdoor fireplace that sat within the deck.

Indoor and outdoor living, she thought, knowing that at some point in her future, she'd be entertaining friends.

That brought her to reflections on the kitchen. It also made her happy. A single piece of grey, concrete-like-stone with a bright sheen to it formed an L-shape in the center of the room. White tile backsplash and matching white cabinets above juxtaposed with black cabinets below. Sleek, narrow metal fixtures with rounded edges set off the stainless-steel fridge and other European appliances. It was a small kitchen but every space was efficiently used so it didn't feel cramped at all. To her, it seemed like a mini-commercial kitchen a professional chef would use, and that fit her perfectly.

The original owner wanted to leave the furniture with the home which Danielle considered a blessing. The man had minimalist taste, using Phillip Stark designed products throughout the home, including metal stools at the kitchen counter and a matching metal dining room table and see-through ghost chairs. Custom rugs of cow-hide were dyed to match each room, protecting the floor without detracting from the view or the design. He'd even gone so far as to match the tones of the furniture with the rock, using the neutrals while bringing out the blues and red hues.

Once the tour was finished, she asked the agent to write an offer. Now, all she wanted to do was share her good news with Lars.

Back home with Monroe, the little girl crawled up and over Danielle's stomach as she lay on the living room floor, motoring towards the table, happily emitting drool. Reaching the coffee table, the little girl frowned in concentration, doing her best to pull herself up.

Her phone rang and Danielle picked it up, staring at the ceiling. "That was fast," Lars said.

She exclaimed in exasperation. "How did you know?"

"The home you selected belongs to another friend of mine. Your agent called him with the offer, and he reported back to me."

Danielle laughed. "This town is wired and you are the central operator."

"Now I'm only a mere operator? My career path continues to decline."

"True. And I'm getting tired of feeling like I'm always intruding on your personal space."

"Don't."

"Don't what? Call?"

"No, don't worry about my personal space."

"That's rather insensitive to your love life, don't you think?"

"Not when I don't have one anymore."

Danielle missed a beat. "How's that?"

"My fiancé is no longer talking to me. I had that conversation about ice climbing. The one where you recommended I take the honest approach. I told her I didn't want her there and that I needed my alone time."

Danielle, sat up, crossing her legs. "That was it? It's over?"

"Well, technically we remain engaged because she still has the ring I gave her, but the not talking part doesn't bode well."

"I'm sorry I gave you bad advice."

"I'm not sure I am." He didn't sound unhappy at all.

"Well, if it was really bad, she'd have hurled the ring at you or something."

Lars gave an easy laugh. "Hard to do over the phone. Besides, I'm taking the pragmatic approach. There is that notion that one should experience all the holidays with family and that sort of thing, which we hadn't done before, at least while being single. I have been told the holidays are supposed to bring out the best or worst in people."

"Hold up. *While being single?*" she repeated. "Is this the woman you were with when she was a client at MRD?"

"The very same."

She whistled. "Oh, man." Her hypothesis had been correct. His fiancé was the woman with whom Lars had an affair with while he was the managing director and she was a married client. The couple had left MRD but stayed married. It was that situation which caused Lars to write the clause in the employee contract about not cavorting with clients. At some point, a divorce must have occurred, Lars and Danielle ended their relationship and he hooked up with his former flame.

"Look at the bright side," she offered. "Now you can go ice climbing on New Year's weekend without distractions and see where you land, literally and figuratively."

"Indeed. What will your plans for that evening entail?"

"I was originally going to be at the restaurant but now I'm not so sure. Lani may already be gone, Max will no longer be a customer so I might just stay home rather than be alone."

"No dancing with Johanne?"

"That's a little premature for me at this stage. I'm not really interested in dancing with a stranger in a cage." She then turned serious.

"Lars, as a friend, are you sure letting things go with your fiancé is the right thing? I mean, perhaps compromise should be employed and you have a heart-to-heart. The two of you do have a past, after all."

"Maybe under normal circumstances I'd agree. But being with

her through the holidays produced red flags I'd not previously seen. This last incident left me feeling like I was looking at the opening ceremonies of a UN Convention in Brussels. It was just too much."

"Oh, no!" Danielle said, doing her best to submerge her humor while maintaining an empathetic ear. "What do I say, I'm sorry or congratulations?"

"Neither. Say you'll meet me at Stars & Stripes for New Year's, because if we are both without something do to, I propose we meet up at the restaurant and at least have a good meal."

With his words, she felt a sense of elation.

"Sounds like a deal."

CHAPTER 28

Once Danielle had the paperwork for selling Andre's portion of the restaurant, she called up Georgy. She felt it was only right to involve him in the decision.

"I'm grateful and supportive," he said succinctly. Danielle asked for his permission to place him and Layda on the trustee paperwork for her daughter. This time around, she was going to have every last bit of documentation in place, just in case.

She then called up Stephen, gave him the news, and also a chance to bid on the shares. "Georgy was completely amenable to you making this purchase, just so you know."

"That's very kind of him, and you," he replied, "but I have other financial obligations that are taking precedent." He didn't sound bitter or resigned, but matter-of-fact.

"No other restaurants for you, I hope," she gamely replied.

"Hardly. Do what you need to do, Danielle. We will be in business together for the foreseeable future, right?"

She scoffed. "And friends much longer than that."

Layda arrived early the next morning so Danielle could continue packing the boxes before the movers arrived at eight. Rushing between rooms, she felt grateful the buyer wanted a fast close, that she had cash and had successfully coordinated taking the keys and arranging the movers.

It was meant to be, she thought to herself.

By ten, she was placing furniture in her new home. She

prioritized Monroe's room, forgetting how hard it was to set up a crib with one set of hands. Several hours and many curse words later, the crib was assembled, and the credenza and bookshelf were in place with the books on the shelves. Her phone rang and she put in her earphone so she could keep working.

"Already in your new place?" Lars asked.

Danielle lifted out a handful of clothes from a box. "Did your friend install cameras?"

"No. I just got off the phone with Georgy. He says Layda truly adores watching Monroe."

"She does, and yes, I'm here unpacking the first of many boxes."

"Alone?"

"As always. Everyone I know works, including you."

"Well, it's lunchtime, so I can take a break. Are you hungry?"

"I am," she huffed. "But I can't leave, just in case you were offering to meet somewhere, which is a gross assumption on my part, but my diplomacy has taken a back seat to moving."

"No, I knew better than to take you away from your work," he said with a laugh. "I was thinking along the line of bringing over some take-out."

"Can the managing director leave the office during the middle of the day?"

"I can, although I mostly choose not to do so." She smiled.

"Well, if you are choosing to take pity on me then you are welcome to come over."

The knock at her door came a little before one. He was knocking a second time when she pulled open the door.

"Greetings! I don't dare touch you with my dusty hands." She stood back so he could walk through. "Come on in."

He smiled and walked through the door, a bag in each hand.

He gave her a kiss to the right cheek. *Tuscany*, she thought to herself. A tingle went up the side of her face and down her neck.

"Can I take your coat?"

"Sure." She then realized her dilemma. Danielle hesitated, feeling a bit dumb. "I have no hangers."

He smirked. "The couch will work just fine."

"It will have to," she shrugged. She draped the garment over the couch and joined him in the kitchen. "I know it's bad form to apologize for my living space, but I can't help myself."

"You think I'm that shallow?"

Danielle reached inside the first of the two sacks. "No. It's a small home and I'm being insecure. How about if you pull out the food and I'll see if I can find us some silverware and plates." She went to the corner of the room where boxes had been haphazardly placed and began opening one after another. Lars soon joined in the search, and it took a few attempts before he achieved success.

"Found them," Lars announced and deposited the utensils in the sink before washing them.

Danielle was torn between mortification and humor. "Can I at least offer you a glass of water?"

"Is that with or without ice?"

"Without." They laughed together as Lars stopped to search for a towel, leading to another quick reconnaissance mission. By the time they dried the forks, got the drinks and sat down, the food was lukewarm and she didn't have a microwave.

"I'm so sorry," Danielle said, embarrassed. "I'm completely unprepared for guests."

"Yes, you are, but that's not necessarily a bad thing," he said, examining her carefully. She wore old jeans and a long-sleeve t-shirt and socks without shoes. "I've never seen you this casual."

"You've never seen me move before," she responded. "Now

I'm afraid you are going to have to finish off your cold food and run."

"I'm an efficient bachelor. Cold food doesn't bother me." They ate, making small talk about the area until she pointed her fork to his tie. It was racing green with a speckled diamond pattern.

"You're really mixing it up with the New Year."

Lars shook his head. "I must be unbelievably dull to elicit that kind of comment over a tie."

"Or you can be appreciative that I notice, *and* that I can complement you on your good taste. It's not just the tie, but the whole combination. I like those cuff-links too. Very classic." His smile was easy, his dark hair, now a little shorter on the top and sides, as she remembered it.

"Any movement on the sale of restaurant shares?" he asked her.

Her mouth was full of food but she nodded. "The bidding started this morning. Two offers outstanding and several more expected. I'm a bit surprised. One is a thirty percent premium."

"Not bad. And then what? Lani goes off into the sunset with her new restaurant?"

"Yep."

"Would you like my humble opinion?"

Danielle coughed unnecessarily. "Isn't that an oxymoron for you?" He grinned. "Absolutely, oh Zeus of the Mountains."

"It's going to play out like a Greek tragedy. She has now lost Stephen, though I'm sure she thinks he'll come back to her when she wants him. She'll go forward with the new restaurant and realize that you were actually the brilliant one to come up with the name, marketing and position of the cuisine. She was just the cook."

Danielle's mouth dropped and her hand went down to the

table. "That might be the harshest thing you have ever said in my presence."

He thought for a moment. "Do you think it's wrong or unjustified? Or that I am being harsh?"

"Actually, no. It's all accurate, and you—well, you have always been direct, but firm and fair."

He nodded, pleased they agreed. "Lani herself isn't a celebrity chef, so that won't initially be part of the draw. Her biggest fault is naivete. A winning combination of food, atmosphere and style have given her a bona fide hit. She's not considering the other half of that success is people and management. Renaldo slip-streamed in to her role and the volume of business remained the same, didn't it? Proving the point that once the reputation is made, a restaurant can continue to innovate without the founder."

"I feel bad for Stephen."

Lars folded his napkin. "Stephen is a smart, handsome man. Since Lani has been foolish enough to walk out on him, then he will be another woman's gain. Who knows?" he said, his voice lightening with humor. "Maybe my former fiancé."

"What? You mean it's officially over, over?" Lars stood, pushing his chair back in and picking up his take-out boxes. She followed, feeling a strange calm as his expression remained neutral.

"As official as giving the ring back can make it." Lars scraped the uneaten food in the trash compactor.

"Shouldn't you be upset or something?"

"No, she didn't hurl it at me," he said with a smirk. "It was couriered over, so we didn't even have to say goodbye in person."

"Wow, that's brutal. After all you and she have been through."

"Length of togetherness has no indelible tie to the strength of the relationship. Besides, I'm a pragmatist. I'd rather wait for a great thing than settle for a good thing." Although he said it without any emotion, the comment hit her like the heat from a laser.

"Men like you don't need to settle, you know."

"No, we don't," he said so blandly that she couldn't but laugh.

He picked up his coat and gave her a peck on the cheek, all done with the ease of a good friend who'd stopped by for a meal. Danielle stood at the doorway, waiting until he'd gotten in his car before she waved and shut the door.

I'd rather wait for a great thing than settle for a good thing.

Lars was single now. He wanted the best for himself. His words replayed in her mind as she continued to put her new home in order.

What did someone do when a former love came back, and all the caring, passion, respect and friendship were still intact? It wasn't a question she should answer at that moment, but oh, how she wanted to.

CHAPTER 29

By four p.m. the following day, Danielle accepted an offer for Andre's share of the Stars & Stripes. It was a forty-five percent premium on the initial quarter of a million he'd invested. She called Georgy and told him the news.

"Thank you for calling, but we already knew."

"How?" she demanded. "I'm seriously beginning to question this whole Swiss-secret-keeping thing."

Georgy chuckled, his deep rumble moving through the phone lines. "My dear. We were the anonymous buyers." Danielle started to protest that she couldn't possibly take the money, when he told her the deal was done. "The check has already been cut, Danielle. What better way to take care of our daughter-in-law and granddaughter than continuing Andre's legacy? He loved the restaurant, and so do we. Of course, someone else was trying to outbid me, which drove the price up, but I could afford the premium."

Danielle's throat closed. It was an unexpected and beautiful gesture.

The moment Danielle was off the phone, she called Lani. Her friend was overjoyed to learn of the quick sale of Andre's portion, speed talking through her plans for the new location and interior design.

"Lani, I do have a few things I want to discuss with you, as friends. First, I'm asking that you don't poach away the staff, and that means Ivan or anyone else. Second, I figured you know you can't use the name, but I wanted to bring it up. It's trademarked and held by the corporation, not us individually. Lastly, while I hope you won't compete directly with us on the American food, there is nothing I can do to stop you, other than ask you make it different."

Lani laughed. "You are so business-like!" she teased. "Don't worry. I have no desire to serve straight American food, no offense to how well the current menus have gone over. I've always wanted to do new-American, fusion, with lighter, spicier items that I came to love at cooking school in Sonoma." She didn't want to use the name or anything else, including the music.

"You will officially be entering the New Year with a clean slate," Danielle said, projecting an excitement she didn't feel.

Lani yipped with joy, then spoke sincerely. "I don't know what to say, other than thank you. Thank you for all you've done."

"You're welcome. Lani," she said, the changed the tone of her voice. "I have something else to ask. Have you been seeing Max on the side?" She had been suspicious of her friend's motivations and couldn't resist asking.

"What? Did you get that from Stephen?"

"Stephen? Are you kidding me? He and I have only spoken once since our last meeting, and you never came up, just the paperwork. This is me asking, because all the signals point to it. The boat. Max hanging around the restaurant under the guise of learning more. Your opinions on kids. It just wouldn't surprise me."

"Are you mad at me?" Lani asked quietly.

"Not mad, but the thought of you sleeping with him while still being married to Stephen makes me sad, even if we both heard him say that that Europeans are more open-minded than Americans on the subject. Please, please tell me you aren't going to hurt him unnecessarily."

A short pause preceded Lani's answer. "It...just happened."

"Stephen doesn't know?"

"I'm sure he suspects, but he's so private he never asked, and I don't expect him to. One day we just stopped sleeping together, then stopped sleeping in the same bed."

Danielle closed her eyes as her heart ached for Stephen. "How long has it been going on with Max?"

"It all started on the boat, emotionally, that is, so before the funeral."

Danielle felt another pang of regret. While she'd been grieving about Andre, hoping that his death might have brought Lani and Stephen closer together, Lani had been hooking up with Max.

"I love you no matter what, Lani. Life is too short not to fulfill your dreams."

"But you're disappointed in me."

"I'm disappointed in the situation and yes, you could have executed on this a little better, but I'm not a person to judge. I will say that Stephen is a good man. A stable man who has loved you for over a decade, and if you want my opinion, I think he still loves you, tremendously. But you don't want the same things anymore and ultimately, you can't force something that is no longer there."

Danielle thought she heard a sniffle. "You know, I thought love would last forever with him, that we could handle anything, and we did, everything but getting what we wanted. It changed my dreams, Danielle."

"Isn't that the irony," Danielle asked. "We spend so much time in relationships preparing for the worst, that we never prepare for the best."

"Thanks for understanding. It means the world to me. I love you, Danielle."

"I love you too, Lani."

Danielle fed Monroe and read her stories, lulling her to sleep as the rocking chair moved back and forth. Quiet music played in the background, this time, a station from Austria. Danielle could understand most of the words now, singing softly as she closed the book. She stayed in the chair until the song ended, then put her daughter to bed.

She'd tell Lars about Lani when she saw him next, maybe on New Year's Eve.

CHAPTER 30

The following day, she called Stephen and they agreed upon a protocol for running the business portion of the restaurant and how and when to best communicate. "Let's do this now, and get it in writing before an unknown third party comes on board and wants to change things," she said. Stephen fully agreed. Danielle didn't bring up Lani or her emotional state, nor did she console Stephen. He was acting stoic in the face of a break up.

The following day, Lani informed her she'd received the paperwork and check for her share. It was far less than what Andre's portion had commanded.

"It's not enough to run the restaurant myself," Lani said, sounding unhappy but undeterred.

"Between that and what you have saved, isn't it enough? Even with Max's investment?"

"Not quite. I want to make this huge. Bigger than Stars & Stripes."

Danielle found herself cautioning prudence which went completely unheeded. Lars' words came to her mind, and she hoped Lani wasn't making a decision that would lead to her financial demise.

She called Stephen back with the update. "Keep an eye out in your mailbox, because we should know shortly who we will be working with."

"Will do. By the way, I scheduled the staff meeting for Friday to communicate the changes, right before closing."

"Super. I'll be there." Danielle was looking forward to the

meeting. Ivan in particular, would be shocked and thrilled to be receiving a share of the profits. Lani had been opposed to the idea. Now that she was gone, it was the first change she and Stephen had made. It was a morale booster and it was smart; well paid employees were less likely to defect to Lani's restaurant. Although they'd asked her not to poach, they could do nothing to prevent their staff from quitting on their own.

Twenty-four hours later, Danielle found herself bent over the toilet, sicker than she'd been in years. Her legs were aching and she felt shooting pains along either side of her throat. She called Stephen and cancelled.

"You go ahead and do it. My guess is they will be so thrilled at what you are saying, they won't care if I'm there or not." Danielle swallowed. "Is all officially over now with Lani?"

"She moves out the 29th. I offered her the apartment, but she didn't want it."

Danielle winced. "How'd she find a place so fast?"

"Max had an extra place in a building he owns."

"That's convenient."

"To say the least. Her things are packed and in the garage and we will go into the New Year without one another."

"You sound better than I expected."

"My life isn't all bad, Danielle. In fact, I have a lot of things to be grateful for. Unexpected, but good." A cough caught in her throat and he finished by saying, "I'll let you go, and hope you get better, at least in time for New Year's. It would be nice to see you."

With her head pounding and body aching on Saturday, she called Layda, telling her that she was too sick to go out on New Year's and would be staying home with Monroe. "You and Georgy can make plans of your own."

"You might have the flu. If you don't mind, can I come get her?" Danielle started to disagree, but Layda kindly interrupted. "I really do think it would be best."

Thirty minutes later, Georgy stood by Layda's side at the front door. Danielle greeted them and backed away while doing her best to express her appreciation and gratitude. She kept a hand half over her mouth, gesturing to the bedroom.

"Monroe hasn't displayed any signs of being sick so we might be in the clear." Layda left to get the baby and Georgy picked up the overnight bags. The large man glanced around.

"This is quaint."

"Yes, it's small," she acknowledged, "but it's all we need. It has the bonus of being close to you and in my price range. We can't all live like our clients," she said with a lopsided grin.

Layda emerged with Monroe in her arms. "On the topic of homes, did Georgy tell you? We've decided to sell the house." Layda meant the home Danielle had shared with Andre.

Georgy bounced the baby bag in his hand, the action a telling sign he had strong feelings about it but no outlet for the emotion. "I'll wire you the money we receive and it can go into the trust you already have."

Danielle's chest pressed inward at his tone, which reminded her of a mountain man looking up at his hill for the last time before moving to the city. As she nodded, she felt a flush of warmth over her forehead, and she leaned against the credenza.

"Don't call us unless it's an emergency," Layda said with purpose. "We will keep Monroe until you are better."

Danielle felt worse right up until the late evening when she experienced fever-induced cold sweats. A few hours after that, her fever crested and broke. Sunday morning, the pain in her legs had receded and by the afternoon, she kept down a cup of soup. After a long bath with Epsom salts and lavender, the last of the pains dissipated and she got a full night's sleep.

Monday morning, she called Layda, telling her she'd improved, but Layda insisted Monroe was doing just fine. "Take two more days to ensure you don't relapse, until Wednesday evening."

Georgy then got on the phone, echoing Layda's instructions for her to rest. "No matter what Monroe does, Layda treats her with the care of an angel," he told her, his gruffness not hiding his deep affection. "Rest easy."

Danielle didn't stay in bed, but she did take it easy. She called Stephen, who told her the employees were ecstatic to be in a profit-sharing pool, an unheard of perk in the restaurant culture in Zurich.

"Does ecstatic mean they actually raised an eyebrow or exhaled in exuberance?"

"Well, a few of the more boisterous ones were heard to utter "that's awesome."" Danielle laughed and told him to have a good New Year. "Danielle, before you go, I want to say thank you."

"For what?"

"Remaining consistent throughout this entire ordeal."

"I'm never going to change, Stephen. College, marriage, kids, a business, divorce..." Danielle couldn't stop from laughing. "Man, that makes us sound so *old*!"

He joined her. "No. Just wiser."

Danielle showered, thinking that she was getting wiser, and she was truly aging. As she dried her hair, she reflected that March would mark two years of living in Zurich.

So strange, the thought, snippets of her time coming to her mind's eye with each stroke of the brush. Arriving at her apartment, seeing Andre for the first time, going to the Lichtenstein Castle, when he broke up with her, falling in love with Lars, the gondola ride, learning she was pregnant, the ring Lars gave her and the promise they both made. His engagement falling apart.

Lars! She'd completely forgotten to call him about tonight. She was reaching for the phone when it rang.

"I'm so sorry," Danielle said quickly. "Are you actually at the restaurant?" Lars laughed easily, a sound that carried a warmth through the phone. She heard noises in the background.

"I am. It was Stephen who told me you'd been sick."

"I feel terrible. In my defense, it's been a rough few days, and I just started feeling better last night. I think it's too late for me to get dressed up but actually, I'm not sure I want to reinfect anyone with my presence."

"Reinfect? What about a person coming over with a batch of food, this time New Year's party fare?"

"Seriously?" she asked. "I can't guarantee I'll last all night long, or even until midnight."

"I'll leave the moment you start yawning. Do you want to assist me with the menu or have me surprise you?"

"I like surprises. Go for it."

Danielle glanced at her reflection in the hallway mirror. Clear skin, straight hair, combed over from a part on the side.

Out of nowhere, an image of Andre's smiling, carefree face came to her, when he stopped his motorcycle to say goodbye after their first afternoon together, the midafternoon shower drenching them both. He'd slipped his fingers under her jacket and pulled her close, gently licking the rain drops from her lips, holding her so tight she almost couldn't breathe.

Four months since Andre died.

With resolve, Danielle slipped on a red, angora sweater, black corduroy leggings with peak-a-boo flats and made her way around the home, straightening and adjusting everything to her satisfaction. When the knock on the front door finally came, Danielle took a deep breath, then blew the air out through her mouth in a thin exhale.

"It's only dinner," she said out loud, lighting the candles. Crossing the living room, she glanced in the mirror.

You're a terrible liar, especially to yourself.

CHAPTER 31

"Happy New Years," Lars greeted her.

"And to you," she said, feeling relaxed until she inhaled. The cologne was a familiar one, and it made her hand shake. "Turn," she said, using the excuse to brush the snow from his shoulders to conceal her wavering fingers.

He removed his coat the moment she was done, examining her. "You don't look like you've been sick. Are you sure this wasn't a ruse to skip being at the restaurant tonight?"

Danielle smirked. "A ruse to avoid you? Definitely not. I would have come up with something far more insulting than being sick to dodge being in your presence." She walked into the living room, catching him glancing around. "Are you finding everything in order this time?"

"It's a little more put together than my last visit."

"Just a little." Red candles burned on silver coasters on the mantle. In the fireplace, the golden embers pushed warmth through the joining rooms, and holiday music played in the background. On the coffee table, a square silver platter held several candles, the décor nearly identical to the one in the dining room, save the holiday-print plaid runner that stretched the length of the table.

"I like your jacket by the way, but am surprised it doesn't have fur. What was that material on the collar?"

"It's from an animal called a vicuna," he said, helping her

remove the coat. "An orange llama-like animal with white stripes." Danielle grimaced.

"And you pay good money for that?"

"It's rather rare so the money has to be good." Danielle laughed at the peculiarity and suggested he give himself a tour of the home, but he stayed in place. "You didn't let me do that at my apartment on your first visit."

Danielle instantly replayed the highlights from that first visit, from standing in the kitchen, watching him make the food to sitting on the chaise lounge, their toes touching and then finally, at the piano, where he'd unclipped her hair…

"True," she said, unable to stop the heat that had moved up her neck. "But technically, this is your second visit, so I'm not sure the same rules apply." Seeing his resolve, she gave in without another thought. "Okay, after dinner, I promise. Did you bring your own wine? You know I don't have any and am clueless in that department."

"You can make it up by having us go completely untraditional by eating in the living room."

"Why not?"

She handed him a large serving spoon and they took turns on the ad-hoc buffet line, dishing up ham and scalloped potatoes, yams with a maple syrup and butter topping and a cranberry salad with cream cheese topping. In the living room, Lars carefully pushed the glass coffee table a foot closer to the hearth, took off his shoes and sat on the floor with his legs stretched out.

Danielle joined him, sitting down on the rug, unable to keep from smiling.

"Yes?" he asked.

"I never would have imagined you eating on the floor," she said, motioning her hands to his feet. "But then, I don't know anything about you at the holidays, so I should refrain from making assumptions, shouldn't I?"

"Let me educate you, then," he offered, lifting his knife, his slight formality making her giggle. "When I was a child I eagerly awaited the start of the holiday season. A month with decadent food and presents from the first of December until New Year's."

"I'm right with you."

"But, as I learned, not everyone gets into the Christmas spirit. My former fiancé was one of those people. It just didn't resonate."

Danielle shook her head with mock pity. "How good food, presents, singing carols and wearing furry clothing cannot resonate is beyond me. In our family, the holiday season started in October."

Lars cut a piece of ham. "As was identified by the witch's cauldron full of M & Ms."

She tilted her head happily. "When I was a kid, my parents always put up the tree right after Thanksgiving and left it up until the day after New Year's. In February, our neighbors replaced the Christmas ornaments on our tree with Valentines hearts, mom ended up buying eggs for Easter ornaments and stars for the Fourth of July. My father let it be, never saying a word when the tree ended up being there year-round. He contended Americans could make a holiday out of any event for the purpose of making money."

"Now that's a principle I can get behind." Danielle snorted rather ungracefully. "I'm glad I can still make you laugh."

"Because you can so easily poke fun at all that us Americans hold dear, especially days manufactured by advertising geniuses."

"I lived in New York, remember? Fifth Avenue is seared in my mind."

His warm eyes pulled at her, the emotional equivalent of the tug from a bungee cord on the side of a bridge, her heart pumping with the idea that the experience of going over would be as scary as hell but exhilarating.

"You know that material on your coat? Can I get a sweater made of it?"

"Sure. There's a place in town," he said vaguely. Something about his manner and tone caught her attention, and what was a simple question turned into something more.

"Do you not recommend it?"

"No, I have one. It's just extremely expensive and not sure it's a wise purchase. I wouldn't have one but it was a gift." Danielle thought about the type of person who gave expensive sweaters. Her money was on the former fiancé.

"Well it is very soft, that's for sure," she remarked, hoping her insecurity hadn't revealed itself.

"Your turn to update me on Lani."

Danielle revealed her friend's involvement with Max. "She's even living at one of his apartments. Stephen agreed it was convenient, but he didn't say a word further and I wasn't going there."

Lars' eyebrows had creased with the information, then went flat with acceptance. It was the kind of quiet understanding that only came from making his own series of bad judgments while he was married.

At the end of their meal, Lars took his plate in to the kitchen and rolled up the sleeves of his sweater.

"No," she said, touching his arm. "You are to be a proper guest and sit on a stool."

"Who defines what makes a proper guest?"

"Are you kidding me? It's my home, it's New Year's Eve, and you brought dinner."

"Yes, it is and I did," he calmly agreed, turning on the water. "I distinctly recall a time when you sat at my bar counter, watching me do dishes, wearing not much more than a bathrobe. You were perfectly fine with my role as a dishwasher then. Why don't you make your homemade whipping cream for the pie instead of chastising me?"

"Wha...?" she gasped, catching a laugh in her throat wide enough to match his smile. "Well, there was that," she responded suddenly, wanting to run her fingers through his hair. Instead, she turned around, unable to stop herself from replaying the scene Lars had brought up. She had felt so comfortable in his kitchen, watching him do the most mundane of activities. It was fun and easy. All that a relationship should be.

In her reverie, Danielle hadn't noticed the water go silent.

"Danielle, are you okay?"

She glanced over her shoulder. "Of course. Just getting this going," she answered, lowering the handle on the mixer, pouring in the whipping cream. "You all done?"

"No, but I saw you stopped and was wondering if I said something to upset you."

She felt his fingers on her hand. "Not at all."

"Then what is it?" His fingers moved within her palm. With only the slightest of movements, she could have intertwined her fingers with his.

"I was thinking of that time in your kitchen, the one you just brought up."

"I'm sorry..." He started to remove his touch.

She turned toward him, touching him with only the tip of her finger, the grip as tenuous as she felt. Danielle's eyes flicked between his, hoping for a signal of emotions that matched her own. "Don't be. It was a lovely time, like all that we spent together."

Lars' thumb barely moved on her skin, his eyes intense and full. "Do you want me to go?"

In that moment, she felt all the conflicting emotions of past and present, hurt and hope, pushing against one another like magnets unwilling to be apart. Very slightly, she shook her head no. "Do you think badly of me that I want you to stay?"

"No." The soft caress of Lars' thumb along the inside of her palm left her weak. Heat from his fingers moved up, along her inner arm as he traced her bloodline. He glanced at her eyes for permission as his fingers reached her neck, where he gently pushed back her hair. She instinctively knew that he was testing her barriers, watching for signs of discomfort. She had none.

"Are you sure you don't think I'm bad?" she whispered to him.

"Bad that you still love me?" She held her eyes steady, suddenly unafraid of being on the receiving end of all that he was silently telling her. "Danielle, I promised to never stop loving you when I left you in the hospital room, and I never did."

That knowledge was within her, as surely as stone lay within a mountain. Deftly, he drew her against him. First, his lips brushed her forehead, then the sides of her temple. He hummed with pleasure, the sound of a person relishing the touch of a loved one long absent. She unconsciously pushed her hands to the collar of his sweater, gripping the soft material as though it were the only thing holding her steady. Just being near him again was more than she'd dreamed.

"Monroe," she said quietly.

"Who I loved when she was inside you, when I felt as though a part of her belonged to me, even after we learned she was Andre's."

Tears rolled down her face and Lars kissed her wet cheek.

"I've always thought you are very sexy when you cry. It's about the only time you are completely vulnerable." Danielle wanted to respond but couldn't. She was floating through successive waves of love and desire.

As he slowly covered her mouth with his lips, her breathing went shallow. It was possible that they could be together. No outside issues, no barriers, just the two of them, starting tonight.

CHAPTER 32

Lars led her to the couch where the last twelve months rolled up like waves on the water. Danielle faced him, knee against the back cushion, toes curled under his thigh. His arm rested behind her shoulder, touching her hair. He'd put a finger through a curl, twist, then let it unwind and drop.

"I've done a lot of thinking about us, Lars. We could have made it work. I don't think it needed to be all or nothing."

Lars removed his hand from her hair and rested his head on his fist, the somber expression giving her a degree of comfort. "When you left for your father's funeral, the same thought hit me. I bought a ticket to fly over and see you and talk it through. That plan, and my hopes for us, were gone when I learned Andre and Georgy had already left to see you."

Her hands started to fidget in her lap, anxiety growing like a weed in a field of spring flowers. "How did you find that out?"

"Glenda needed to get in touch with all of your clients for the end of the year reconciliation. She informed us Georgy and Andre were out of the country attending family business. It wasn't a big leap to draw the natural conclusion they'd left to attend the funeral. I had nothing to do but wait and see you back at the office. By the time you returned, you might as well have had a plexi-glass shield in front of you. As time went on, it never went away."

"Life could have been very different."

"Andre would be alive and we would be together, perhaps

even married. We would have been a blended, unique family unit. Would I have hated it? Yes, but we could have coexisted."

"Just like Andre had hypothesized."

"Turns out he was smarter than I was." Regret was so embedded in Lars self-recrimination she took his hand.

"I'll only let you take so much responsibility for this," she began firmly, forcing him to look her in the eyes. "He gave me his own ultimatum, remember? It was either him or my job."

"You do have a hallmark of keeping promises."

"Which threw me out of a perfectly good relationship and into the arms of another, which is what I told my dad." She let out a small burst of laughter. "Why did I get two men, so headstrong and determined, so righteously justified in their own motivations..." Lars smiled and tenderly stroked her hand.

"It was good Andre got to experience a wonderful, full period of love in his life, at least for a matter of months, wasn't it?"

"It was," Danielle answered. "My father said things always work out as they were intended to, whether we plan it or not."

"I am a big believer in plans, even if they sometimes fall apart."

Danielle grinned. "Of course you are. It's a control thing."

"As if you know nothing about control." Lars pulled her close. Her cheek lay on his chest, her forehead against the skin of his neck. Her right leg was looped over his, their bodies in unison.

After a moment, he spoke again. "Danielle, are you really sure you want to come back to work?"

"Yes. Should I be worried you don't think I can handle it as a single mom?"

"I'm only looking out for you, something I do for all my employees."

"Yes," she said, nuzzling against him, "just like this."

Her tease had the desired effect. They talked of other things, including Emma working full-time and Johanne's previously undiscovered natural ability to manage clients. Then her thoughts turned back to Andre.

"Lars," she said quietly. "Do you want to know what I'm thinking even if might be hard to hear?"

"Absolutely."

"Why are so many of the memories I recall are about my time spent with you, not Andre?"

"Probably because reliving the memories of someone who has died is painful since there's no going back. Recollections of someone who is living and present has a measure of hope."

"Does that make me a bad person?"

"This is the third time in two hours that you've asked if you are bad. Why and where does 'bad' enter the equation? Do you feel like you are being judged by me?"

"No. If I did, I wouldn't be so open."

He tenderly stroked her neckline. "I think you're being hard on yourself. The mind can only take so much grief before self-preservation kicks in. It's likely subconscious and perfectly normal. It's not being disloyal."

Danielle let out a breath of guilt that had been harboring in her lungs. "Andre said it once, and now I will. I don't know if I could be as kind and understanding if the roles were reversed."

"Lucky for you, we will never have to find that out."

CHAPTER 33

Lars lay next to her on the couch. It was the final position of many that they'd enjoyed as they refamiliarized themselves with each other's touch. His lips were buried in her neck and she was gently running her fingers through his dark hair. She inhaled, the scent of Paco Rabonne giving her several flashbacks of her time with him.

"You always wear this cologne on special occasions," she murmured. He kissed her neck and gave her a little nibble.

"I wasn't sure you'd get close enough to notice. I'll admit to wearing it far more than I should have over the last few months. It was like having a mental affair. Since I couldn't have you, I wanted the memory of you."

She relished the image. "Did you think of me a lot?"

"Yes. I kept wondering what you thought, if you liked the sights. It became…more distracting as time went on. I missed the little things, like your penchant for chocolate."

That gave her an idea. "You know what I want to ring in the New Year? The world's most decadent hot chocolate."

"Now?" His hands moved up and down the small of her back until his thumbs found her hips and she squirmed.

"What better time? Especially since I can't have you, I might as well substitute four types of chocolate, a bit of bourbon vanilla and Himalayan salt. It's an amazing concoction."

His finger ran down her hip, traversing her thigh. She shivered.

"And why can't you have me?" His look, combined with his

touch and tone, gave her a thrill so intoxicating she felt lightheaded. Still, she kept her wits about her.

"Because I'm not about to get pregnant again and I doubt you came prepared for bedroom excursions, or did you?"

"Danielle, we fell in love once before we ever took our clothes off, and it didn't take away the absolute sensuality of it all. And after enduring the last twelve months, I'm not going to risk you and I for the immediacy of gratification."

She kept a straight face. "That was a lot of words to simply say we aren't going to sleep together tonight. *Ouch!*" she shrieked, as Lars' fingers dug into her sides.

"I always try to be serious…"

"You deserve it and I can't help it!" she laughed, squirming. In a flash, she lifted one leg up and over him, sitting on his lap, her arms on either side of his neck, her eyes consuming him. "I also suspect you want to see what happens with the three of us—you, me and Monroe—for a while. It's all a part of what a *planner* does." Danielle felt the bright joy behind her words and the overwhelming feeling of happiness and excitement that continued to build.

"It's wonderful to be on the receiving end of that," Lars said quietly.

Danielle leaned close. "What about being on the receiving end of this?" She lowered her body to his. Lars slowly began moving up, against her, the intimacy increasing with the pressure of his hands, slow and cautious. Danielle's breath turned uneven, and she dropped her cheek to his face, groaning softly with pleasure.

"I've missed you, Danielle," he said, his voice husky.

Danielle had long since promised herself not to use the words never or forever or always, even in the quiet of her mind. There were no absolutes with love; there were only times and experiences, some good, others not, each connecting to the next, creating a journey of emotional development. She wasn't ready to let herself go completely, nor was Lars taking her to the point of physical release. He was building upon what they had started, one bit of intimacy at a time. She cherished his approach, feeling safe in his grasp.

"Don't let me go, Lars," she said, her words layered with meaning.

"I don't intend to."

Long after the New Year's had rung in, Danielle finally rose and made her hot chocolate.

"Is that bourbon going to knock you out?" Lars called from the living room. She watched him pick up the remote and surf the thousands of internet music channels.

"The alcohol burns it out, oh ye of little culinary knowledge."

When the hot chocolate reached the rim, she lifted the pot from the stove, added the vanilla and salt and filled two cups, bringing him one as he sat on the couch.

"It will send you to the moon, but as you were already there…"

"Orbiting," he responded, wincing at the hot temperature. "Good thing I have a couple of days to drink this down."

Danielle felt her eyebrow rise inquisitively. "You do? I thought you had work tomorrow."

"When New Year's Eve falls on a weekday, companies anticipate their employees might overindulge and give an extra day for recuperation. At MRD, we throw in another day. We have until Wednesday."

Two full days. She took another sip of her drink. "And then what? You turn into a pumpkin?"

"Almost. I disappear into the black void called work."

"Is this your deal taking priority?" she asked thoughtfully.

"Half of it. The other half is what I'd call cautiousness," he said. "You do have two weeks before you start work, and now that we are…"

Danielle refrained from making a quip. It was her first glimpse of insecurity in this man of stature, the one who ran a multi-billion-dollar firm, climbed slats of ice in his spare time, who raced cars and seemingly never misjudged a person or an incident. She was infinitely comforted to see he was human, just like her.

She put down her cup and rested her arms over his shoulders, touching him as though she couldn't believe he were real, this ghost of the past now come back into her life.

"If you are wondering whether I'd like to spend as much time with you as possible during the next two weeks, the answer is yes."

"You do agree it's wise to take it slow, don't you?"

She looked deeply into his eyes, flicking to his lips and back. She tenderly touched his lower lip with her thumb. "As much time as possible while taking it slow? That will take some control."

"Something you and I have much of."

She escorted him to the door, watching him walk into the falling snow and drive away. Danielle hummed as she put on her nightgown, catching herself mid-verse. She'd not sung or hummed to herself since Andre died. On the first day of the New Year, Danielle felt peace at the thought.

CHAPTER 34

The next morning, Danielle spoke with Layda to get an update on Monroe, then made eggs benedict and hollandaise sauce before Lars arrived. She toasted the English muffin and as he sat down behind the counter, she drizzled thick, yellow topping on the layered breakfast, adding a sprinkling of Hungarian paprika for flavor.

"A man who gets to spend time with the owner of a restaurant essentially wins the lottery." She preened, reaching for his empty plate. He touched her left hand, making her pause. "I haven't asked you about this."

She stretched out her fingers. She told him about the man in Hawaii, their conversation, and his recommendation she change the ring to her other hand.

"Sage advice, even if he was hitting on you." Danielle swatted his arm good naturedly. "And you've been wearing it all this time?"

"Yes. When I returned Layda noticed and asked about it. I only told her the *other* part of the story, where that same man suggested it was like Kryptonite to Superman. When she heard that, she encouraged me to leave it on."

"And this man. What was his story?"

"I thought it was rather sad. He's a divorced father of two who said the separation occurred because he and his wife were too stubborn to compromise over little things."

"But there was regret?"

191

She nodded. "Definitely. I found myself feeling envious that he had at least a few years of happiness with birthdays, Christmas caroling—you know. All as a family." Danielle stopped talking, looking down, fighting the unexpected surge of emotion. "I'm sorry. That can't feel very good. And after such a lovely breakfast."

Lars put his palm on her hand. "Don't apologize. I'd be a pathetic individual if I were so weak-minded and insecure that I couldn't hear you were sad to miss enjoying experiences with Andre as a family. Look at me," he requested, touching her face when she didn't look up immediately. "From now on you won't be alone for life's milestones."

"Feel like a walk?" he asked. "It's gorgeous outside and I want to take you to a place just down the road that's got great pastries."

"But I'm not hungry."

"Humor me. It's so tucked away you'd never find it and it's likely quiet today."

Sure enough, down a side street and behind a door that looked more like a butcher shop, was a dining-room sized bakery, the stout, but kindly owner talking in an accent so thick Danielle couldn't make out more than a word or two. "Did you order ham and cheese and chocolate?" she asked Lars under her breath.

"Just a nibble," he said. Lars paid and thanked the man for the pastries and milk before they both sat at a long, family-style wood table, complete with bench-style seating.

They were alone in the quaint place, the privacy allowing Danielle to ask more about the timing of his engagement ending and if it was just all about ice climbing and holiday traditions.

"She didn't know of the extent of our relationship until I attended Andre's funeral without her. She was irritated but let it go. Then when I took your first call, she was in the room and I left. She didn't take too kindly to that."

"It's never a good sign if you have to leave the room."

"Hmm, yes, but it didn't occur to me to do otherwise. The next month, by Octoberfest, making myself available for your calls was more important than having her over at my home, or me being at hers. That meant fewer nights together."

"I'm sorry. I—"

"No," he said abruptly. "I told you to call. I *wanted* you to call. At some level, she connected all the dots."

Danielle felt sympathy for the woman. "To be in the shadow of a person loved by your man is not a good feeling."

"There was another fundamental character flaw on her side that I couldn't accept. In the early part of our relationship, she showed her irritation at sharing me, for lack of a better description, with relatives or friends. I mistakenly took this as a desire for more of my time." Danielle smiled impishly. She could understand that notion. "It turned out I was wrong. The quiet hours she spent alone drove her mad."

"And you hadn't noticed this before?"

"No, which says something about my own work schedule. After being with you, I kept busier than normal." In some small way, the notion that Lars hadn't been as invested in this other relationship gave her a bump of happiness. "I wouldn't have ever sought her out, actually, but her divorce had been final for a year. She traveled abroad for some time and contacted me when she returned to Zurich. She bought an apartment down the street from my place and the timing was right. You had just become engaged."

"I bet it made you feel good," she said. "You were the first man on her list."

He tried to look modest, but failed. "She pursued me like I had pursued you. And yes, it did feel good."

"In more ways than one," she said with a sly look.

"I told you in my apartment the first time you came over, no one comes close to measuring up to you, in any category. Still, she is beautiful and very smart. In fact, I'd not seen many flaws until they all appeared, seemingly at once."

Danielle sensed there was more. She forced herself to eat, one small bite at a time as Lars continued to share.

"Compounding all of this was my memory of you with Monroe at the funeral reception, playing and bouncing her on your lap, all the things I remembered as a child. Having fun, making things silly and joyful, not always being wrapped in a mohair sweater, worrying about lip liner and stains on a shirt. To her, children meant nannies, daycare and boarding school, standard child raising for the affluent."

"But not for you?"

"My mother was and is a traditionalist. She liked staying home making bread. I understand times have changed, but if you can't have fun, what is the point?"

His dark eyes met hers, seeing she agreed.

"How'd she handle the final ending of it all?"

Lars almost laughed. "Angrily. I think she actually used the words, her 'time with me had a high opportunity cost,' or something like that."

Danielle had a hand to her mouth, stifling a snicker, as she looked to the doorway. An older couple in their late sixties walked through and she leaned closer to him. "That's so awful it's funny." His life had evolved on its own, through a natural course of events, their reunion unforced.

"The truth is, I had been trying for months to turn off my love for you, and I believed myself to have been mostly successful. I thought of you as the past love who would always be dear to me, but had moved on. When she came back into my life, I probably pushed myself out of the gate earlier than I would have, but she provided a very nice physical enticement. Sorry to be so crass."

"Don't worry about it," Danielle said sincerely. "You have great taste in women and she was clearly and fully enamored of you."

"And I was caught up in it all. In hindsight, I was probably trying to make things as exciting as I thought your life was."

"Having a child?" she asked, somewhat surprised.

"And a family in a new home. That was wonderful to me. It was all I wanted with you." Danielle got a very real sense of his heartache as he looked at her. "One day, we were going by a jewelry store and she threw out the notion that she'd never find a better match than me. At the time, I felt exactly the same way. You were taken. I had to follow my own advice and move on."

They finished eating and walked outside.

"Do jewelers here give full refunds?"

Lars chuckled and kissed her cheek. "No. It's more about trade-ins for something better." This got her laughing and she couldn't resist teasing him further.

"You know, the Swiss have a reputation for getting you coming and going when it comes to money."

"It's well-deserved, I assure you."

"On other, less dramatic subjects, do you have to pay a cancellation fee for missing yesterday's event or is it the potential prize money you forfeit?"

"No prize money or award. It's the glory factor." She laughed heartily before turning serious.

"You said the last event was indoors. That sounds a lot safer than outdoors. Is that true or a misconception?"

"It's more controlled, that's true," he acknowledged. "The indoor ice walls are kept at a specific temperature. Outdoors, the ice is always tested and the event is cancelled if it gets too warm."

Danielle walked in silence. "Did that question make me come across as needy?"

"Aren't you?"

"Ohh!" she growled, hugging his arm.

Lars pulled her to a stop, releasing her hands and finding her face. His palms were warm to the touch. "Know this. I'd rather have a person need me tremendously than not at all. Sometimes it's the only way a person understands he's loved, especially if the woman is strong." He kissed her. "And independent." Another kiss. "And a little in need of reassurance herself."

Back at her home, she asked him to find that great dance music he'd had on the night before. Lars obliged, finding a station out of Belgium that mixed ambient music with electronica. She admired his figure, one hand in the pocket, the slim cut outline of the grey jeans over his lean legs, his olive-green cashmere hoodie both urban and elegant. The sky behind him was still grey with clouds, the water gloomy and dark, but it could have been the blueish turquoise hues of the Caribbean given the happiness she felt.

"Dance with me," he invited.

She rose. "You've never asked me to dance before."

He held out his hand. "We have a world of things we've never done before."

"I'm not sure how much we can pack into twelve days."

"Then let's make every moment count."

CHAPTER 35

They ordered in Chinese and watched German television until Lars' phone beeped around eight p.m. He glanced down, his fingers moving rapidly.

"Do you mind if I check my email?" he asked, looking up. "I'd only do this for one reason."

"The deal?" she asked, not caring a bit. She went into the kitchen and loaded the dishes in the dishwasher. A glance out her window to the lake made her long for the spring time and warmer weather.

Life always seems better in the spring, she thought. New beginnings, fresh starts. She wondered what life would be like with Lars in it, for the spring, then the summer. They'd never had either season together. The entire time would be new.

Danielle poured herself hot water with lemon and joined Lars on the couch. He was still typing away and she flicked through the television channels.

"Would it be better for you to go to your desktop computer? Carpel tunnel syndrome isn't helpful to me or rock climbing. Me being more important."

He flicked her an appreciative look at her innuendo. "Agreed. I do need to send this along to the partners. Just a few more minutes."

Danielle slid herself down to the end of the couch, pressing her toes under his thighs, the heat warming them nicely. The snow had started to fall again and she realized she missed Monroe. Four and a half days without her little appendage in the house had made her feel an emptiness she'd never experienced.

Lars put away his phone and took her foot out from under his leg. He began rubbing the. "Would you be interested in taking a trip to Geneva at some point?"

"Sure, I've never been. Are you thinking of taking me on one of your business trips?" Lars rubbed his thumb along the base of her heel, making her twitch.

"Not at all. I was thinking about you meeting my parents." Danielle's mischievousness turned to disbelief. "And bringing Monroe of course."

"Wow," was all she could get out. It implied so many things. She smiled, a goofy, I-can't-image-it kind of look, which she tempered with a reality check. "We'd need to tell Georgy and Layda about us first, you know."

"My parents aren't in the same social circle as they are." That little fact didn't matter to Danielle. Her first order of business was going to be talking to Georgy and Layda. It was a matter of love and respect, not convenience.

Lars told her of his father. He had declined rapidly after his stroke, and as Lars spoke, she sensed a sadness she'd never seen in him before, as though a great man of industry was forced to leave it all behind, and the money, position and surroundings of success had given way to premature aging and decline.

"It bothers you, doesn't it?"

"Very much so. I've always envied Georgy, and by association, people like Andre, who had vibrant fathers who could enjoy all they created in the prime of their life. In my early twenties, all that was taken away from me. He basically became a recluse and my mother doesn't do anything without him, or very little."

Another part of his world opened up with his words. He had no siblings and never mentioned cousins or extended family. His network of friends…well, she didn't even know what that consisted of.

"It sounds very lonely being at the top in your business. And your age doesn't help. You're not part of the older generation with adult kids, but you aren't a young trader either. You're stuck in the middle."

He tilted his head. "A no-man's land."

"Speaking of adult children, I am going to speak with Georgy and Layda as soon as the opportunity presents itself."

"Are you sure now is the right time?"

She took a breath. "As opposed to what? Another month? Two?" It was going to be hard, she was sure, but she also knew they loved her and wanted her to be happy. "There is never going to be a right time, Lars. But I certainly won't let them find out from someone else. That would be so hurtful. Besides," she continued on a lighter note. "It would be really nice to go out to dinner without worrying who might see us."

Lars gently moved her foot off his leg and slid towards her, his look fixed. "Did you know that my apartment is only seven minutes from here? And factoring in time to change, I can do a turn-around in less than thirty minutes."

Danielle bit her lower lip, the notion of falling asleep in his arms divine. "Stay and sleep with me," she said softly. "I won't even tempt you."

Lars stood up, bringing her close. "Just being with you tempts me, but I do holding really well."

"Prove it."

CHAPTER 36

At a quarter to five the following day, Danielle arrived at her mother-in-law's home. She had been coaching herself through what she was going to say. All she needed was the right moment. When Danielle walked through the door, she felt Layda scrutinizing her the way a mother-in-law should.

"You look much improved," Layda pronounced, inviting her to sit in the kitchen area.

"The last forty-eight hours has helped," she replied, the air in her chest feeling constrained from anticipation. Monroe came around the corner in her walker. "She doesn't seem any worse for being away from me," Danielle remarked dryly. "Which I'll try not to take personally."

"Georgy had more than one phone call interrupted, but he proudly announced it was because of his granddaughter. He can tell you himself." Georgy entered the room, assessing Danielle from top to bottom.

"I understand my daughter punctuated your business discussions with her own opinions."

Georgy waved away the comment. "Which didn't hurt the conversation at all," he said blithely. "But Layda and I have been talking. Since this unplanned time with Monroe went so well, maybe you should take advantage of it. Perhaps you would like to go skiing or have some additional adult interaction. It's been months now, Danielle. It's time."

She couldn't believe Georgy and Layda were making it so easy. "Are you really encouraging me to go out, on the town or with other people?"

"Consider this a gentle invitation to do just that," he suggested.

"Nothing with you is gentle, other than perhaps the way you hold Monroe."

Layda laughed in agreement. "How about we take her this weekend and the one following? That will give you two before you start back to work full-time."

Danielle took a quick breath, swallowed and spoke. "Lars has—come back into my life. Just recently, in the last few days. Now seems like the perfect time to bring that up." Georgy scrutinized her with his dark eyes. "More than simply telling you, I guess I'd like your approval. Layda?" she said hesitantly, waiting for a word or a reaction. After a few awkward moments, Layda attempted a smile. "As I said, I wanted to speak with you, to be sure it was..." Okay? Not offensive?

Georgy's eyes went down to his hands, the thumbs slowly crossing over one another as though he were pondering what to say. After a few more moments of silence, he spoke.

"Lars is a good man. He has integrity." The words rumbled from Georgy's mouth like gravel falling down a hill.

"Georgy, he's engaged to be *married*," Layda said, her voice soft, but clear, the emphasis on the last word.

Danielle belatedly realized his love life and the appearance of how things would look to outsiders hadn't even occurred to her. "He was, until recently."

"Did it conveniently end with Andre's death?" Layda's voice was still quiet, but rang like a bell tolling at end of a long, cold walk.

"No, Layda, as I understand it, she broke it off with him a week ago, right before Christmas, giving him the ring back."

"That was fast," muttered Georgy. "But not unexpected."

Layda's hand was at her heart, then her mouth. Both unusual mannerisms for a woman so perennially stoic, even in the face of death. Danielle reached to put her hand on Layda's, and the woman retracted it.

"Layda," said Georgy, his tone disapproving. "We have just been encouraging Danielle to move on with her life. To be happy."

Layda lips pressed together, then inward, struggling to hold back all she wanted to say. She looked at Danielle, her eyes controlled but forced.

"I agree, Lars has integrity, but he must have done something to cause his fiancé to leave him and so soon. It doesn't look good," she added. Danielle's stomach was acid, the roiling of nerves moving up her insides.

Georgy turned to Danielle. "Looks don't always translate to intent."

"There is no intent here," Danielle said fervently. "I am very sensitive to both of you and would never do anything to hurt Andre's memory or the family. Layda, you have to know I'm sincere about that." Layda raised her eyes, still flat and dry, but not as cold as they had been. "If this relationship progresses, and there is no guarantee, I promise to be discrete, until it's appropriate."

Layda didn't respond, but Georgy did. "Thank you my dear. That would be appreciated."

Things remained awkward until Danielle left, the plans for a meal cancelled when Layda announced she was going upstairs to lie down. Danielle quietly gathered Monroe's things and Georgy helped her to the car.

"We both knew this was coming," he told her. "But it suddenly becomes reality when it's thrust in your face." She cringed at his choice of words.

"I really am sorry Georgy, but I was absolutely sure it was the right thing to approach you both immediately."

He lifted the car trunk. "Which I appreciate. Yet I do agree with Layda in that it would have been ideal if Lars had formally announced the engagement was off, or at least put the word around town, but these things..." *Can't be helped*, she said mentally. Georgy closed the trunk and took her arms. "Live your life, Danielle. I'm sure your father would have said the same thing."

On the drive home, Danielle was unsettled. The conversation had not transpired as she hoped, and the future of being out and about with Lars was now going to be postponed, at least until she got a sense of what appropriate meant in the Swiss context of going public with a new relationship.

Her phone buzzed.

How did the conversation go? She wasn't going to distract Lars while he was at work nor was she going to text while driving. She waited until she pulled into her garage.

Call me after work and I'll fill you in

Bad?

Unexpected

Danielle put Monroe in the walker so she could make beef stroganoff and mashed potatoes, every so often repeating the single, syllable words in German that Monroe would most assuredly needed to know. By six, Danielle had fed and bathed Monroe and thirty minutes later, she'd read two stories aloud. Wrapping her under the covers, Danielle thanked the gods above her daughter slept twelve hours on a full stomach of potatoes.

A beep from her phone broke her train of thought. She reached over and read the text message.

Now?

Yes

Her phone rang seconds later. "Want to tell me about it?" Lars asked politely.

"How about you start," she responded, feeling sad and weary.

As if sensing her mood, he turned serious. "I'll keep mine short. One client left, taking several hundred million with them, unhappy with the performance of the trader."

"One of my clients?"

"Technically, your clients are the clientele of the firm."

Crap. "So that's a yes."

"The gap will be filled soon enough, I'm sure." At Russelzs, she'd witnessed high net worth clients shift money to and from management companies for no reason other than greed, thinking a different trader would bring in better results. Sometimes they were right, other times not. Most eventually came back around.

"Now tell me about Georgy and Layda." Danielle replayed the conversation word for word.

"You were right," he said. "There was no good time. Take heart that this conversation only needed to be had once. It's over now." She wanted to feel his arms around her and told him so.

"Falling asleep with my head on your shoulder." In the warmth of his love, she closed her eyes, waiting for him to say goodbye.

"With me caressing your back." She imagined him on his couch, legs up, phone to his ear, the soft fur of his blanket under his feet.

"Lars…" she said.

"I'll make you a deal," he said in a persuasive tone. "I'll talk, you listen. If you fall asleep, I won't be offended."

"Deal," she whispered. Lars resumed talking and she did indeed listen, but sleep didn't come until well after they'd gotten off the phone.

Danielle woke at five-thirty a.m., showered and ate, working dutifully on the computer until Monroe stirred. Emma came over at six, a little later than she would normally during a regular week. Danielle went back into her office and made several calls, one resulting in an unexpected appointment that caused her to leave the house and go downtown to the medical center. She was back home by one and called Johanne, knowing he'd be at his desk during lunch.

"Hi mom," Johanne greeted her jovially. "I understand you are officially returning on time as planned."

"Ready or not."

"So what's with Lani leaving the restaurant? And Max? *Seriously?*"

"Word travels fast in this town."

"No, she was out dancing with Max and I was slightly drunk and asked her directly what was going on. I just wanted to hear it again from you because I didn't believe it. What really went down?"

"Not much, other than she didn't want kids or Stephen but she did want a new restaurant."

"And Max," Johanne hissed. "Don't get me wrong, Max is hot, but he's loose like a cut rubber band dangling in the wind."

Danielle couldn't contain a laugh, but did soften her reply, hoping to strike a diplomatic chord. "Max…well…" she trailed off.

"Was convenient," Johanne finished for her. "I hope Lani doesn't get too attached."

"Speaking of being attached, do you ever speak with Dario?"

"Yes. He periodically sends me notes asking about your well-being and wishing you the best." Danielle's heart was touched. "If you can make it through the death of a man you love and the father of your child, I'm not one to complain about losing the love of my life."

"Moving on is good for both of us. See you in two weeks."

CHAPTER 37

Danielle was in the kitchen doing the dishes and Monroe was starting to issue tired complaints when the phone rang. Seeing it was Lars, Danielle picked up Monroe, hoping walking around would soothe her. Over her daughter's squawks, she heard commotion through the phone.

"Are you at an airport?" she asked him.

"Yes. Geneva. This afternoon a dinner meeting was scheduled followed by an early meeting tomorrow morning. I should return late afternoon."

"Lars," she laughed, "it's completely unnecessary to give me your itinerary."

"I do it out of a desire to share things with you, not out of a sense of obligation."

She let out a happy sigh. "I miss you."

"I waited a year to hear those words from you."

That evening, as Danielle rocked Monroe to sleep, her mind wandered to Lars. She envisioned him in an elegant Geneva eatery, at a table with two men and perhaps a woman, all dressed in custom, hand-made clothes, sipping expensive wine while eating small amounts of delicately prepared food. He would manage the table, engineering the conversations to his desire, flattering his guests without being condescending. The meeting would end, and he would drive back to the hotel.

For some inexplicable reason, at that point her thoughts went dark, just as they had the night before when he offered to go home and get his clothes. The snow falling on dimly lit roads, a car coming around a corner and hitting him...

No. That will not happen, she told herself. He'll show up at the hotel, get on his computer, work until midnight, then go to sleep, just as he said.

It took a few moments before her heart rate slowed. She lightly moved the hair from Monroe's forehead. The visual of Lars being in an accident was unnerving, but not unexpected. The books on grieving all included a section stating that many who lost a loved one suffered deep set fears associated with loss. It could handicap them to the point of being unable to create a new relationship.

Not me, she thought stubbornly. The trick was to let it go. *I have and I did.* Lars was alive and well, and their emotional threads were growing more intertwined by the day.

Friday, Emma arrived at five-thirty a.m. and Danielle went back into her home office to work. It wasn't until she heard Monroe stirring that she looked at the clock. 7:15. Lars would have already started his breakfast meeting.

Her fingers tapped quickly, her eyes darting on the screens before her, catching up on the industry shifts, refamiliarizing herself with the current movements of the major players. When her stomach grumbled, she saw it was after eleven. Her next thought was not of food for herself but of Lars, getting on a plane and coming back to Zurich.

The phone rang and she looked at the number with disappointment but answered anyway.

"Hey Lani, what's up?"

"Nothing," she said glumly.

"What does that mean?" Danielle turned away from the figures on her computer, swiveling in her chair to look out over the lake as her friend shared her situation. The bank would lend her half of what she needed for the new restaurant and she'd need to put in all her cash on hand and savings.

"I didn't figure for taxes and then what I needed to pay in commission," she admitted. "And I guess my estimates for the build-out were too low, along with the figures for the design plans." In fact, she was already short a hundred grand.

"What happened to Max? I thought he was all in."

"He was and is all in for the business, still at a quarter of a million." She grunted then. "But he's not in to me, which he made abundantly clear when I was at my apartment and saw him come home with a girl."

"Did you ever think it was exclusive with him?"

Lani hedged. "No, but I hoped it was."

"Okay, are you asking for my opinion or advice, because if not, I'm going to keep my mouth shut."

"No, I mean, yes, I want your thoughts and no, I don't want you to keep silent."

"Separate your personal and professional life," she advised. "Max is a financial partner, an investor and manager, period. Acknowledge that you and he share some level of physical compatibility and leave it at that."

"I'm not sure it will be that easy."

Danielle shook her head. "Not in all the time Andre has known him did Max have a steady girlfriend. He said as much to you during the boat trip."

"And after."

"Detach Lani," she advised. "Look at Max for what he is. A nice looking, smart guy who likes your company and wants to be your partner in business. If you aren't okay with being one of many girls, then tell him so and be prepared for disappointment."

"Okay," Lani said, sounding a bit brighter. Danielle coached her to get the partnership paperwork for Max written up and signed.

Danielle went back to her own work, her mind still on her friend. She had miscalculated the initial estimations of her new business venture and worst of all, relied upon a man who she'd been sleeping with.

Lars might be right again. Lani could lose it all.

At the end of the day, Danielle's lower back felt stiff and the space between her shoulder blades burned. She was out of shape and unused to sitting for hours at a stretch. Perhaps it might do her good to get out walking more in the next nine days. After Emma left, Danielle bundled up Monroe in her chest harness and went for a walk. The phone rang and she inserted the node into her ear.

"Ready to come home?" she asked brightly.

"More than," he answered, "but my meeting ran over, giving just enough time for a storm to come in and ground the flights. The earliest doesn't get in until noon tomorrow."

"That is a complete, and total, bummer," she said, slowly emphasizing each word for effect.

"Your response, being uniquely American, has lifted my mood. But what about Saturday night?"

Danielle thought of Layda and her offer to watch Monroe for the next two weekends. That was before the conversation about Lars, and now Danielle certainly wasn't going to take her up on it.

"My place?" she suggested. "I'll make dinner and you can stay until work calls again."

Saturday around noon, just about the time she thought Lars would be getting on a plane, he called again. He greeted her in a tone Danielle immediately knew meant disappointment for their evening plans.

"A meeting has been called with the partners," he explained. "I'm doubly sorry."

Danielle rubbed her fingers along the drawer top. "But you're on your way back?"

"Yes, I will arrive in an hour but then head directly to the office. I honestly have no idea how long this will take."

"I can only say I'm *not* a woman who is thankful for your work activities, but such is life of dating Zeus. You know, if it were the summer, I'd be on the lake sailboarding and you could have meetings to your heart's content. I wouldn't even miss you."

"That must be American for 'I really need you,'" he chided good-naturedly. "Still, I don't want you to stay in limbo waiting around for me."

Dinner was spent with herself and Monroe, the lasagna savory and sourdough bread moist on the inside and crusty on the outside. She had classical music playing in the background, the only sounds other than Monroe's periodic chirps, which she made when she got stuck in her walker. Danielle envisioned Lani in Max's arms, Johanne at the club dancing and Giles off skiing somewhere. Andre's other friends, Lucas and Christian would be playing hockey. The only other person in her network was Benny. She missed his smooth voice and wise comments. As the musician at a jazz bar she and Andre frequented, and who was also periodically hired by MRD to play at company events, his insight into her life was unique, fun, and confidential.

Almost without thinking, Danielle called Emma to see if she was available to watch Monroe that evening. Danielle went into the bedroom and searched for an outfit. She was going to take Georgy's advice after all.

CHAPTER 38

On the cab ride down to the jazz club, she was grateful for the leather pants, a nice barrier against the cold, and her short-heeled, shearling boots felt cozy yet sexy. She snuggled within the layer of her rabbit-lined black rain jacket.

Danielle heard Benny before she saw him, singing a piece perfect for his mid tenor, stretching up into a low alto but then going deep to hit several base notes. He gave a nod to a man sitting at one of the VIP tables in the front, an indicator the song had either been requested by him or for him. The host, a tall man with dark blond hair clad in all-black stood by her, helpfully pointing out a seat at the bar counter.

"I actually came to say hello to Benny," she told him. "Do you know when he goes on break next?"

The man looked at his watch. "He just came off it, so another thirty or forty-five minutes."

She smiled at him, taking in his smooth skin and light eyes. "I'll be taking that seat then." Sitting at far end of the counter, Danielle half-turned on the stool, observing the room. It had been many months since she'd been here. She recalled the scene. Andre's arm had been around her, her hand on his leg, laughing and talking, their enjoyment of each other and the music all that was necessary to have a good time.

Danielle then remembered another time when she'd seen Benny playing, when her personal life was very different. Andre had brought Eva, a beautiful woman who had long desired Andre's attention and had gotten none until he'd wanted to get back at Danielle for not marrying him. She'd been at a company hosted function, in a bar at the top of the mountain resort in St. Moritz. Lars had been making small talk about drinking, and she'd had her first Mexican coffee.

The combination of the memory, Benny and being alone gave her a desire for the tequila coffee drink and when the bartender came by, that's what she ordered.

Benny bantered with the crowd, playing random chords and transitioning the melody by modifying fifths. He hummed when he liked an answer and scowled with mock severity when he didn't. The crowd good naturedly laughed, the room becoming a bit louder as it filled to capacity. The host returned, telling her he'd let Benny know he had a guest waiting during his break. She thanked him, expecting the man to leave, but he lingered, asking how her drink was.

"Very good," she answered.

"I don't believe I've ever seen you order a drink."

"No, I guess I haven't."

"I'm Robin." Danielle shook his outstretched hand.

"Danielle."

"It's been a while," he continued. She nodded, wondering how long it was going to take him to ask about Andre, somewhat surprised he didn't remember her former fiancé or know of his death. "Have you been too busy to see us?"

"Busy with my daughter, yes."

A heartbeat of a pause before he responded. "Lucky her." Danielle smiled pleasantly, and he left shortly thereafter. It proved her theory: having a child was a faster deterrent to a flirtatious man than being married or in a relationship.

Benny finished his song and Robin leaned over to him. Benny glanced to the bar, lifting his head in acknowledgment, beckoning. Embarrassed, Danielle smiled, gave a little wave and declined. The bartender put a water in front of her and another Mexican coffee.

"Compliments of Robin," he said. Danielle thanked him, purposefully ignoring the smile of interest that accompanied the gesture.

I guess having a child wasn't as much of a deterrent as I thought.

When Benny finished his set, he came to her. The patron next to her graciously gave up his seat.

"Hi beautiful," Benny said. He gave her a welcoming hug and two cheeky kisses. He saw what she was drinking, smiled and asked for one himself. They raised their glasses and had a reunion drink.

"To the New Year," he said. The Moroccan man's dark looks blended in almost seamlessly with the silhouettes of the crowd behind him. He took one of her hands in his. "Now, tell me. How have you been? What have I missed?"

"Seriously?"

He shrugged. "I only have so much time."

Danielle told him of her forced time off, the travel and the evolution of her relationship with Andre's parents, right up to their admonition of getting out more.

Benny's clay brown eyes bored into hers. "You are here because you had a date and got stood up?"

"I find it curious you aren't asking about the person I was supposed to see."

He took another drink. "No need. Allow me. The one in St. Moritz who set Andre off. The boss man."

"What?" she practically squeaked. "No, no. It was my *drinking* that set Andre off."

"I may be old and wise, but I am not a fool, nor am I blind."

Benny took another sip as the phone vibrated in her purse. She glanced at it and pressed her lips together. "Excuse me just a second." She rapidly typed, put the phone face down on the counter and took another sip of her coffee. "You aren't going to dig for details?"

The jazz-man's eyes peered over the rim, a look that told her he'd taken in a thousand gestures and auras, synthesizing mannerisms and making guesses, a good many of which probably turned out to be true.

"That night I observed two men in love with the same woman. Your body language told me that you were trying to get over Andre, just as he was trying to do the same with that arm-candy. But baby, you were chemically attracted to the boss-man."

Danielle unconsciously leaned forward, her nerves like pin-pricks at the surface of her skin. "You think anyone else saw that?"

"Other than Andre, I doubt it. People are in to their own issues." Benny glanced at his watch, took a long drink and set the cup down. He put a hand on her shoulder to keep her seated and bent down to her ear. "I'm glad you are happy. The boss-man makes you glow brighter than a super nova."

A thickness in her throat prevented her from responding. Benny's analogy wasn't that far off, although she felt that being on the other end of receiving Lars' love was like being in the way of a glowing star. Hot and bright, ready to burst, inflaming everything in its way, casting the radiant heat to all around it.

Danielle drank half her water before she started on the second drink and was mid-sip when she heard Benny call her name.

"Danielle Grant, I won't be leaving this stage until you come up here and sing with me." His arm was in the air, and the front portion of the room seemed to turn as one toward her.

"I'm drinking," she said, loud enough for those close by to

hear and laugh.

"Then do it fast," he drolled. First one, then another man in the audience said 'Danielle,' and she feared the room might start chanting. She took two large swallows, set the glass on the counter, slipped out of her coat and weaved her way through the packed tables. She expected Benny to slide over on the bench and make room, but he lifted his right hand, gesturing her to stand. Before she had time to register her shock, he started on *At Last*, made famous by Etta James.

"How's that?" he murmured. She could only smile as she lifted the mike out of its holder. As she inhaled for the first note, Danielle turned to the crowd, her hand on the black piano. In the dark, she felt the eyes on her,

"At last my love has come along/ My lonely days are over and life is like a song...."

The first line moved into the next, the words taking on a meaning that she couldn't have understood two weeks prior. She felt her voice deepen, the notes moving up and into her head where the comforting vibration told her the sound was true.

"You smiled oh and then the spell was cast..."

Danielle looked beyond the eyes in the front row, to the back bar, and then around the room, as though every man was Lars, because that's who she was thinking about. She closed her eyes and sang the last line, holding the final word.

"And here we are in Heaven/ For you are mine at last..."

The applause was loud and appreciative. Danielle smiled and gestured to Benny, ready to take a seat when a waiter came up and handed a white note to Benny. He leaned to her and she nodded, looking up and around for the source of the anonymous note. When Benny began playing the notes for Fever, the crowd quieted and she sang.

"Never knew how much I love you/Never knew how much you care..."

This time, she moved around the platform, touching her hand to the piano, reaching Benny, her hand traversing his shoulder. All the while, she searched for the man she knew was out there, in the dark, watching. The one who had likely sent the request.

"Fever when you hold me tight..." It wasn't until the last line of the song that Lars stepped into the light and she sang to him.

"What a lovely way to burn..."

Danielle kissed Benny on the cheek. "That was fun." She stepped off the platform, her eyes focused on one person.

CHAPTER 39

Danielle had started to feel the effects of her second drink by the time she reached Lars. He leaned into her neck, breathing a kiss that moved down her throat and chest. "I'm so glad you came," she whispered, inhaling his cologne.

"My God, you are unbelievably gorgeous."

Danielle giggled, rubbing the unusual scruff on his face. "You've gotten used to me in pajamas and ponytails."

"Which I adore."

"When did you get here?"

"Right as you got to the stage. Sensually delicious, I might say." Danielle felt a moonshot of happiness at his words. He glanced inquisitively at the empty cup. "Have you actually been drinking?"

"Yes. Two Mexican coffees but not a gondola or steep drop in sight so you don't have to worry about me."

A hint of controlled passion crossed his angular face. "You sure you are okay?"

She lifted her lips to his ear, her words an intense whisper. "Are you going to sit and join me or stand and give me a lovely lecture?" She felt Lars' cheeks tighten with a smile. She gripped his hip with her thumb and forefinger.

"I'm sorry we aren't at your home," he said.

"We could leave now," she offered, her eyebrow arched.

She looked him up and down, his dark leather coat, a deep brown mock sweater, an ivory t-shirt underneath, the contrast hip but elegant.

"Or I could order a drink and we could sit for a while," he

countered. "It's dark, we are in a corner, and are relatively hidden." In other words, they could be out in the town with little risk of offending Layda or Georgy. She leaned into his cheek, inhaling and kissing. He put his hand on her back, touching so lightly she shivered.

"Tell me about your trip." He glossed over the business aspects, instead telling her he disliked the salmon at dinner but it was made up by chocolate mousse that had Grand Marnier in it.

"Switching subjects, where is Monroe?"

"With Emma." Lars countenance showed concern. "I wasn't going to have her with Layda, even though she offered. It's too soon." Thinking of her daughter, it made her consider the life of an only child, which she was.

"Lars, this is out of the blue, but I'm wondering if you are interested in having another child? Not right away, but in the future?"

His brown eyelashes lowered as he assessed her. "As an only child, the notion of having a playmate has always been appealing."

"What about other reasons to have a child? I mean, not just for Monroe, but..." She trailed off, suddenly insecure about revealing herself.

He leaned to her. "Danielle, listen very carefully. I don't need to create an entity that has my blood running through it to be closer to you or feel any more love than I do right now. One child, a daughter, that we would raise together, is more than enough." He emphasized his remark with a kiss so strong and sensual to her cheek that she didn't inhale. "If, at some point, we wanted to add to a family of three, then we could consider it, but I think that's a long way off, don't you?"

"Yes."

Lars' warm breath cloaked her neck and he twirled the ring he'd given her. "May I ask where this came from?"

"I always wanted a sibling. Knowing I can carry a child, I'd definitely try for another."

"But?" he prompted when she stopped.

The words had to be spoken, and they might as well be done now, before they became even more invested in one another than they already were. "The doctor told me I needed to try relatively soon, because, and these are the doctor's words, 'the plumbing is cleared out.'"

"What does that mean?"

"One or two years at most. And the other element is Georgy and Layda. You'd have to be okay with them, as their grandparents and in-laws. Seeing them all the time, sharing them with your own parents."

Lars touched a piece of hair against her cheek, moving it back as though seeing more of her meant he had a deeper view into her mind and heart. "I thought you knew my evolution on this topic. I truly respect and admire both. They are essentially your parents, and that's how I look at it."

"Really?" she whispered.

He spoke very clearly. "Do you remember the elation and joy and fear that I had when we thought Monroe was ours? Take away the fear part, and it leaves elation and joy. You and I. Together. A child, a sibling to Monroe. Our family unit."

Danielle was oblivious to the bodies and movements around her, grateful they were at the end of the counter, in a dark bar, where the attention was on Benny at the stage, not the darkened corner where they were consumed with one another.

With some difficulty, she pulled back and smiled.

"I have someone I want you to meet when it's convenient." She directed him to Benny. "He already guessed about you." In response to Lars' look of doubt, she told him of the man's observation in St. Moritz. "Was I really that obvious?" she inquired. Lars' smug smile made her feel faint. The notion of her peers seeing her attraction to the boss momentarily jolted her out of her sultry mood.

Lars laughed easily. "Don't worry. Benny is right. The others were all drinking, involved in their own affairs. If I'd been concerned about it reflecting badly upon you, me or the firm, I would have stayed away. But you know the rule, regardless."

She nodded. "By heart. Interoffice relations are not an issue. This is Switzerland, not America," she repeated in a fair imitation of the attorney from MRD. "*Shit*," she muttered under her breath. Lars let out a bark of laughter, covered only by Benny's singing. "Well I should take heart that no one in the office said a thing for two months while we dated, so I can't have had it written all over my face."

"True, and to my knowledge, Johanne never even knew, which mildly surprised me."

"No, I told you before I never said a word."

Danielle turned back to the stage and saw Benny looking her way. She waved and then pointed her finger at Lars' chest. Benny nodded and smiled, continuing his song.

"It's official now," she muttered, her hand going under his leather coat, pinching his side. "We can leave."

"Do we have to leave? I like being out with you. I haven't been used to my date receiving this much attention."

"Date?" she repeated.

"Ahh," he grinned knowingly. "I seem to recall you preferring the term girlfriend over companion."

"I've never understood what's so odd about girlfriend to you."

He gave a dismissive scowl. "It's temporary, like it's on the road to being something permanent but not quite there."

"Well, we *are* on a journey," she said, tipping back her mug.

"True, but all journeys have an endpoint, and when it comes to a man and a woman, much of the time it ends with some sort of major commitment to one another."

Her slightly foggy mind recalled they had just talked about

having a child together. It was inevitable.

Lars lifted his shoulders a bit higher, playing with a curl of hair on her shoulder. "I'm thinking that after Benny's next set we grab a snack then I take you home."

Danielle didn't know whether to laugh or cry at the oddity of the situation. The closer they got to being intimate the more cautious Lars seemed to become. "Why are you doing this?" her vulnerability exposing itself in her words.

"Emotional precautions."

"But we…" she stopped, so frustrated with the obvious she couldn't finish.

"I want you to be in control of yourself, your emotions and your sexuality when we are together, especially for the first time since Andre's death."

In the dimly-lit room, Lars' eyes were there, on fire, burning bright as they gazed at her with the fierceness of a man in love. He was also a man aware that the unexpected could occur at any time.

"You're worried I won't be able to handle it, or have some kind of breakdown?" Her voice had unconsciously risen while she shrunk away from his touch.

"Danielle, you read the same thing about physical interactions following the death of a loved one that I did. Intense emotions trigger fears, doubts, anger, guilt and a list of other things. On top of all that, you start work in eight days. If something…unconstructive happens, we may need some time as a buffer."

Danielle turned from him, trying to get the attention of the bartender. *What a load of crap.* She felt Lars place his hand on her shoulder and she stiffened. Against her desires, he pulled her close, into his chest, her body so stiff it was like a plank leaning over.

"Danielle, if we had been at your home, you would not have been drinking. That emotional volatility would not have come into play. Can you think objectively enough to consider that anything

I'm saying has merit?" Danielle didn't say a word, unwilling to admit he was factually correct. "Well if you can't look at me, listen to me. We just spoke of having a child together and of our future state of being. That doesn't sound like a man wanting to orgasmically frustrate his girlfriend."

"Who even uses the phrase orgasmically frustrate?" she grumbled.

"Your boyfriend, that's who." He said it with pride and without hesitation. "And this very *serious* boyfriend of yours, who is also the managing director of the firm where you work, has certain obligations to ensure his trader—his top trader—as we all know you to be, remains mentally stable after she returns."

"You speak so objectively about our status and my well-being it's almost robotically impressive." Even as she said the words, she felt her anger dissipating, being replaced by a sentiment closer to awe. Lars noticed and allowed himself a half-smile.

"It's like orgasmic frustration," he said. "A wonderful skill I have to objectify that which needs to be reasoned with."

Danielle rolled her eyes to the ceiling. "Personally, I want nothing more than to experience a wonderfully fulfilling and sexually satisfying moment, if not tonight, sometime in my immediate future, preferably before Monroe turns sixteen."

Lars chuckled, assuring her she was the sole recipient of his complete love and attention. Comfort overpowered her disgruntlement when Lars walked her to the door and gave her a loving, passionate kiss. They spoke Sunday, but he didn't come over. Once again, he counseled caution and patience.

"Monroe needs your attention, not mine." Danielle was forced to put her own desires and wants behind a door that she slammed shut, knowing Lars was right but not liking it one bit.

CHAPTER 40

The following week, Danielle and Emma modified the schedule. Emma arrived in the morning and stayed until noon. Although Danielle had originally arranged for Emma to be full time, she realized that she wanted and needed to be with Monroe as much as possible. As her father once told her, she had the rest of her life to work.

Wednesday at three, Lars called, inviting himself over for dinner. "No need to make anything," he said proactively. "I can always bring food."

"I was already in process and would love to have you here." Dinner, her home, the three of them. She was thrilled.

When he arrived, he kissed her forehead then rested his cheek against hers. "How have you been the last few days?"

"Good. Missing you." They went into the kitchen, Lars greeting Monroe, who was teetering on the edge of the couch, her big, hazel eyes looking up at him. "Watch this," Danielle said. She lifted Monroe and put her in the walker. Soon the little girl was zooming up and down the concrete hallways like a driver in a Maserati.

"Just like her mother," Lars noted.

She offered him food and he accepted a bottled water, sitting at her counter. "Have you spoken again with Layda?" Danielle admitted she hadn't. Lars encouraged her to do so. "She's probably feeling as insecure and unsettled as you are. More talking is better than less."

"I'll call tomorrow."

Danielle had prepared a simple meal of spaghetti with meatballs, along with French bread from the bakery Lars had introduced her to the week prior. She slathered it with soft butter, adding garlic salt and seasoning before she wrapped it in tinfoil and put it in the oven to broil. She diced a salad, asking if she was adding vegetables he disliked. Lars laughed.

"I like everything you create." He encircled her with his arms. A quick kiss on her neck and then he released her.

He seemed humored by Monroe's puttering about, encouraging her to move and adjusting her walker when she hit a roadblock. She felt Lars watching her intently as Danielle lifted Monroe out of the walker and placed her in her high chair then put on the bib.

"Get ready," Danielle told him. "Meat sauce stains. Would you like to sit on the opposite side or wear an apron?" Monroe, who was observing him with wide, hazel eyes, watched in silence as Lars elected to sit straight across from her.

"She's not sure of me," Lars said honestly.

"You're big and you're a man. I wouldn't be either."

Dinner was served, with Monroe getting more spaghetti and meat on her face and bib than into her mouth. Lars asked about her sleeping patterns, what kind of food she ate and the various stages of development. At one point, Danielle started teasing him. "I could give you the book if you want to get the reader's digest version."

"I've already read it, but each child is different." Danielle decided to challenge him on this, quizzing his knowledge on the terrible two's.

"Conventional wisdom is that you can avoid the terrible two's entirely by refusing to use the word 'no,'"

"Is that right?"

"It's what my mom did. Apparently, I never had a tantrum."

This bit of insight set her laughing. "I'm going to validate this fact with your mother the first chance I get."

Lars grinned. Probably sooner than she expected.

Bit by bit, Danielle learned more of Lars' perspectives and opinions on children and parenting. In some ways, this was far more advantageous than being married and then having kids. With Lars, it was like they were speed-dating but it was about parenting styles, getting it all out on the table before they were ever committed to get married. With Andre, she supposed they were lucky, because they'd agreed on most everything.

Danielle twirled the ropes of spaghetti on her plate, wondering when Lars starting viewing Monroe as a daughter. Was it weeks or months after Andre died, or after she started calling him at all hours of the day and night, seeking advice? What if it had never stopped, from the moment he left the hospital room?

She watched him surreptitiously. Lars dished up the food, taking a piece of noodle from Monroe's chin and pressing it into her mouth. At that moment, they made eye contact and he smiled, a genuinely happy expression of being content with her and Monroe in her home.

She felt content the first moment, and sad the next. Andre should have been here, but he wasn't. Another man, in his chair, loving her child with all the caring of a biological father. She bit her lip, holding back the tears. Lars saw her and lost his smile.

She flapped her hands by her eyes. "Happy tears. These are happy tears, not sad ones."

"Isn't that an oxymoron?"

Danielle shook her head, taking several quick breaths before she regained her composure. "Yes, but you think I'm the queen of the oxymoron so it doesn't matter. What does matter is seeing you, so completely happy with Monroe. It was too much. All good, just a lot to take in at once."

Lars was thoughtful, his tone subdued. "It's hard."

She nodded, once again unable to speak. "I know you will tell me this is normal, but what's normal about my life Lars? Nothing. Not since my mom died when I was in college."

Lars extended his hand to her, palm up. She placed her hand in his, feeling his love before he ever said the words.

"I consider this a crucial, wonderful phase, one that I wouldn't skip just to save a few tears."

"You like the way my tears taste," she whispered. This brought humor back into his eyes.

"That's not the only thing."

They cleaned up the table, Lars insisting on doing the dishes as Danielle gave Monroe a bath and dressed her for bed. In the rocking chair in her room, Danielle sat with Monroe on her lap, wrapped in her favorite blanket. Danielle read *The Red Barn*, improvising the words around the pictures. She didn't notice Lars at the doorway until she placed Monroe in her crib. He was standing quietly, observing her with a look that would have assured her father she was in good hands.

Danielle turned on the classical music. "It plays on a timer," she whispered as she met him in the hallway.

Lars touched her hand. "This went well." She nudged him slightly as they walked to the entryway.

"A little emotional, but not as bad as it could have been."

He stopped her in the hallway, leaning into her. "What do you consider bad, a word I dislike but am forced to use?"

She rested against the wall behind her and looked at him carefully. "Let me rephrase. Tonight was emotionally intense for me. I find it very strange and difficult to comprehend that certain things you do remind me instantaneously of Andre, but they're not images of what he did, because he never had the chance. It's images of what might have been, but will never be—because you are here, doing those fatherly things. So it's not bad, it's more emotionally impactful, like a bullet going through me that I feel, but when it goes out on the other side, there's no hole. Just the memory. Does that make sense?"

"A great deal. Thank you."

Danielle placed her fingers on his chest. "Lars, I miss feeling you and being next to you. I want you to know that if you didn't have to be up so early, I'd ask you to stay the night."

The moment his fingertips met her wrist, she closed her eyes. Her fingers reflexively twitched as he followed her bones up the soft skin of her forearm. To her elbow, then down to her palm, rolling out every finger, up, around and over, before going back up her arm. His fingers moved up to her neck and face where he crisscrossed her cheek, side of her eyes and forehead without a pattern, caressing her lips that opened involuntarily. She kissed his fingers as they passed in front, then back down her neck and to her arm.

His touch then turned to a clasp, and soon he was leading her down to the master bedroom. He slipped off his shoes, and pulled her next to him, putting the comforter atop their feet.

As his fingers went down her arm, Danielle lifted her camisole top above her belly.

"I love how you smell," she murmured.

"The feeling is mutual."

"How long can you stay?"

"Until you fall asleep."

CHAPTER 41

Thursday at ten, Danielle called Layda and asked to come over. Danielle could tell Layda was dreading the interaction as much as she was, but it had to happen. Andre's mother was gracious when she opened the door, kissing Danielle's cheeks like she normally did. In the kitchen, over mushrooms stuffed with salmon mousse, the words came. Danielle started, her apologies followed by Layda's admission of feeling torn in two directions: happiness for Danielle and sadness for herself. Between the two of them, they filled in the blanks Andre had left in their lives

"Layda, did you know Lars is an only child, with no cousins to speak of?" Layda shook her head no. "His father's stroke left him disabled. His parents now live in a flat and rarely travel. I know he admires you and Georgy so much. More than anyone else in his acquaintance, I believe."

Layda looked conflicted, as though she too wanted to be open minded about Lars, but she had her own emotional barriers in place.

In time, thought Danielle. She hoped Layda would come to realize that she'd gain much from having Lars in her life as an adopted son-in-law, one who had the benefit of knowing her for years, as opposed to someone else new with no background or history they already shared.

The conversation moved to the easy subject of Monroe and Layda's plans for the new year. She was going to take a position as board member of another charity, this one that supported young children battling cancer.

"I'd been approached several years ago and declined, but now that I have a grandchild, the topic tugged at my heart a bit more."

On the way back home, Danielle called Lani. The phone rang through the speakers. The roads were slick and she wanted to both hands on the wheel. When Lani picked up, Danielle greeted her pleasantly then ribbed her for not calling. "What happened with Max? Are things moving forward?"

"I thought you'd know."

"Know what?"

"Stephen? Eva?"

Danielle had no idea what Lani was talking about. "What? I just said Max, not Stephen. And who's Eva?"

"Eva, the woman Andre dated after you and he broke up."

"What about her? What's going on Lani?"

"She's pregnant, Danielle, with Stephen's child." It was a good thing Danielle had both hands on the wheel and she was concentrating on the road.

"Come on, Lani. Are you kidding around?"

"Do you think I'd kid around about something like this?" Her words sounded like bullets coming through the speakers in the car.

"No," Danielle responded automatically. "That's...crazy."

"Well, did you know?" She asked the question accusingly, as though Danielle had been hiding information.

"Lani, I don't talk to Stephen a lot and when we do, it's about the restaurant, not his personal life or mine. This is the first time I'm hearing any of this."

"Are you sure?"

Danielle was exasperated. "Lani, the answer for the final time is no, I didn't. But since you are acting irritated at me, why do you even care? You were done with Stephen before the paperwork was complete. Not that I'd expect you to be happy for him, but really, can you be all that surprised? I mean, he's been wanting to have a kid forever."

"Yes!" she practically shrieked. "With me!" Danielle let Lani rant as she navigated the snowy roads. When Lani was done, Danielle asked if there was anything she could do for her. "Help me figure out how to fund my restaurant."

"Come again? Max doesn't want to invest?"

"Sure he does, but for his money he wants the majority ownership, not minority."

"Where does that leave you?" Danielle asked, worried she already knew the answer.

"It leaves me angry and in a position of asking you for help." By this time, Danielle had pulled into her garage. She turned off the car and pressed the garage door.

"I'm so sorry to do this, but I'm just pulling in and Emma needs to go. Can I call you back?"

"Sure, but what I'm wondering is if you can invest one hundred thousand?"

Danielle felt a push through her gut and down her legs. "Lani, what I told you months ago still holds true. I didn't want to invest in a new restaurant, even with you as the chef and Max as the manager. But now you don't even have that. I'd be the only investor, the numbers are all wrong. It's—"

"I can do it, Danielle!" Lani interrupted.

"I'm sorry, Lani. But I can't."

Danielle heard her take a few concentrated breaths, as though each inhale was swallowing the rejection. "Wow, okay, I understand. We'll talk later."

When she and Lars spoke that night, he was pleased to hear about the conversation with Layda and less so about Lani.

"She did it to herself," Lars maintained. "Regarding Stephen, are you curious as to how that came about?"

"It doesn't strike me as all that odd," Danielle answered. "She was a regular at the first restaurant with Andre. She's gorgeous and single. They might have even known one another before, so at least three years, maybe more, but Stephen was married. We both know how things change when people break up. ”

Danielle went back to the situation with Layda. “I still think it’s awkward to have her watch Monroe for the weekend, but Emma did mention her husband is traveling, and that she’d be available.”

A short pause followed her comment. “Does that mean you’d be interested in a weekend in Zermatt?”

“Absolutely.”

CHAPTER 42

Friday afternoon, Lars arrived in black jeans and a charcoal leather coat, all that was handsome and rugged, an eager smile on his face, the one a man wears when he's preparing to go on trip of a lifetime.

"Aren't you divine?" she admired. It had now been two weeks of seeing one another, each moment strategically placed like the squares on a quilt. Outside, Dominic was waiting by the car.

"Good evening, Ms. Grant," Dominic said as she approached. The man knew more of the details of her relationship with Lars than any person alive.

"Hello, Dominic. It's nice to see you." The man nodded his head. He was as formal as ever, and Danielle was rather grateful for it.

It had been dark for two hours by the time they reached the outskirts of Zermatt, and all she could see of the famed Matterhorn was the angled peak.

Dominic stopped the car in Tasch at the main Matterhorn Terminal for the twelve-minute train ride in. They walked along the wide streets, sharing the roads with modified horse-drawn carriages. It was still holiday for the many Europeans who visited the small boutiques of the famous city.

Danielle had to duck once or twice to miss the low-flying Swiss flags flying from first floor overhangs or below the chalet-style porches above. Lars led them off the main street and along a waterway filled with rushing grey, glacier fed water. Subdued lights shone at an angle, giving the running water an exotic effect. They had dinner at Findlerhof and Lars introduced her to the owner and his wife. Danielle felt oddly scrutinized, as though it were an anomaly Lars had a guest, but then another thought occurred to her. On the return drive, Danielle asked if he'd taken many friends to that restaurant.

"Are you really asking if I'd brought my former fiancé there?"

Danielle grimaced. "Got me."

Inside Lars' house, Danielle followed him up the stairs into the main floor, refamiliarizing herself with the home she so fondly remembered. In the living room, the black Bosendorfer grand piano was in the same position, beside the all-glass and steel windows, with the large deck beyond and the Alps in the distance.

Lars stood beside her. "Can I can get you anything? A stress reliever?" She glanced at him inquisitively. He turned her around, resting his hands on her shoulders.

"How about I go make some hot chocolate?"

"How about you answer the question? You haven't made eye contact with me since we arrived at the house. Just now, your gaze skipped right over the piano when you saw it, towards the view outside, as if it weren't really there."

Danielle gave him a weak smile. "My counterproposal is you let me make my hot chocolate first and then perhaps we talk over everything else afterward?"

He pursed his lips. "That was a lot of words for you to tell me no."

Danielle let out a hearty laugh, applauding his imitation of her words the week prior. "Touché. Go start a fire. That would be divine."

She went into the kitchen, searching for chocolate. "Awesome," she muttered to herself, pulling out three kinds of dark and milk chocolate, all different brands than she'd previously used. Then it was the fridge for milk, vanilla extract and salt. By the time she went in search of him with two mugs in her hand, Lars had changed into long, loose pants and a button-down top, so soft it had to be some type of cashmere, cotton or wool blend. His eyes were alight as he glanced at both her drink and lips.

"You look very at home in my home."

"Enough to raid your cupboards," she said, extending him a cup. "You have different chocolate than I do, but it should be just as decadent." The activity of making her drink was all the time she'd needed to synthesize through her emotions. She had arrived at a point of peace. They'd waited two weeks, when in fact, she could have made love to him that first night, New Year's.

He stood by her, took a sip and handed it back to her. "It's all mine then."

The intense emotion Lars displayed at her words told her that everything he had would be hers if she wanted it.

"I love you, too," she said softly, holding the warm cup very still.

Lars carefully took it from her hands. With the sensation of Lars' lips on her skin, followed by his fingers on her blouse and pants, and the rustle of his own clothing coming off, Danielle knew she was ready. Her past love, hopes and fantasies came together like beads of energy uniting, binding tight then exploding into a new life as she experienced Lars in his entirety as they were meant to be. Together, completely and fully.

In the middle of the night, Danielle was staring at the ceiling, her eyes stinging from tears and her head aching. She tried not to make a sound when she sniffled but failed. Lars stirred, turning to her.

"Hey," he said softly, immediately touching her face, pulling her to him. "What's going on?"

The closed off sensation in her throat told her words weren't going to come out right, no matter how hard she tried. Danielle touched his cheek with the back of her forefinger.

"I don't want you to think badly of me."

Lars took her fingers and pressed them against his lips. "Did I hurt you?"

An absurd thought. "No, and before you ask, what you are seeing are happy tears. A phenomenon I told you about. It's…" she stopped, struggling. "There are so many things, all of which are …good. Better than… " Her voice cracked. Lars stayed quiet. "It's just that on every level, it's like this is a better fit, tighter, in a way. He and I shared common interests in food and music, but not to the degree you and I love both. He had a nice, modern decorating style, but yours is elegant and timeless."

"Like yours," he added softly.

"Exactly. Do you remember when you told me that you loved that woman in New York while you still loved your wife? You said you loved her more, or differently." Lars nodded. "I feel so…bad, is the only word I can think of. I did love him. I still feel love for him. But Lars," she said, her voice shaking. "I just love you so much more."

Lars said nothing as he gathered her into his arms and she sobbed. It was as though the grief of Andre's death had risen from the ground, coming back into her life, a specter haunting her because she cared more for this man than the one she lost. Lars held her tightly, stroking her hair and kissing the top of her head.

Eventually, they lay still, his warm hand in the center of her back, moving gently back and forth, the way one instinctively comforts a child. She tried to relax, but found another swelling of grief building within her.

"Do you know what else is killing me?" she whispered. "I feel like I haven't felt as bad as I should, but at the time, I did. My heart felt like it was going to break and I couldn't live, but then…I did. And I was doing fine until you came along…"

"And changed things."

"No. *That's the point.* You didn't change what was there. You just moved it up, like the volume on a stereo. And it's so soon, but it's really not, and even Andre had said you were the best guy a woman could have all things considered. Georgy wanted me to start going out, and even now that Layda seems okay with it, it's so hard and guilt-inducing."

"Slow down," Lars said gently. "You have to let the guilt go. Georgy always knew of your feelings for me, and me for you. I don't honestly think he believed that went away, and he must have spoken with Layda about it, or else they never would have created the rooms for you and Monroe in their home. So while they didn't anticipate it happening so soon, they certainly expected us getting together. They said as much."

Her voice was almost inaudible when she spoke. "That's true."

"Lucky for you, those who love you want to see you fulfilled, not torn apart." Lars placed his fingers under her chin. "We have *earned the right* to be together, Danielle. If anything, we may, at some point, give them another reason to celebrate. I'm convinced your new Swiss family will be there for you more than you can possibly imagine. Maybe even this weekend had you given them a chance."

He drew her to him again, and this time, she felt like the arid, Oregon fields at the end of a dry, hot August, when the crops had been harvested and to regenerate for the next season, must be lit on fire. Eventually, the blackened field yielded to the green life springing forth underneath, giving life where none had existed. Danielle felt her own thrusts of new life from within Lars' arms. Her guilt and grief were finally burned, the ashes of pain going in to air, the black grief within her gone. Now the shoots of love erupted all over her, first in her chest, then up the back of her neck, cresting at the base of her skull. A wave of desire moved throughout her body.

They fell asleep as the sun rose behind the Alps, the image of her heart rising with it. She'd never felt closer to another human being in her life.

CHAPTER 43

Monday, January 15th, Danielle arrived at the office at a quarter to six, greeted the security guard and receptionist, waiting once again for Jacqueline Lader, the third such time she'd done so during her tenure at MRD. The head of human resources met her ten minutes later, and the process for acquiring updated security cards was familiar and fast. By six-twenty, she was behind her computer, running through the clients in her accounts, along with the totals. Over her holiday, she read that Blackrock had an astounding three trillion dollars under management. A single family had eleven billion placed for currency alone. Compared to that, MRD was boutique.

But we stomp them in returns.

She heard the ping of an appointment reminder. Fifteen minutes until her session with Ulrich. Seven-forty. Only the Swiss and airlines used strange times to meet, knowing it was because odd numbers tended to stick in a person's memory better than quarter of the hour intervals.

Danielle flicked her eyes between two screens, capturing the research she'd assembled from the previous two weeks. She was mid transaction when the two taps made her jump.

You would think that after all this time, I'd be used to it she thought as she lifted her hands. She met his eyes. *No. I'll never get used to the frisson of heat that Lars creates inside of me.*

"Good morning, Lars." Dark, charcoal suit, white shirt and an

238

azure tie with a shimmer. Gorgeous.

"And you," he said. "I see you have everything operational." A movement took her eyes from Lars. It was Glenda, waving with a smile before she turned to her desk. He noticed the woman as well. "I won't keep you. I just wanted to say I may be stopping in briefly during your meeting with Ulrich."

Glenda came by to welcome her back and hand her a folder. "This is for your meeting. The client roster and a few policy changes that were recently implemented."

Danielle thanked her and flicked through the pages. On the right side were half a dozen pages of updated certifications, and she noted several courses she'd need to take over the next six months to remain compliant. She was on the last page when her eyes stopped.

Desk leads, managers, traders, roles and expectations. She skimmed through the details on the page and closed the folder, waiting for Ulrich. What she'd just read was a great example of the very thick and clear lines of propriety that weren't ever going to be crossed in the off hours between she and the managing director.

She was already in the conference room and re-reading the materials again when Ulrich entered. "Good morning," she said, rising to shake his hand. "Are you tired of welcoming me back to my place of employment?"

"It is becoming strangely familiar," he said dryly. He looked unchanged, his whip-grey hair slicked back, the widow's peak on his forehead blending into taught skin, a shade darker than many of the Swiss she'd met. Ulrich took the seat next to her at the round conference table. "You've had a chance to review the items with in the folder? Good. Let's go through the client situation first, then the new policies and procedures." Then it was her financial goals followed by a new process for compliance training and testing.

Finally, the changes in positions and roles. "Are you comfortable with what you've read?"

She nodded. Johanne had been promoted to desk lead and Ulrich was promoted to an associate partner. Johanne would now be setting her numbers, not Ulrich.

"My only question is if I've actually chased you out of this position?"

Ulrich sat back just a bit, twirling the pencil in his fingers. "I will admit that the series of client discussions haven't always been pleasant, but that's our world." Danielle suppressed a smile. Her interaction with Ulrich as a boss had been largely relegated to him handing out bonus checks and covering her accounts when she'd been absent. Oh, and that little issue around dating a client that nearly cost her a job.

"Lars concurs that Johanne has a good style with the clients and certainly enjoys the interactions with them much more than I do." He paused as Lars entered the room and took a seat across from Danielle.

"I was just about to ask her about her thoughts on inheriting Johanne's account load?"

Here she was, a twenty-nine-year-old American about to have the bulk of gold trading accounts at MRD. "No different than when I first entered this room," she answered honestly. It truly was only more zero's. "As long as he takes more of the mandatory meetings so I can trade."

The men confirmed that was the case and Lars spoke. "And on the currency? Would you like to wait or take it on now? It's at ten billion," he added.

When David first told her of the opportunity in Switzerland, he'd challenged her to move mountains, not the course of a river here and there. Now she wryly wondered if that included separating and conjoining continents.

"Danielle," Ulrich began, leaning forward, a serious look creating wrinkles on his face where none previously existed. "Lars has always maintained you put more pressure on you than we ever could, or would." Danielle glared good-naturedly at her managing director. He sat looking smug and proud, his mannerisms suggesting this conversation was playing out as he presupposed. "With all you've been through, I feel compelled to ask you the same question I did when we faced your father's health. Are you sure we shouldn't change your quota?"

"No. Leave them." Her father would be proud, and she would be successful. "And on the currency, I'm comfortable with you giving it to me now, two weeks or thirty days won't make much difference."

The meeting over, Danielle walked briskly to her desk. She stopped by Johanne's office to congratulate him, but he was the one making effusive compliments to her.

"No one in this office has ever had so much under their management," he said "Congratulations. I certainly don't want it."

"I know, you want a social life, but the override on my returns won't hurt, will they?" He winked and she left.

Back at her desk, she put on her headset, her fingers were already on the keyboard and mind on the screens in front of her. The ferocity of her desire to achieving her goals was eerily reminiscent of her first day at the firm: she had a lot to prove, to herself, and everyone else. Again.

At one, Danielle put on 1 FM, an 80s Euro channel based out of Switzerland, the ambient noise pop electronica a necessary distraction from the numbers that went up and down on her screens. She was now eternally thankful she'd spent a portion of her time at home conducting research before returning to work. In spurts of reflection, she thought back on how busy Lars was during that time.

Lars. He'd been scheming the entire time. No wonder he wanted her rested, satisfied and ready to return.

That night, Danielle had Monroe in bed promptly at six and she began her second bout of trading. The phone jolted her at eight and she felt a ping of guilt. She'd not thought of Lars once since she got home.

"Are you calling to apologize?" she asked archly. "Because if you aren't, you should." His response was a low laugh so sexy she felt a spike of passion that she dutifully ignored.

"I can't apologize for being the managing director."

"Oh, no. Not that. You should apologize because the events of today have effectively killed every moment of my free time for the foreseeable future." Even as Danielle said the words, she was smiling.

"Perhaps I should have brought up that fact to the partners."

"Absolutely," Danielle laughed. "Excuse me, gentlemen, hundreds of millions of dollars are nothing compared to my sex life, so we need to keep Danielle's numbers down for the time being." Their laughter ricocheted back and forth until she spoke.

"On a serious note, Lars, I completely support that you didn't tell me what to expect. You have your role and I have mine. That said, I did spend more than a few seconds in complete shock between Johanne's volume and the currency you gave me to trade."

"To which you recovered quickly."

"Maybe," she hedged. "But I'm sure of one thing. Our time together is going to take a serious nose dive for a little while. I hope you know that and are OK with it."

"Yes, and yes."

She glanced at the clock as she now did constantly. "You may go to bed knowing that I miss you, love you, and would like to be with you here, in my room."

"Perhaps a date night in at your place this Friday, since no one trades at that time, anywhere in the world."

Danielle accepted his proposal and said goodbye. Fours later, she fell asleep, exhausted but happy.

During the week, Lars dropped by her office once a day, short interludes of levity that lasted only minutes, but were like cloud bursts, the electricity hanging in the air long after he left. Her conversations with him at night were equally short. Both knew she needed to focus, not be distracted.

Keeping to that philosophy, Danielle and Johanne didn't have a real conversation until Friday afternoon and even that was truncated by an off-site training he had to attend.

"How's the week been?" he asked congenially, still her peer and friend while displaying the professionalism of her new boss. "Your numbers are fantastic."

"Like being at a Formula One race, this being my tire-rotation pit stop." Johanne smiled, inviting her to have a seat. His office was arranged with his desk towards the wall, his right side, where she sat, faced the water, his left the hallway. He could easily glance in either direction, but while he worked, he wanted no distractions. He didn't even have a picture above his flat screen.

Danielle thought Johanne looked tired and drawn.

"So, is being a titan-in-training everything you imagined it would be?" Johanne rotated his neck around, stretching it out, the motion moving his ear-length wavy hair.

"A desk lead is not quite Thor, but it's been interesting actually."

"Did you want this? Or rather, had you suggested it?" she asked.

"Suggest, no. But I was open to the possibility that less trading might yield benefits in other areas."

Danielle applauded his wording. "Well, for the record, I'm thrilled for you and don't even mind you being my new boss. My deal is that in turn for treating me well, I will try not to give you any of the unexpected surprises my predecessor had to deal with."

"Thanks for that," he said, using the phrasing and intonation she'd used with him several times before. They both smiled, the comradery based in mutual admiration and a real sense of friendship.

At home, Danielle sat on the floor with Monroe, removing her daughter's soft-soled shoes, tickling her feet then checking the new nubs of teeth in her mouth. Monroe constantly tried to push and pull herself up from the ground to the coffee table, dropping down on her wobbly legs, barely missing the corners. Thankfully, Emma had purchased rubber corners made to adhere to glass and wood, placing them on all the sharp corners of the end tables. Danielle made a list of remaining corners in the other rooms. It was after six when the phone rang.

"Another late meeting in Geneva this wonderful Friday night?" she asked Lars.

"No. I'm purposefully giving you time to be with Monroe and relax."

"Lars," she began hesitantly. "Perhaps you're the one who needs a break this weekend, and I am happy to give it to you."

"I don't recall saying I needed one."

"I heard from Glenda that you have an ice climbing event, but you hadn't told me about it and I felt—well, I hope you are going to go. I'm perfectly fine with staying home and not distracting you."

"I like you distracting me."

"Lars, I'm serious. Go climb."

"I'd rather spend the day with you," he insisted.

Danielle deflected the statement. "That's great, but I disagree with changing your life or lifestyle to be with me. No, listen," she stopped him when he started to speak. "Integrating three lives doesn't mean you should stop living your own. Furthermore, your season only lasts a few more months, so you should take advantage of it."

"Hmm. I'll agree to be away from you Sunday but not on Saturday, and only if you promise to spend time with Monroe and not the computer. Maybe even go see Layda and Georgy."

It was a good idea, and she did that on Saturday morning, staying for lunch. The conversation wasn't forced and they didn't ask about Lars. Baby steps, Danielle told herself, knowing it would continue to get easier with time.

That evening, Monroe was already asleep by the time Lars arrived. After a snack of cheese, meats and crackers, he asked what she was going to do the next day. "You promised no work."

She kissed him. "I have already arranged for us to go with Georgy and Layda to the Asper Family Home tomorrow. You are rendered completely unnecessary." He kissed her in such a way that he thought was necessary, his hands moving along her inner thigh.

"I can't do this in public," he murmured.

"Because it's not *discrete*."

"You have gotten so much use out of that single word," he teased, biting her lip.

She pulled back in mock anger. "And I should, since you used it within the first five minutes of meeting you and consequently, it was indelibly seared in my mind."

Lars ran his fingers up and down her arm. "Those first five minutes when you described sailboarding? When I was nearly overcome with your looks and brilliance and briefly thought about making love to you."

"You did not." The slightest curl formed on his lips. "Did you know how I felt? What was going through my mind?"

"I could tell you were surprised when you saw me. Even then, you glanced at me in a way that was a little more than investigatory."

Danielle smiled mischievously. In hindsight, the memory was exhilarating.

"I thought you were the most magnetic person I'd ever met. How you looked, spoke, the energy that exuded from you. Had it not been for me being slightly offended by your pronouncement regarding inner office affairs, I would have had a much harder time keeping my thoughts professional."

"You tried so hard," Lars added, "but didn't always succeed. Remember when we had the intense discussion about your position with the firm after the situation with Andre was exposed?"

"I was sitting there, waiting for you to fire me, but all I could focus on was how gorgeous you looked, even in your controlled fury. Then at the end…"

"What?"

"When I gave my commitment to the firm, you said there were plenty of smart, attractive men who were willing to go out with me. My last thought was that 'yes, and one is a coworker sitting right in front of me.'"

A pleased smile formed on his lips. "I couldn't be sure of what you were thinking, but I saw something in your eyes. I wanted to take you to the couch and push you down right then."

Danielle's inhaled quickly. Lars slid her legs to the side, and moved his body fully over hers.

"You sat there, angry at me but also wanting me," he said with confidence. "I imagined one hand above your head, holding you still." He took her hand, raising it above her head, fulfilling his fantasy.

"And you knew I would respond to you," she murmured, as she arched her back to get closer to him.

He released her hand, burying his face in her hair, gravitating to her neck then down to her chest, just above her breast, licking and biting her skin. She was unable to restrain her hips from rocking back and forth, holding him tight as she did so. "I would say your name," he murmured, "and in that moment, you would know what would happen next."

Danielle groaned with desire, envisioning the scene happening in his office. She slipped off her bottoms then unbuckled his belt, pushing off his pants, hooking them with a foot and dropping them to the floor. She lifted her top past her belly button and pulled up his shirt, simultaneously wrapping her legs over his, curling her toes underneath his calves. Legs intertwined, the heat between their bare stomachs increasing as they breathed each other's scent.

"Is this what you imagined?" she breathed. He nodded, biting her neck harder as she arched her head back, rolling her pelvic bone upward, capturing him as he moved his body along hers. He pushed into her, and heat rushed through her inner thighs, over her breasts and down her arms. Their rocking motions were as one, and she felt the flex of his legs and sweat on his lower back.

Lars' breathing intensified as her fingertips pushed him even deeper. The friction gave her a double pleasure that came so quickly she emitted a faint cry of surprise. He realized the source and perpetuated the movement.

"You are more...so much more than I ever imagined." His words were cut off as he gave a strong exhale and she knew that they were both reaching the top of the waterfall. He clenched her shoulders, his back starting to arch but he channeled the movement down, into her, shuddering, sending a final ripple through her, and she involuntarily exclaimed. They had gone over the edge together.

CHAPTER 44

Sunday morning, Danielle called Stephen, who willingly agreed to have Renaldo make food for the retirement home, further suggesting it could be a regular donation on Sundays. If Danielle wasn't available to be there, he'd have the food delivered regardless. She was thrilled, and then took the opportunity to congratulate him on the baby.

"When were you going to tell me?" she asked.

"When it was convenient. Honestly, I didn't think word would get around that fast, but she has family in town, and some of them knew as did her friends. That includes Max and the other guys, who have been tight for years. Apparently, Lani and Max got into an argument about something, and Max threw it in her face."

Danielle closed her eyes to the image, and encouraged Stephen to tell her more about Eva. "There is a lot to say about Eva, but the most important is that she's a lovely individual. Not nearly as bad as we previously hypothesized." Danielle laughed at the obvious understatement.

"If Andre was with her for an entire month, the sex must be good."

"Danielle, it's a lot more than that," he said seriously.

"Stephen. I was joking. All I want to know is if she's going to be nice to me."

"Of course. She was in love with Andre, and when it became clear he didn't return her affection, she was crushed in her own way. Then you became pregnant and it was salt in her wound."

"She wanted a family?"

"And a home. We are both very traditional in that way." Danielle waited for the change in the tone of his voice, the one that would express thrilling excitement or plummeting worry, like the rollercoaster of emotions that naturally occurred when learning of a pregnancy, but didn't hear it.

"Stephen," she began. "Are you in love with her?"

"That's a big question," he hedged. It was all she had to hear.

"What are you going to do?" she asked quietly.

"For now, let it play out. I like her a lot, and we are matched on so many levels…"

"But you're still in love with Lani." His silence was another confirmation of his emotional state. "I haven't known you for a dozen years without being able to read the tea leaves."

"How about you? Is there something you need to tell me regarding Lars?"

"Yes, we are back together."

"I already anticipated that. I'm talking about him buying Lani's portion of the business. I will personally thank him the next time he comes through the door." At her silence he said, "You didn't know?"

"No." That sly man. She had no issue with his purchase, whether he was active as an investor or passive. He was brilliant, knew the industry and certainly would help in any fashion she and Stephen required. That evening, she found a moment to share the news with Georgy and Layda, confessing she had no idea of what he'd done.

"Smart investor," Georgy said, as though he could take partial credit.

"He's watching out for you, which I like," added Layda. So did

Danielle.

For an entire week, Danielle kept her knowledge of the information to herself, which was made easy because Lars was in Geneva the entire time. He'd phoned her every night, their conversations glossing over work and focusing on Monroe and her own activities. She told him Lani had called her several times, inquiring about her request for money.

"She sounds like she's getting desperate." Lars asked if Lani had shared all the details of her situation, and Danielle admitted that she hadn't asked. She didn't want to know. Lars counseled her to find out.

"Subtly, if you can."

"Are you thinking I should invest as well?"

"No, but if you have the facts you can at least address this and move on. Having a one-way dialogue on money doesn't make for a fulfilling friendship, and she's your one true friend in town." Danielle took his advice to heart and made a mental note to call Lani on the weekend when she could have a substantive phone call without the pressure of the clock.

"Lars," she said quietly. "Why did you purchase Lani's portion?"

"You know the answer."

"Because you love me."

"And I would do most things in my power to make your life a little easier." Danielle felt a surge of gratitude mixed with her heightened desire to have him come home to her.

"Will you be climbing this weekend?"

"Sunday, if you don't mind." She didn't and confessed she might even go to a club with Johanne.

"Although I'll be parked at the bar, probably talking to Dario rather than dancing in the cages." She had no desire to be hot and sweaty with anyone other than Lars.

Lars thought he might be home Saturday and could see her, but if meetings ran over or he were delayed, he'd travel directly from Geneva to the ice climbing competition.

Friday at two-thirty, she stared at the trading boards that showed trader results for the week. She glanced around and seeing no one, removed her phone and took a picture. As she walked back down the hall, she wrote a few words, attached the photo and sent it to David. He had to see this.

"Hummer girl," called Johanne from his office. "Danielle."

She laughed as she poked her head in the room. "Hummer, like the car?"

"No, as in, you are constantly humming, though I can't place the tune. Is that something from Benny's playlist?"

Danielle felt her face go warm as she blushed. "I think it's an amalgamation of several songs." And she was completely unaware she was doing it.

"Your numbers are outstanding," he said, tapping on his computer, followed by the screen going dark. "My former boss Ulrich thanks you, as do I." Johanne had a mischievous light in his eye. "You've been wearing your hair differently this week as well."

Danielle rolled her eyes to the ceiling, as if looking for guidance. "You have way too much time on your hands in this new position if you are noticing my humming and hair styles. But then, you are more of a fashionista than anyone else around here. I have a question. Can my boss go meet me at the dance club?"

"Definitely."

Layda enthusiastically agreed to having Monroe stay over on Saturday night, suggesting Danielle come by at noon so she could have a day for herself.

She was at the grocery store around one in the afternoon when her phone buzzed. "Yes?" she answered in a low voice.

"I'm in town. Where are you?"

"Shopping."

"Fantastic. Can I join you?"

"To buy asparagus?"

Lars laughed. "Actually, I have a friend who's having a baby and I need to buy a few things."

"You aren't talking about Stephen, are you?"

"No, but you can give me input and I'll do the same, just in case you want to purchase something for him."

He met her in the parking lot and they took his car, driving to the Swiss equivalent of Babies-r-Us. She'd answered all his questions about form and function, style and comfort of a car seat before giving her opinion on the best one for a girl. It was twice the cost of her own, but told him that since money was no object, he might as well get the best. He agreed. She did tell Lars he went a little overboard when he purchased the sheepskin-lined model, but he countered the baby should be warm and cozy. They went to his apartment to unload the items, and she was confused when he started to take the car seat of the box. It wasn't until he started to place it in his own car that she realized it wasn't a gift for anyone but himself.

"You wicked man!" she exclaimed.

"If I'm going to have Monroe in my car, she needs to be safe. And warm." Danielle was practically speechless. "Let's go. We have more shopping to do."

They went from store to store picking up other necessities that make up a room for a little girl. At first, Danielle expressed disbelief, then discomfort, then elation. When Lars asked for input on furniture, she had a moment where she nearly broke into tears and couldn't speak.

"Happy tears?" he asked quietly. Danielle put a hand to her mouth. This was his chance to be a father after the fact. "Shall we keep going?" he asked. "My short list got longer when I saw what was in her room at your house."

They picked out bedding, wall coverings, matching floor rugs and a custom rocking chair that Lars had previously tested for comfort. Danielle felt like she was an angel being asked to jump from cloud to cloud, each time picking up a bit more happiness and sprinkling it all around her.

They finished out the day by purchasing airtight disposable trashcans and baby wipe warmers. Lars had done his homework on what was technically the best, but willingly listened to Danielle's real world experience of what worked and didn't and why. They debated and she laughed, willing to give in to his extravagant purchases but telling him the temperature of the baby wipe warmer didn't really matter.

When they got hungry, the decision of where to eat wasn't even a question. Stephen held the door open for them and smiled wide.

"Out for a bite?" he asked as he guided them to a table.

"Shopping for car seats and cribs, actually," Lars answered. Danielle winked and went with it. Stephen gave Lars the man version of a 'you-did-good' look and left.

Ivan came over to say hello and stayed so long Stephen had to come by and nudge him along. Between appetizers and the main meal, Danielle went to the kitchen and said hello to Renaldo, receiving handshakes and hugs from various members of the staff.

"You know, it seems things are slowly but surely working out for some people. Even Dario and Johanne have resumed talking." This intrigued Lars, because it had been under his watch that Johanne went through the same dating gauntlet as Danielle, ending with Dario leaving as a client but remaining with Johanne.

"I felt personally responsible for their breakup you know," Danielle said, taking a bite of crab cakes. "It was all the stress he felt from my leaving that caused them to split."

"Does that mean you can take all the credit for them getting back together?" His sarcasm was obvious, but his smile gentle.

"Only half. You get the other half of the credit for making him a manager. By the way, did I tell you Lani called me back? She found a new investor for the business who wishes to remain anonymous." Danielle eyed him warily. "Was that you, again? I mean, wasn't purchasing her share of the restaurant enough?"

He cocked his head back and laughed, then leaned to her ear, sensually caressing the area with his warm lips. "I'm not investing in any other woman, in any other way, other than you. Good enough?"

The air felt electrified as she let herself absorb his energy. When he pulled back, his eyes were deep and focused. The topic transitioned into his schedule for the next few weeks.

"Two working professionals who blend right in with everyone else."

He shook his head and smiled. "We will never blend in, anywhere. Not with your beauty, my career and a gorgeous little girl." He raised his finger off his glass, directing it to her.

"You know, this whole uber-confidence-smug-side of you is rising to the surface more frequently."

"Can you blame me? We are together. As a family or individually, we will always stand out in a crowd." Danielle's felt elated, as though his statement and look of confidence had sucked the air out of the room, replacing it with helium.

"We will," she said on a whisper.

CHAPTER 45

At the office, Danielle tried very hard to blend in and submerge her feelings of emotional exuberance, saving that energy for her time with Lars. They alternated days between her home and his apartment, sharing cooking duties. As a three-person unit, they did normal family activities: watching television, taking walks and occasionally eating lunch out. Monroe had several meltdowns of epic proportions, but as Danielle belatedly realized, they occurred when she had failed to adhere to Monroe's normal sleeping routine during the day, causing the little girl to be overtired. The cycle of crying, fussing, then taking even longer to fall sleep was a lesson Lars got to learn with her.

"This is my first time, too," Danielle said one Saturday afternoon as she held a crying, squirming daughter who wailed unabated for the entire ride back home. Lars took it in stride.

"There's nothing we can do but put her to bed, right?" Danielle stared at him, then laughed. He was exactly right, and no amount of getting irritated about the situation was going to change a thing.

Periodically, they drove by Lani's new restaurant, watching the progression of the buildout. Max had hired the staff and the official opening was scheduled for three weeks out. Lani had invited Lars and Danielle to attend the soft opening, which she planned for a Monday night. Danielle had agreed to go, as would Lars if he was in town. He knew Lani was hoping for good press, and Lars was willing to put the word out.

SARAH GERDES

"Assuming the food deserves it," he said with all the seriousness of delivering a quarterly report. Danielle was nervous and excited for her friend.

On Tuesday, Johanne entered her office with the look of a manager with an agenda. She removed her hands from the keyboard and sat back in her chair.

"Ulrich is right," he noted, taking the seat in front of her desk, crossing his legs and adjusting his glasses. "You look positively uncomfortable when you have to talk during trading hours."

"Only for my bosses do I lift my fingers from the keyboard."

"I'm here out of courtesy, not obligation. I thought you'd like to know you are going to be invited to a partners-only meeting next Monday. I won't be there. I don't know the specifics, only that they are trying to get you to stay."

She tilted her head. "But I'm not going anywhere."

"That's what I told them, but they clearly want confirmation of your intentions." He then got a quirky look on his face, one that belied his position as her boss. "I suspect it has something to do with whatever has been going on behind closed doors, but that's only a guess."

"Hmm. That sounds intriguing."

"No more than you." Danielle looked at him, bemused. "Oh, come on," he said, leaning forward, as though his proximity would get her to reveal all. "You'd have to be blind not to see that you are in love. Not that any of us mind, but I think the partners are scared shitless you're going to leave again and our clients will revolt."

"That's an awfully un-Swiss way to talk," she hedged, glancing up into the hallway, grateful no one could see her. "No, I won't leave," she said cautiously. If she'd been that easy to read, she would be even more so now.

Johanne's lips moved, and she could see him working through

his next words. For the first time since she'd returned to work, her heart felt constricted. "Dario thinks it's the man who came after Andre. The one who you originally thought was the baby's father."

Danielle felt a wash of fear jolt from her chest to belly. "Dario spoke to you about this?"

Johanne's eyes bored into hers. "Yes and, I can go now, since your avoidance confirmed his guess." Danielle threw her head back and laughed. Johanne glanced over his shoulder and back, his gaze wicked. "He's got to be out of his mind over you, isn't he?" Danielle closed her mouth and tried hard not to smile. "Another yes. Well, then," Johanne said, firmly putting his hands on his knees and stood. "I guess you will be here for a while. Excellent."

He didn't wait for a response before he left, which was just as well. Danielle didn't have one.

Danielle wanted to ask Lars about the partners meeting but knew he wouldn't tell her anything. The most she could do was tease him, which she fully intended to do when he came over Saturday. That evening, she watched the interaction between he and Monroe. Her daughter played around him or with him, comfortably sitting on his lap while he read stories. Later, Lars had Monroe bouncing on his foot, up and down as he held her hands out to the side. She was laughing as he lifted her up and down.

"I loved this as a kid," Lars called out.

She wiped her hands off and joined him in the living room. "Is your deal any closer to being wrapped up?"

"A few lose ends that have to do with personnel but nothing too difficult. This week should conclude most of it."

"Does the partner meeting I've been invited to attend Monday have anything to do with that?"

"It shouldn't, but then I can't predict the future."

"That was a suitably vague response," she teased, sitting on the edge of the couch. "I saw that it's scheduled at the end of the day. Can you at least tell me if it might go much later than four? I'll need to call Emma and make sure it's okay for her to be with Monroe a little longer."

"That might be wise. I'd suggest two hours if possible."

Monday, Danielle chose a slate grey pantsuit that was an anomaly for her, but she liked the straight leg cut and heavy wool blend. The cropped jacket, its high collar stylishly tailored to round on lapels, and the embroidered buttons were a pop of fashion. As she approached the conference room, the men stood when she entered. Unnecessary, she thought. She was a trader, not an honorary member of parliament.

"Thank you for joining us," Lars said, indicating she take the available seat at the end, near Ulrich, who stood to her left. He shook her hand and smiled. She had met the partners before, though had limited interaction outside the general meetings. It simply wasn't necessary to anyone's task, and the office culture didn't support idle discussions.

"Danielle, you have been asked to participate in this meeting as a matter of distinction," Lars explained. "To date, we've never had a trader holding 14.7 billion under management for gold and twelve in currency. You've earned it and we, the partners, want you to know you have our complete support and confidence."

Danielle kept her breathing even and her eyes steady, rewarding Lars with a smile she deemed appropriate for the setting. She then glanced around the room, making brief eye contact with each man.

"You may someday be sitting here in this group," said a man named Gabriel.

"Or leading it," remarked the eldest of the group, a man she recognized from his founder portrait in the hallway, Noel Garman.

"I'll remain right where I am for the time being, thanks very much."

Then Ulrich spoke. "As your former, direct manager, I've conveyed how your loyalty to the firm has been unshakeable."

"Remarkable really," interjected Noel. "Just ask all those associated with Georgy. You might as well have tapped into a blood red vein that stretches throughout Switzerland." A rumbling of agreement echoed throughout the room, augmented by a few head nods.

Lars leaned forward, hands on the table. "What the partners are getting to Danielle, is that we want you to stay with us for the foreseeable future. Is there anything that you need or want to assist you in your efforts to ensure that you remain here?"

"How about a private plane and chalet in St. Moritz?" she said, pausing fractionally for effect. A chuckle emerged from Noel. She'd struck the right chord. "In all seriousness, gentlemen, my support staff is excellent so I don't require a thing. You've exercised immense patience with my personal issues. The least I can do is remain here and produce."

"And there is nothing that will compel you to stay or propel you to leave?" Noel pressed.

She'd worked her entire career to arrive at the point where she was being asked to stay.

"Noel, my commitment is to MRD. Only a non-business related situation would compel me to leave. And if I have any more of those, I have much bigger issues than a trading goal."

After her statement, she noticed the tenor of the room shift slightly.

"Thank you for joining us, Danielle," said Lars. "And once again, congratulations on your achievements. You've earned it."

Danielle smiled and left.

Just another day at the office, she thought abstractly. Although perhaps she'd call David and share the news of the crazy numbers she had in trading. He'd predicted at one point she'd make it to twelve billion under management. Now, approximately twenty-one months later, she'd surpassed it.

"Pardon me." The voice made her jump and she peered around the door.

"I just lost a week of my life," she said quietly. Lars smiled pleasantly, a little twitch on his lower lip immediately capturing her attention. She turned back to her wardrobe, retrieving her purse. "May I help you?" she said, closing the door.

"Yes, you may. I need an hour of your time. Maybe two."

"Now?"

"Yes, if that's possible."

"It is possible," she said, looking at her watch. "It's a good thing I asked you about staying later." She started to replace her purse back in the closet.

"You will need that," he said.

"I will? But I thought you said…"

"I said I need you for an hour or two. I didn't say where. A congratulatory dinner is being extended to you, compliments of MRD."

"Excellent!" she said, keeping her voice low. A dinner date on the house with the man of her dreams.

Danielle said very little in the elevator, answering his innocuous questions about the week's activities until the metal doors shut. She peered up at the numbers above the door, watching them descend. She wasn't sure if the compartment had audio along with video, and she wasn't going to utter a word that could be recorded. They remained silent as they walked to his car, and he held the door open for her. "Thank you." She kept her hands on her lap, unconsciously sucking on the inside of her lower lip. The garage door lifted and she watched it in silence.

"You're awfully quiet," he remarked.

Danielle looked over at the brilliant, charming man beside her. "Can you please drive out now? At least in the darkness of the streets, I don't have to worry about cameras and I can love you at will."

He pulled out of the garage and on to the main road and a second later her fingers were in his hair, her lips on his neck, sensually running her tongue along his skin, up to his ear. She loved him so madly, she wanted to touch and bite and kiss all of him. She felt his hand go into her hair, removing the clip, her dark curls falling around her shoulder.

"I'm so proud of you, Danielle," he murmured. "The partners wanted me to reinforce that you are valued and appreciated."

"I hope," she mumbled through her kisses, "that you take your responsibility as the managing director *very* seriously." She placed her right hand just below his tie, unfastening three buttons, sliding her hand through the opening.

"I promised to take you out," he said firmly, as though he were saying it to convince himself to stay on course.

"Just drive around for ten minutes," she requested, scratching his chest.

He did as she asked, and after a few minutes of intense touching, spoke. "It's a good thing that driving while sexually intoxicated isn't illegal, because I'd be in jail for life."

"Okay," she said laughing. She did have a daughter waiting at home and couldn't be gone all night. When they stopped, she asked him where they were eating.

"A place called LaSalle that us locals love. You will too."

"As much as I love you?" she quipped.

"No. Not even close."

CHAPTER 46

For the first time during their acquaintance, Danielle and Lars had dinner together in downtown Zurich. "Although I'm not sure this counts as being in town," she observed. The area was industrial and the restaurant was within in a former ship building factory warehouse. The inside ambiance was a contradiction in appearances. Massive, Venetian style crystal chandeliers hung from the ceiling serving as a striking centerpiece visuals the strong wood grains of the walls, white table linens and floor. They sampled the varied cuisine of French and Italian, but it wasn't until dessert had been served that Lars brought up work.

"Now that we've enjoyed a wonderful meal on the house, I can tell you the real reason we are here is you struck the right note with all the men, particularly Noel. He has a few things he'd like me to offer you to convince you to stay on." A glimpse of the managing director broke through Lars' personal charm. "Think of it as insurance to keep you nicely insulated from those who may try to take you away."

Danielle could only think of one real possibility. "Like Georgy?"

"They know each other. Most billionaires do."

She sat up straight, her eyes flat and all business. "I'm ready. What does MRD consider enticing enough to keep a profitable trader?"

"An annual override bonus of five million francs, two more

weeks off at your discretion and use of the company chalet in St. Moritz, in accordance with its rules of use and availability." A flick of humor crossed his face. "You gave me the same, unimpressed expression when you saw my apartment for the first time."

Danielle shrugged. "The partners at Goldman had perks of private planes and getaway vacations and top sales people at every firm received incentive trips. Why not the same here?"

"But?"

"But you can tell them the best thing for me is to get your damn deal done so I can have you to myself full time."

A slow, wonderful smile pulled his lips back. "I'll be sure to pass that along. Actually, I'm pleased to say we are on track to complete the paperwork for the end of next week. And although you will likely maintain your rigorous schedule, I can assure you, all of my personal, non-office hours will soon be yours."

Danielle gave him a look that should definitely never pass between a trader and boss. "Not all. Don't you still have a few ice climbing events left?"

"Yes, this upcoming weekend is one of the biggest. Would you like to go?"

"No," she said. "You are on a streak that I don't want to be responsible for breaking."

"Fair enough."

Lars paid the bill and they were soon in the car. He took her face in both palms and covered her lips with his own. "I love you completely," he murmured.

The following night, she left work right after closing time. She had planned to spend the weekend with Layda and Georgy at their home. As the glass-fronted elevator descended, she said a prayer of thanks that her relationship with Layda had returned to normal. The awkwardness had dissipated, and their conversations included

Danielle's life outside work life, from cooking to kids and new restaurants. She never had to use Lars' name, but it was implied and understood that he was her companion.

Once outside the building, Danielle called Emma and asked if she could spare another hour. "I'd like to stop by the restaurant and see how it's running."

"Take your time," her caretaker said. "I'll feed Monroe and put her to bed if it gets late."

Stephen gave her a massive hug and she sat the bar while he went around the counter and poured her a soda with lime. He inquired about Lars first.

"We are dating but I'm not pregnant. How's that for the summary?" They laughed. "And Eva. How far along is she?"

"Three months, so it's early yet." Danielle did the math.

"I'm proud of you. You waited until after Lani told you she was leaving."

"No," he corrected. "I waited until Lani stopped wanting to have sex with me, but even then it wasn't enough to push me away completely. That happened when Lucas let me in on the fact Max and Lani were sleeping together. The mystery of her disinterest solved."

Danielle bit her lip against the pressure of the guilt she'd been harboring about keeping silent. "When she told me she wanted out of the business, I guessed. She admitted to the situation with Max, but it wasn't my secret to tell. I didn't want to hurt you, Stephen. I'm sorry."

"You've been through a death of your fiancé. I'm pretty forgiving." His tone told her his mind, or emotions, were not on her.

"Does Eva know how you feel about her and Lani?"

Stephen's elbow was on the counter, his fingers touching the glass. "Strangely, she is in the same situation. She still hasn't really gotten over Andre."

"So both of you, attractive and alone, not in love with one another…but having a baby," she whispered in a humored yet serious voice. Stephen nodded.

"You know what I feel most often? Disappointed that after all the down times Lani and I went through we didn't make it through the upswing, to plant the flag on the top of the hill."

"Are you sure divorce was the right thing?"

His ear nearly met his shoulder as he shrugged. "What does it matter? Where I saw a new horizon, she saw a sun setting."

"And what if perspectives changed?"

"You mean if she came back around and wanted to reconnect? I don't know. The situation is radically different. I will always be the father of a child that's not hers. She'd have to do some serious maturing to handle that."

She touched his hand. "Yes, and in the meantime, think of yourself on top of a hill, by yourself, with your own flag. You're looking across to a new woman, who is at the top of her own mountain. Both of you are alone but you enjoy one another and you're having a baby together. Love can straddle many mountains."

"Yes, with serious valleys in between."

"So," she said pragmatically, "get yourself a few zip lines and pullies." Stephen laughed and hugged her, ending the conversation with a kiss.

Saturday morning, Danielle took Monroe over to her grandparents where she witnessed a sight she never thought possible. "Jeans, Georgy? Really?"

"They've been in the shop for years," Georgy said with the tenor of a man wanting to escape scrutiny. "It was time." He excused himself, going out the back door and into the garage.

"Andre was always happier when his fingers were a little dirty from working on the bikes or the boats," said Layda, standing beside Danielle and looking out the window. "It helps."

After Danielle had set the table, she went out to get Georgy. She'd never been in the garage before, a building hidden from the house on the other side of twenty-foot privacy hedges.

"Knock-knock," she called, peering in the door. The workspace was the antithesis of what she'd expected. The floor was rough cement. Tools hung on metal hooks attached to a board with holes, the type that had hung in her father's garage at home.

"Lunchtime?" he asked, sliding out from underneath a car from the seventies.

"Yes. That's quite a vehicle you have there."

He wiped grease from his hands. "It will take a year or two, but it will be perfectly restored when I'm done."

"You guys and your muscle cars." When Andre died, Danielle had insisted Georgy take back the red Mustang Andre used to drive, along with the remaining motorcycles. It hurt too much to drive them herself, and as she pointed out, she had nowhere to park the car or bikes in her new home.

"When I was a teenager, my father took us to the States. We went to Los Angeles, saw cars the length of boats and I fell in love. It's where Andre got the bug, early on, us working on the cars together." He turned off the light, shutting the door behind them. "You don't have to wait for this one. I still have Andre's Mustang. It's in the main garage and will be there when you want to drive it in the spring."

Once at the table, Georgy lifted a drink to her. "May I add my congratulations to that of the partners?" His proud smile instantly reminded Danielle of Andre.

"For what?" she asked curiously.

"The fact that Noel had to bribe you to stay at MRD with more bonuses."

Danielle shook her head in wonder. "And I thought all this Swiss privacy stuff was for real."

Georgy gave a derisive scoff. "When you've been friends with someone for nearly five decades, the lines of business blur. Noel did say Lars was going to take you out to dinner in honor of your accomplishments. Did that happen?"

"Yes, right after the partner meeting, and I'm glad it was him rather than Ulrich, who I fear wouldn't have been quite as interesting." It was the closest they'd come to discussing Lars in a meaningful way.

Georgy's wide shoulders rose and fell as he chuckled. "I did tell Noel that under no circumstances was he to increase the stress level of my favorite daughter-in-law."

Danielle looked at her father-in-law. "Seriously?"

"Absolutely," he said with vigor. "I've made no secret of my plan to have you run our trust one day, from outside the walls of MRD. So, it may be years, but…" he raised his hands in a mea culpa. "Can't blame me for trying," Georgy rumbled.

After dinner, she bathed Monroe and put her to bed, following her not much later. She had just turned down the sheets when she heard a soft knock.

"Come in."

"Saying goodnight," Georgy said, his head peering around the door. "I wanted to say thank you, Danielle. For being with us."

She sat on the edge of the massive, intricately-carved bed. "Who would have thought that you, who was so skeptical of me when I first arrived, would become my second dad?"

"The Swiss one you never had," he said, using the identical words she'd said to him so many months ago.

"I love you Georgy. Really I do."

Danielle waited for a few minutes after the hallway light went dark before she called Lars, their conversation hushed and exciting. He loved talking her to sleep, but it was less talk and more verbal caressing, his sensual words and intonation arousing her to the point of satisfaction.

"I have a proposal," he said once her breathing had returned to normal. "I think it's time to inform the partners about us."

"What?" she said, suddenly wide awake.

"It's not required, but diplomacy and courtesy are well thought of. Furthermore, your recent commitment to stay at MRD and this project I've been working make it a relatively good environment for the information to be received without much fanfare."

Danielle felt excitement. It was like a formal coming out party. First Andre's parents, now her work associates, or at least some of them. "Are you sure?"

He chuckled. "I wouldn't bring it up if I wasn't confident in the outcome." He said he'd provide the information at the partners meeting Monday. It brought a gleeful smile to her face.

"Be safe tomorrow," she said unnecessarily.

"I always am. See you Monday."

CHAPTER 47

Danielle arrived at the office three minutes before six, having been delayed due to an overnight snow storm that snarled traffic. She quickly brushed off the snow from her jacket and hung it in the closet before taking off her boots and replacing them with her heels. She didn't notice the package on the top shelf until she lifted her purse.

It wasn't hers.

A glance in the hallway confirmed the others were already at their desks, doing what she should be doing, which was trading, and Glenda was sitting in her cubicle. She turned, shielding her actions, and removed the card.

For all things American, including Valentine's Day. All my love, L

Danielle's felt a quickening, half-expecting him to walk through the door at any moment. She glanced over her shoulder. The hallway was clear. The dark blue leather box had a single word imprinted in the center: Boucheron. Her left hand was shaking as she opened the top. Inside, was a watch, the face a flower with five petals colored with blue sapphires. White diamonds rimmed each petal of the flower. A sapphire bezel matched the deep blue leather band. It was substantial and yet elegant.

Danielle turned the watch over.

I Count Only the Joyful Hours With love, Lars.

She wanted to cry, which she refused to do at the office. She removed her own watch, slipping it in the side pocket of her purse.

Danielle opened her door wide, still expecting to see Lars. When she sat down at her desk, she lifted the phone, dialing his cell. It went straight to voice mail.

"Thank you for the very early Valentine's gift," she said, her full of emotion. "I love it."

Still giddy, she turned on her computer and traded with a zealousness created by adoration and love. It had been only six months six Andre had died, and she felt blessed. More fully than she deserved.

At ten, Glenda told her the management meeting had been delayed until the afternoon. Danielle thought nothing of it until noon, when she walked around the offices and saw Lars' office door shut and the lights off.

"Have you seen Lars?" she asked Johanne.

"Nope," Johanne said, barely lifting his eyes. "But I do know he had the partner meeting over the phone and will be coming in later."

"Oh, great. Thanks," she said, somewhat disappointed Johanne wasn't let in on the secret. She would have loved seeing his shocked reaction.

Danielle shifted her wrist back and forth as she traded, loving the smooth feel of the elegant timepiece on her arm. Out of interest, she looked up the make and model on the company website and gasped. A quarter of a million dollars. Danielle' legs felt like they were standing on a fishing boat in an Alaskan Bay, off-balance and uneven.

Well, she thought with a hint of competitiveness. Lars did have to take back that engagement ring, and he did say the jewelry store had no-return policy. Maybe this was his trade in.

At two-thirty, Danielle took a seat in the conference room near the end of the table, closest to the door. She was speaking with one of the other currency traders when Lars walked in, his arm in a sling. Her eyes went to it, a cold sensation moving from her cheekbones down to her jaw, her thought process interrupted.

Danielle returned her eyes to her peer, willing them to focus, feeling her lips press thin as she maintained her smile. She heard Lars laughing with another man.

He's happy. That's good. It means his head is fine.

The meeting commenced and Lars made no mention of his left arm, nor did he wince in pain. He was right handed and when he used the white board, his manner was unchanged. Noel entered the room, standing on the side of the room, waiting for Lars to finish. He scanned the room, catching her eye and pausing ever so slightly. The smallest of curves went up on Noel's lip before he broke eye contact. Lars must have informed Noel they were a couple.

Of course. He must be thinking I'll trade faster, more brilliantly and will now never, ever leave the firm.

Danielle surreptitiously glanced around the room. The facial expressions of the partners were unchanged, including Ulrich. Further, they'd not looked at her in any way other than normal when entering or making small talk. Her being with the managing director was a non-issue, just as Lars had anticipated.

Lars gestured for Noel to join him. "Noel has joined us today for an announcement that affects the entire firm."

Noel looked patriarchal as he began. "For some time, we have been considering merging our firm with another best-in-class entity. Our goal was to provide the premier trading and wealth management services in Switzerland. Through his vision and direction, Lars has made this happen. This afternoon, we announce the merger of MRD and Velocity Capital."

Whoa. Didn't see that coming. Velocity was the number one firm in Europe for wealth management for corporate investors with over a billion dollars. It was a distant second in commodities though and by merging the two would give MRD access to new institutions while Velocity would have access to MRD's high net worth clients. It was brilliant.

Noel congratulated Lars before inviting him to share the details. The offices of both companies would remain in place, Velocity in Geneva and MRD here in Zurich, but each entity would create space to house specialists from the other firm. The new name of the organization was Velocity MRD.

"The order doesn't reflect anything more than the fact that it sounded best," Lars said. The group laughed and Danielle could guess what was going through everyone's mind, including hers.

"Your position, role and compensation won't change, except for one area, which is bonuses. We will now be sharing the override for profits with Velocity, and they with us." To this, there was mixed responses as corporate returns weren't as high as commodities. Lars proceeded to explain the accounting structure for profits, splits and payouts. It sounded typical and fair according to all Danielle knew about mergers in her industry, but she'd check with David just to be sure.

"The announcement is going over the wire in exactly five minutes, three p.m., so as not to affect today's trading," Lars continued. "The executive team of Velocity will be flying in tomorrow while myself, Noel and select partners will be in Geneva Friday. For the next two weeks, our availability will be more limited than normal, but your trading and desk jobs shouldn't be much affected. To accommodate the integrated staff, we will be taking over the entire floor below us and the build out commences tomorrow morning."

After a short question and answer session, the group was dismissed. Danielle returned to her office, shut off her computer and said goodbye to Glenda. She was walking past the front desk when she heard her name called.

"Danielle, a moment if you can." It was Noel.

She smiled. "I'll give five, just for you." She got the impression he enjoyed her casual banter with him, much the same as Lars had when they were getting to know one another.

Danielle followed him into a small conference room.

"My intent in speaking with you is to affirm I know, and am comfortable with, the relationship between you and Lars. Would you like to add anything to what he said?"

"No," she said, politely inclining her head. "But I am wondering if our status was announced to everyone."

"Only to the partners, six including myself."

"Is this something that will be shared with anyone at Velocity?"

"We see no reason for disclosure. That said, we were obligated to provide a status of our top traders, their level of commitment and investment in the firm, all done with an eye towards estimating the future value of the business. That was one reason we wanted to make sure you were not on the verge of going elsewhere."

"What you're really saying is you owe me another elegant dinner in return for not defecting to work for Georgy?" Noel blanched, then cracked a smile.

"I can see why he likes you." Danielle felt the heat of the compliment going up her neck. "And yes, you will enjoy one, if not many more dinners, compliments of the firm. Have a good night, Danielle."

CHAPTER 48

By the time Danielle reached the metro, she felt a chill down her back. The overnight storm had now moved through the area, and the sky was cloudless, the air not so thin as it had been. A sure sign spring was around the corner.

Perhaps that's why Lars had been hurt. Warmer weather made for loose ice. The initial nausea at seeing him hurt had dissipated. What followed was professional tunnel vision, allowing her to put the sight of his useless arm, in a sling, out of her mind. Now she was left alone with the vision of Lars not only injured, but badly hurt. Or dead.

No. That will not happen again.

Danielle greeted Emma and took Monroe in her arms, wanting a comforting hug but got an eleven-month old's version of a push away. "She's not in the mood, I guess," Danielle remarked.

"She's quite the independent little girl," Emma agreed. "That's good. It will make her strong." Between making spaghetti, Danielle sent Lars a text.

Talk tonight?

Seconds later, came the reply. *Of course*

Later she was in the bathroom, running the brush through her hair as she waited for his call. It had grown long in the last few months and she'd not been to see the hairdresser since Andre died. Just using the word died caused a burst of worry, fear and anxiety that she would not, could not feel. She refused to be another statistic in the books she had read and vowed to be perfectly normal when she spoke with Lars. When the phone rang, Lars greeted her warmly.

"Hi sweetheart." Whether it was his use of a term he'd never used before, his intonation full of adoration or her fragile state of mind, she didn't know. It didn't matter. She couldn't get a word out before she burst into tears.

He was at her house ten minutes later, holding her in the foyer, then on the couch, tight within his one, good arm. The uncontrollable sobbing had been gradually calmed by soothing strokes of her hair and words of reassurance. He told her it was the warmer weather that had made the outer ridges of the ice fragile.

"It was caused by a piece of ice that fell from above," he said, explaining that he had braced against a direct impact with his left arm. "I had to preserve my writing hand, the one most important to both of us," he had joked. She didn't think it was funny, and he apologized—again.

She ran her fingers along the top of his right hand, speaking only when she knew her voice was going to be even. "The sense of dread I had today just thinking about you being on a mountain again was enough to make me stop thinking of you at all."

"I get it."

"Do you? My chest has felt compressed all day today after the meeting, almost suffocating."

He took her cold hand in his, the warmth having little effect. "I'm sorry you had to see me like that for the first time at the conference room. My cell phone died when I was at the doctor and frankly, I knew you'd be working."

"You always have another charger," she said softly. "There are other phones. You just didn't want me to worry."

His eyes were dark. "It's true. I'm sorry, again."

Danielle found forgiveness came easy. Turning off her fears did not. Still, she attempted to be normal. "You are right, though. Telling me over the phone would have made things worse. My trading would have fallen short and then where would we be?" She lifted her finger slightly, keeping only the tip on his skin. "I guess I'm late on congratulating you. The deal is impressive." He lifted his right hand up to her face, caressing her neckline.

"That's not where my mind is at."

"Not until you're out of this sling. How long?"

"A week or two at most. It's basically a really bad bone bruise."

She suddenly felt tired. Her mind was shutting down and her body was following. Slowly, careful not to hurt him, she sat up from the couch. He looked expectant.

"Come on," she said, her arm out. "Time for you to get home."

"It's early."

"I know, but I'm exhausted and you could probably use a pain killer and some sleep yourself." She could see Lars was disappointed and worried, but her response was to help him on with his coat. It was only when she was in bed, turning out the light that she glanced at her hand.

I'm such an idiot. She'd completely forgotten to thank him for the watch he'd given her. It had felt weightless against her wrist, covered up by her precarious emotional state as much as her sleeve. A text would be classless. She'd wait to thank him in person.

CHAPTER 49

The following day was like any other, right up until trading closed and Lars called her internal line. "I will be entertaining our new partners this evening and tomorrow, then gone Thursday and Friday," he told her. "Our evening calls may be sporadic at best."

"Don't worry about me," she said. "You have your hands full."

"I do, thank you." He was off the phone before she could thank him for the watch. It was home, on the bathroom counter.

Friday, she stopped by Johanne's office on the way out. "Feel like going to the club tomorrow night? Maybe with Stephen if I can get him and his pregnant girlfriend to tag a long?" Johanne practically spit out the coffee he'd been drinking, inelegantly wiping his mouth with the back of his hand. "Oh, you didn't know?"

"No, and your delivery is making me wonder if you're kidding."

"I'm not. Actually, I don't know if she's technically his girlfriend, but she is pregnant and has already told a bunch of people, so I figured you might already know." Johanne was speechless, and she laughed. "After nearly two years, I'm finally adopting the dry Swiss sense of humor. Do you like it?"

"It's strange."

"One doesn't always have to be the bull in the china shop. Sometimes, one can be the Limoges."

"Well said, you American siren."

"I will blow my horn tomorrow night around eleven."

Saturday, she woke wanting to explore. Zug was her destination, a small town only twenty minutes away. She found parking along the waterfront and slung her camera around her neck before putting Monroe in her back pack. She babbled happily as Danielle began walking. Now and then she stopped to take photos at the historical buildings along the waterfront, the four and five story structures of white, then orange and taupe linked together, their walls blended seams, holding each up. She looked forward to coming back in a few months with her sailboard. She needed to branch out from Lake Zurich. At eight p.m., she dropped off Monroe at Layda's, staying for another half-hour, doing her best to laugh with Georgy about Noel, and listening to his pleasure at the merger of the two firms along with his fear that his own returns would suffer.

"I'm being left alone for the time being, so my work is completely unaffected," she said.

"Are you okay?" he asked abruptly.

"Yes, of course. I've put on some weight, which seems to be the Swiss' measurement of happiness."

"No, it's not that. I'm just being the protective dad not the client right now." Danielle affirmed she was just fine, using her day trip to Zug as confirmation of her words.

"I don't know. You seem—thoughtful, is the best word I can use."

"And in my thoughtful state, I'll stay here tonight, if you don't mind," she said, hoping to detour his line of questioning. "I'm meeting Johanne at Benny's club then I think we are going to go out with Stephen." Georgy nodded and Danielle said goodnight to him. She found Layda tucking in Monroe.

"See you later tonight."

"Really? I would have thought..."

"I'd like to stay here this weekend. I won't wake you."

Nor did she. It was nearing two thirty when she unlocked the backdoor and was in bed by three. Monroe woke at seven a.m. promptly, but Danielle was so tired, she did little more than take a bottle from downstairs, warm it up and lay the little girl beside her as she pulled the covers back up to her neck. The strategy bought her another hour of sleep. After she'd dressed herself and Monroe, they ate breakfast with Layda and Georgy and on her way home, she confirmed her presence at the Asper Family Home for later that evening. It wasn't until she hung up the phone that she saw two messages in her voicemail.

"Call me when you are free," Lars requested in the first call. The second message was longer. "Please call me when you can. I love you and miss you."

She called him back, but the conversation was short. She first apologized for not getting his messages, explaining she stayed at Georgy's and went out with friends. "Now I'm heading out to the retirement home."

"I'm glad you are enjoying yourself, even if it's not with me. But tell me, how are you?"

"I'm good."

"No," he paused, "I'm not talking physically. How are you emotionally? Has the—worry about me passed?"

Danielle didn't want to have this conversation now. There was nothing to say on the subject. "It is what it is Lars. There's not much I can do, unless you say you will never go ice climbing again, and that's not going to happen."

"How do you know? I've already been considering it."

"No," she said forcefully, even shaking her head, confusing her little girl who heard her tone of voice and looked up. "My father wasn't going to have me live a half-life worrying about him, and I will use those exact words on you now. You can't stop doing the activity you most enjoy because I have some—issues."

"Sure I can. Or I can at least consider a compromise of activity and risk."

"Really Lars? I had a friend whose fiancé was killed in a snow mobiling accident. A couple of years later, she met a new guy who also snow mobiled. They got engaged. Six months later, he had a minor accident, wherein his vehicle was smashed up but he was fine. It freaked her out so much, she realized she could no longer be with him if he continued the sport. At the same time, he loved her to death, but he couldn't change who he was."

"Which was what?"

"A thrill-seeking, adrenaline junkie."

"I definitely share both of those traits, but I have a limit. It's called serious injury and death."

"Lars, what I'm saying is I don't think I can handle the worry over you, not now."

"Danielle," he began, saying her name in the tone he used for his meetings. "I've been thinking about this since I saw your reaction at the meeting."

"Thinking about what? To stop climbing, just like that?" she disputed. "In the two years I've known you, you have enjoyed one thing, and that's climbing. It's exhilarating for you, mentally challenging and physically demanding. What would you possibly replace that with?"

"I don't know, Danielle. A family? A little girl and her mom, perhaps a dog?" Danielle wanted to shout and cry at the same time. Her words came out as a desperate whisper.

"I can't do that to you."

"Then what?" he asked, his calm demeanor becoming slightly challenging. "Are you suggesting we stop seeing each other because you can't acknowledge how much I love you? How much you *mean to me?*" She heard a voice in the background calling Lars' name. "We can continue this another time. I'm getting ready to head out to Geneva for meetings Monday, but this discussion is to be continued."

No, it's not, Danielle told herself. She was not going to be responsible for Lars giving up half his life, half of himself, for her, or them. But if he didn't stop and find some 'compromise' as he called it, she'd worry herself to the point of sickness.

Danielle called up Lani, asking if she had five minutes. Talking at the rate of a chipmunk on speed, she disgorged all that had transpired with Lars, from his injury to his offer. Lani was succinct.

"What have you got to lose? If he gives it up and can't handle it, you might not be together anymore, but at least you have the possibility of togetherness. If you walk away now, you guarantee the ending of your relationship. Why would you do that?"

"Because I'm afraid."

Lani scoffed. "I'm afraid at this very moment too, but I'm not backing down." Danielle didn't get the comparison. "What I'm saying is that I've put my entire savings and other people's money into a new business venture and I'm scared to death, even more so now because I have the soft opening of a restaurant tomorrow and now I learn that Lars can't come, and in your mental state, I don't think you can or should come either."

"I also don't have a babysitter," Danielle added, feeling morose. She'd completely forgotten about the opening and failed her friend.

"Exactly. So, in my time of complete freak out, I'm doing something you would council, which is face it, don't avoid it. Please don't tell me you are going to avoid this, not with Lars. I saw you do that in college, and you know what happened then."

"I got pregnant and he left me."

Lani snorted rudely. "That's how you have always chosen to remember it. Do you want the true-life version of events?"

"No, not really," Danielle admitted.

"Too bad," Lani said, unrelenting. "The father of that unborn child wanted to give it a try and was willing to be involved and pay child support. You were scared like a rabbit being pursued by a fox, darting in and out of your mental hole. He got tired of not knowing what life was going to be like and he left, after you essentially made it so hard he gave up. That's why I think you lost the baby, not because your body couldn't handle it." The revelation was like a bullet going through her stomach.

"You've never described it quite like that," Danielle said, her mind reeling. Was it possible that her emotional state had caused the baby to miscarry?

"You know how you said you're being my friend and talking to me honestly? That's what I'm doing, because you have no one else who understands your history. Above and beyond all of that, I like Lars. He's not some guy you slept with who got you pregnant. This is a guy who truly loves you. Heck, he wanted to marry you even with you carrying Andre's child." Lani slowed her voice had slowed to the speed of a gently moving river. "Danielle, do us all a favor. Don't avoid facing your fear with Lars. Don't head into oblivion forever."

I'm not avoiding it into oblivion, she told herself over and over during her visit to the retirement center. Just until I can sort out my mental and emotional issues.

CHAPTER 50

The following morning, Danielle sent Lani a text with a thumbs-up emoticon and stars, wishing her the best. She also returned a call from Layda who wanted to talk about planning Monroe's one year birthday party.

"I hadn't even thought about it," Danielle admitted. "Do people do that for a one year old?"

Layda laughed lightly. "I would like to." Danielle raised her concern about a lack of people who would be interested in attending. "I have a list already assembled." It included relatives on both sides of Andre's family, from Geneva to Lucerne, neighbors and also Andre's friends.

"Layda, I'm not really sure single men are going to be interested in attending a party for a one-year old."

"My dear, in Switzerland parties are for the adults as much as the child. They will enjoy the cocktails and food and even some of the single women I've invited."

Danielle was influenced by Layda's cheerful manner, sensing that holding this event was as much for her to share her home as it was to be around those who loved Andre. Danielle's optimism lowered a bit when she considered Lani being in the same room as Stephen and Eva, but in all likelihood, the three wouldn't come. Work was always a convenience excuse to avoid personal events.

Monday night she felt compelled to send Lars a text, but hesitated. Text what? I love you and miss you. Thinking of you.

The words struck Danielle so hard her fingers froze on the phone. Thinking of you. The exact phrase she'd once used with Andre.

She opened her mouth on an inhale, her chest expanding and shoulders lifting and falling as she released the memory.

Lars isn't texting or calling me, she rationalized, giving herself a reprieve. He knows where I'm at mentally and emotionally. He could just as easily be sending communication my way.

Danielle made sure Monroe and after hours trading consumed her until she heard from Lani. When the soft opening for Stars & Stripes had ended for the night, Lani called Danielle and proudly proclaimed they killed it. Today the silence was deafening. She waited until Tuesday afternoon to call Lucas, who she knew had attended.

"It was very Swiss," Lucas said, his voice even.

"Lucas, it's me. You don't have to be so diplomatic."

"Let's just say I wouldn't go there unless I had to."

"Bad food? Atmosphere?"

"Not bad per se, but if I'm going to spend a lot of money someplace I want it to be worth it." Danielle felt terrible for her friend but was simultaneously grateful neither Lars nor she had invested in the new venture.

Tuesday night, she was at her dining room table trading when Lars called.

"I'm wondering if I should take it personally that you are posting record high numbers now that I'm not around," he said with a scolding yet playful lilt in his voice.

Her eyes remained on the screen, hoping to close out a trade and speak at the same time. "I always told you it's harder to focus when you're around."

"And I can tell you are still working, aren't you?"

"Yes," she said, almost absently. With a few more clicks, she finished the trade and lifted her fingers off the keyboard. "How's your arm?"

"Almost as good as new. By this weekend, I will be wearing a soft wrist brace. Really, Danielle. It was only a bad bruise. A minor, *minor* bone fracture."

"Sure," she said, going into her bedroom. He asked about the office and she put the phone on speaker as she updated him, stripping off her top, replacing it with her nightshirt.

"Get ready for your brains to be tapped into," he suggested. "You have already attracted quite a following, as I'm sure you know." Danielle sat on the bed then got under the covers.

"No, I didn't," she said dryly, "but I have already begun to experience more interruptions than I'd like during work hours." Lars said he'd speak with Johanne, but for the first month, she should prepare herself for more questions.

"Everyone wants to replicate the best. And in trading, you're it." Danielle thought the words sounded familiar.

"Have you been speaking with David?"

"Maybe," he hedged, deflecting her question. "Tell me about Lani."

After she told him what Lucas has said, Lars responded, "If it was that bad, my presence wouldn't have changed anything."

She adjusted the pillow. "Nope, it wouldn't."

"Danielle...."

"Yes?"

"You're being short and crisp with me."

She turned out the light. "Well I'm certainly not going to purr like a kitten. We are talking about business and Lani. Neither topic conducive to anything sensual."

"You know I'm not referring to that."

"No," she said, slinking down in the bed. "You are trying to fill up a space that's empty."

"How so?"

"Lars, you are gone, entertaining strangers, integrating two teams in the biggest deal of your career. I'm here, working away and trying not to think about things I can't control in a new environment with a man who hasn't told me what the word compromise means."

"You're not giving me the chance Danielle. Just a little more time and I'll be back, things will quiet down."

"Right," she said a little too crisply. "Now, you need to sleep as so I."

"I don't like this Danielle."

"Neither do I, but as you said, everything will quiet down and things will get back to normal."

"I certainly hope so."

In the dark, Danielle tried not to think of the words she'd just said. *I'm lying to him, and I told myself I never would.* But what other option did she have, to tell him the truth? That the fear inside her was like a black, iron ball she was trying to push away, towards the water, where she could shove it in, trusting it would never rise to the again to the surface.

The following day, the black ball was resting on the bottom of the sea floor as she sat with the other commodities traders in a special meeting.

"We have our new compatriots joining us today," Johanne started, "so be ready to answer questions and be called into impromptu discussions about how we do things." He was direct and to the point, like his predecessor had been, but he always infused his remarks with a sense of humor. "Tomorrow night we'll have a group dinner at The Stinking Rose, directions will be provided." Danielle blinked. That was Lani's new restaurant, and she always cringed when she heard the name because it was a rip-off of the famed eatery in San Francisco. Well, nice of Johanne for throwing a bone her way. She probably needed it.

That afternoon, Danielle was distracted from her screen as Jacqueline Lader escorted new faces through the hallway. Then she caught a glimpse of Lars, who had stopped outside her offices with a man who he introduced to Glenda. Danielle wondered if she was going to be sharing her resource. Lars wore a half-smile, his dark hair had a flip in the front, the sides shorter. His stance was commanding, just as it had been when she first came to MRD.

Unconsciously, she felt for the ring on her finger, feeling the heavy metal and diamonds. Lars turned, his smile now wider, his eyes focused on the man before him. He was healthy, happy and for a moment, she forgot all about the anxiety now associated with her thoughts of him.

Then she saw his sling. Danielle felt her eyes drop and her cheeks sag, the emotional high at seeing him falling, tumbling over itself into her chest where it fell and bounced against her heart, settling in her stomach, pressing on her hips and thighs, the muscles cramping. This was not some mental reaction. It was physical; every molecule of her being was tied with his, as if her soul knew that his preferred sport was dangerous and was trying to counteract and protect itself.

I don't know what the word compromise means. I can't do this. My body can't do this.

She purposefully clenched her stomach muscles, attempting to prevent that big, black ball from rising up. It didn't work. She experienced sensations awfully close to nausea, all in the short time it took Lars to say goodbye and leave her line of site.

I will not be so weak as to suffer from these anxiety-like attacks, nor will

I make Lars deal with months of my emotional baggage. She visually placed another one hundred pounds on her black ball in an attempt to submerge her feelings. When that didn't work, she knew what she had to do. She mentally took out her scissors and cut the cord from her worry, at least for now so she could focus on work.

Not from him, she told herself, from my emotions. It didn't consciously occur to her that they were one and the same.

Thursday night, Danielle stood at the doorway of The Stinking Rose and looked around the room in surprise. White linen-covered tables were accented with blue embroidered chairs with wood trim. The windows were partially covered by plush, auburn colored drapes, parted in the center to the far outside of the tall frame, reminding Danielle of Moses parting the Red Sea. The carpet was taupe, not a hint of wood, tile or stone. She thought it looked like it belonged in a hotel and designed for the business traveler, not a hip crowd that wanted ambience and a good time.

"Welcome," Lani greeted the group from Velocity MRD. Waiters dressed in black pants, whites dress shirts and black ties held trays of wine and appetizers. Danielle was standing near the back, beside a man in his mid-thirties, waiting their turn to be seated. Max was speaking to those in the front, smoothly alternating between French and Swiss German as he ushered them to the linen covered tables. Danielle was still in a state of disbelief. Lani had gone right back to the same ambiance of restaurant she had originally created with Stephen, the one that had failed.

She listened for the sound of music and heard barely audible jazz. At least it was something better than the dead silence she'd had before.

"Have you heard anything about this place?" asked the man

beside her whose name she struggled to remember.

"It just opened, Jacob," said the woman in front of him, turning slightly. "But I know the chef is the one who started Stars & Stripes."

"Wish we were there," Jacob said under his breath. "This place feels like a morgue."

Danielle kept her mouth shut, hoping the food was better than the atmosphere. Max saw her at that moment and came over.

"Nice to see you," he said, giving her a hug and kisses to each cheek. "Like it?" Danielle was conscious of Jacob and the woman watching her.

"I'm looking forward to the food," she said, turning to her companions. "This is Max. He is actually one of my clients," she added as if to justify her response to him. Jacob extended his hand, his countenance one of respect, as did the woman, who identified herself as Georgiana. Max invited the three to sit, served the initial glass of wine then left the group to attend to other customers. Danielle didn't discuss Max or the restaurant with her peers, nor did they raise the subject. The food was adequate but not extraordinary. The service was prompt and efficient, but lacked liveliness. Why was it, Danielle wondered, that Lani's vivacious personality did not carry over to her wait staff and vibe of her restaurant?

When the meal was over, Danielle avoided Max on the way out by engrossing herself in a conversation with Georgiana. In the crisp night air, she breathed a huge sigh of relief she never invested in the place and felt sorry for that anonymous investor who had. It had only been open a week, and Danielle was sure it wouldn't last a year.

Friday afternoon, Danielle glanced up at the boards on her way out.

"The Velocity team wants to know what you are eating or drinking that's so different," said Noel. He'd come up beside her.

"Say it's an American thing and let the natural competitive tendencies rise to the surface." Noel chuckled, the flesh of his cheeks pressing up to his eyes, wrinkling his crowfeet, reminding her of a younger Santa Clause. "Or how about you tell all the men to have a baby or find a woman who can. Life comes sharply into focus when one must allocate time so carefully."

His penetrating eyes cut through her glib response, causing a warmth to crawl up her neck. "While plausible, I think the real reason is the one best left unsaid, don't you?" He gave her a wink and left.

The heat was dissipating as Danielle walked by the front desk at which point it disappeared entirely. Lars held the door open for a striking woman who gave him a big smile. She wore a pinstriped suit, pearls and high heels with a herringbone top coat over her shoulders.

"Danielle, have you met Margaret? She's a partner with Velocity and will be here several times a month to work with the operations teams." Danielle extended her hand.

"Very pleased to meet you," Danielle said evenly, feeling an immediate sense of competition. The woman didn't look much older than herself, but she was already a partner? *Damn.*

The woman's eyes and smile had lost a fraction of warmth when she spoke. "Your reputation precedes you," Margaret replied. Her accent was Italian, though it had a hint of French influence.

"It's well earned," Lars said in his matter-of-fact way. Danielle gave a nod of her head and Lars gestured for Margaret to take the lead. She caught the scent of Dunhill as he passed by. Jealousy, insecurity and fear were a dangerous combination.

Once on the street she called Lars, knowing the probability he couldn't answer was high. She said she wasn't feeling well, would be going to bed early and spending the weekend with Georgy and Layda. She'd graduated from one minor lie to a larger one. A bad progressive path, but it worked. She didn't hear from him before turning out her lights.

CHAPTER 51

"Two weekends in a row," Georgy said, closing the massive metal and wood front door behind her. Monroe reached out for grandpa and hugged him fiercely, looking back at Danielle with a 'I'm-never-letting-go' look.

"You can see she's where she wants to be," Danielle responded, giving Georgy a kiss. Georgy bounced Monroe in his arms, making her laugh, and then he glanced over to Danielle again.

"You were putting on weight for a bit but now you seem to have lost some. Would going to Stars & Stripes do you some good tonight?"

"No, but thank you for the offer. As to the weight, I need to fit in my wetsuit, oh favorite father-in-law."

Monroe squirmed in Georgy's arms, her head craning towards the kitchen. Georgy set her down and she was immediately tottering towards the other room.

"Don't tell me," Danielle began, her voice a warning. A child's playhouse, built to resemble a Swiss chalet was in the corner of the large kitchen area. It had dark brown shingled accents, dormers and lattices, shutters and rectangular flower pot holder dangling outside the windows. Walking around it, Danielle saw it had a front and back door and a side stairs to an upstairs room. It made the Cinderella's Castle playhouse she had as a child look like a shack in comparison.

Danielle washed her hands and set about making dinner. Layda was at a charity event, giving Danielle the chance to make chicken cordon bleu and scalloped potatoes. She poured the thick whipping cream on the top of the sliced potatoes and added dollops of butter, "just for you," she called out to Georgy.

Over dinner, Georgy wanted to hear her thoughts on the merger, her impressions of the Velocity employees and if any of the changes had caused disruption at the office

"None, whatsoever," she answered. "In the US, we have an oft-used saying that applies to anything that works as it should, 'with the efficiency of a Swiss watch.' It's immortal, and more important, it's the truth."

"And Lars? How has he been?

"No different than Ulrich, Johanne or Noel. Meetings are held as usual, and I don't even hear the build out being worked on downstairs. Other than learning new names, it has had zero impact on me."

"Zero impact, huh? Noel did tell me the other traders are envious and, in awe of your knowledge." She deflected the compliment, instead savoring the rosemary she'd put in the potatoes.

"So far, it's been manageable. But over here, I don't have to worry about my tires being slashed, if that's a concern you had." He raised a bushy eyebrow, like it was a real possibility, the reaction making her laugh.

It felt good. She hadn't enjoyed much laughter lately, and with the way things were heading in her personal life, she didn't think that was going to change soon.

After Monroe was asleep, Danielle started the gas fireplace in her room. Curled up in her comfortable, richly embroidered chair, she read a worn copy of a book from her teenage years, one that she'd pulled out of a single box of books she'd saved. When the

DESTINED FOR YOU

phone rang, she took the call.

"Hi, Lars."

"Where are you?"

"At Layda's, in my pajamas, reading a book by the fire. And you?"

"In my apartment, alone."

Danielle thought of him opening the door for Margaret.

"You get a reprieve then, don't you?"

"For tonight, yes." More out of duty than real interest, she asked about the week and if everything had gone as expected. As he answered, she fiddled with the pages of the book and looked at the fire. She added a word or sentence here and there, finding the conversation as awkward as the dialogue. She wanted to end it but didn't find an opening. A third lie, she thought to herself.

"I'm so sorry, Lars, but I think I hear Monroe in the other room."

"Isn't the policy to let her cry herself to sleep?"

"It doesn't hurt to check her diaper."

A pause followed, and she had the eerie feeling of knowing what was running through his mind.

"Right," he finally said. "Have a good night."

"You, too." She didn't say she loved him or missed him or needed him. But then, she told herself, neither did he.

Saturday, she spoke with Lani for the first time since the opening of her restaurant.

"You came to the restaurant and didn't come to the back and say hello?" Lani asked in disbelief. Danielle started to defend herself but Lani cut her off. "I totally get it. Max said you were with your co-workers and Johanne told me it might have looked bad, like you had influenced the firm into giving business to a friend."

"But Johanne chose it, not me. Way to work the system."

Lani laughed. "After the poor showing on Monday, I had to do something. Well, did you like it? What did you think?"

"I thought it was all you, of course."

"Elegant, wonderful and refined?"

"To be sure," affirmed Danielle, seeing no reason to point out the downsides of those adjectives. "And how's Max? Treating you well?"

"He's been very professional and had all his hockey friends come in, plus many of his extended business associates. It might be enough so we can save the money on a publicity firm." Another mistake, thought Danielle, keeping her mouth shut. If Lani wanted more advice that she'd likely discard, she'd ask.

Saturday night, Danielle went appetizer hopping with Johanne and Dario, which meant having one plate of food and a drink at each location before moving on to the next. It only took three stops for the boys to become tipsy and Danielle full. They skipped the club scene entirely in order to catch Benny's early set. The wonderful jazzman gestured at her through the crowd, and the maître 'de escorted the three to a prime table near the front. Her singing evidently had the same impact on him that it had on Lars. The man stood in the corner, watching, sending a drink her way when she finished. A Mexican coffee. He'd remembered.

On her way out, she thanked him and he responded by touching her lower back, leaning toward her, inviting her to return soon. Johanne and Dario flanked her, escorting her through the doors.

"Your mystery man will thank us," Johanne said protectively. She was home by twelve-thirty, checked on Monroe and looked at her phone. Lars had called an hour before.

"I hope you are out having fun somewhere, and not alone, as I am," he said. "Spreadsheets don't make good bed companions."

Her stomach churned. She heard an unfamiliar hardness in his voice. Given the lateness of the hour, she decided not to call him back. No need to wake him.

After Danielle ate breakfast with Layda and Georgy, she called Lars as she was headed to the zoo. His phone went directly to voice mail and she envisioned him on a plane to Geneva. After penguin watching and seal feeding, it was time to head to the retirement home. All afternoon, she'd expected a return call. When it never came, she was relieved and distressed. She felt the distance growing between them, and it wasn't due to physical miles.

CHAPTER 52

The next day started with a wet snowstorm that washed some of the snow from the ground, revealing green shoots with yellow tips. Giles called her, announcing he'd returned and the shop would be open to the brave and crazy the following month. Lani called her twice that week, once with news that business was up and down. The second time she asked about Lars. "Are you doing what I told you to do?"

"What? Tell him to stop climbing or we need to break up? No, I told him I'm fine and not to worry."

Lani whistled. "Well he is brilliant. Maybe he'll figure it out for himself and won't go get himself killed on a mountain." Danielle was slightly appalled at her friend's insensitivity, but then it was Lani.

Johanne was at her door, gesturing. "Sorry, Lani, but I have to get back to work," Danielle said. From the look on her manager's face, she knew what he wanted.

"Again?" Danielle asked him, irritation scraping through her question like a blade on concrete. He shrugged helplessly.

"You are a victim of your own success," he told her. Members of the Velocity team had called, stopped by and interrupted her office so many times she was on the verge of rebellion.

"When is this going to end?"

"As soon as they have sucked you dry." Danielle removed her ear piece and stood. "After you," he gestured. An hour later, she was going back down to her office, annoyed. Why they couldn't do this after hours was simply inefficient and dumb.

"Danielle, a moment if you would." She turned at the voice that always caused her heart to beat unevenly, like a gas pedal being pushed down fast and hard.

"You're back in town."

"As evidenced by my standing in front of you," he said blandly, the twinkle in his eye missing. He gestured to the glass-enclosed conference room. The bright afternoon sun glared off the lake and she a seat on the far side of the table. Feeling the heat against her back, she looked expectantly at Lars who took the end seat. "Actually, I've been in town for the last two days, but you haven't noticed."

Regret, shame and fear pushed her to a take an offensive stand. "The Velocity traders aren't giving me time to think on my own and I'm not getting paid to train, but to trade, which has been adversely affected by this deal."

He crossed his legs, tapping a finger on the table. "You should be flattered the other traders are so complimentary of your working process."

Within the steel and concrete walls of this building, he was the boss, she the trader, and business was business. Danielle glanced up at the clock on the wall. Twenty-five more minutes of trading. "Anything else?"

"Yes. I just noticed you aren't wearing your gift." *Oh, damn.* It was the conscious, unconscious part of her that had removed it.

"I tend to take showers with my watches on, and I can't take the chance of ruining an incredibly expensive timepiece." It wasn't the full truth, and if she knew it, Lars probably did too.

"I'm sorry for the toll this has taken on us."

"There is never a need to apologize for business Lars."

"I wasn't speaking of business, Danielle. I added the *us* part for a reason. You haven't looked at my tie once since we've been speaking, and you always notice my ties." His fingers ticked off his points as he spoke. "Your voice is monotone instead of vibrant.

Your countenance is drawn. I've actually had several partners ask me if I'm putting more pressure on you now that the company has increased in size."

"And?" she queried. His chestnut-colored eyes grew darker at her tone. "Look, I'm sorry, but I've just given up an hour of my life to other traders who are only bringing my numbers down. Now you are telling me about the partners discussing us, which is wasteful gossip I could do without. I have only twenty minutes left of trading and I want to end on an up note."

All his fingers stopped moving at once, lying flat. "What about us ending on an up note?"

Danielle glanced at his left hand. It was encased in an ugly, soft black brace, strapped over his light blue dress shirt. "Ending?" she repeated.

"It will happen if you continue like this." She forced her eyes to remain even, not widen in anger or nor narrow in skepticism.

"Me?" she queried calmly. "What about if you continue like this? Climbing now, then car racing in the summer."

"Those are my hobbies of choice, which you have known about since we first grew close. Nothing has changed on my part."

"And that's the problem." She glanced again at the clock. "May I go now?"

His eyes held her. "Certainly." He held the door for her as she walked by him and down the hall to her office.

When the day was over, she refused to think about their conversation They didn't speak for the next two days, and she didn't hear from him over the weekend. If this was his strategy to letting her figure things out on her own, then she hoped he was doing some soul searching as well.

"We are both figuring out how we are going to handle this," she told Stephen one evening when she dropped by on the way home from work. Eva had been at a table with a girlfriend, and the two had made brief eye contact as Danielle sought Stephen's advice.

"Independently, not together," Stephen observed. "You told me what Lani suggested and I must say I agree with her. What does avoiding the hard conversation get you? And more importantly, why are you doing it? You love this man, and he has loved you since you first met." Danielle didn't respond. "You're so scared of losing him and going through the hurt again, you're making it happen on your own."

"I can't help it," Danielle said weakly. Stephen leaned forward, his hand on her forearm.

"It's only been a few weeks Danielle, but I'm telling you, for your own sake, don't do what Lani did to me. Every man, no matter how strong and how much in love he might be, has a limit."

"But what about him?" she asked, her voice fervent. "Why isn't he helping me out?" Stephen patted her arm, familial and kind, not condescendingly.

"He tried, and you rebuffed him. A man keeps hope only so long, and then pragmatism sets in. Maybe Lars has already reached his limit."

The following week, in the midst of her struggles with fear and uncertainty, Lani called her relentlessly. Initially, she asked about Lars but then brought up her financial situation. The Stinking Rose had already burned through forty thousand francs, more than double what she had estimated.

"How long can you go at this rate?"

"Max says three months without a new influx of money."

"Lani…" Danielle half-whispered. She'd lose the business and the investors would take a total loss. "What are you going to do?"

"Ask friends like you for more money. It will give us the additional time we need to build the business."

"What do you need?"

"If we had two-hundred and fifty more, that would give us six months." Lani sounded like an actual business person now instead of a chef. Max must be rubbing off on her in ways other than physical.

"And what's the contingency?"

"Max doesn't think we will need more than six months in reserves."

Danielle could see Lani's education had only gone so far. "Lani, most restaurants in the US take three years to reach profitability. Are you sure it's not closer to that range?" Lani admitted she didn't know, and both of them knew Max was flying in the dark. This was a first for him too.

"If you are asking me to invest Lani, my position hasn't changed since we last talked about this."

"But you've seen the restaurant, and you said it was elegant and refined."

"Yes," she hedged, wanting to spare her friend's feelings, and their friendship.

"What?" Lani said, her voice growing hard.

"I'm not comfortable investing. That's it."

"Give me one good reason, or two if you can think of them." The challenge and belligerence in Lani's tone pushed Danielle to a breaking point.

"Lani, elegance can be found anywhere in Zurich. You need to be different, dramatically different, not the same. You said you were going to do fusion, but it's gone so far I'm not sure which fusion you were using, Asian? Italian? Mediterranean or French? I couldn't describe the cuisine if I tried—"

"And that's the point. It is *different.*"

"Lani, I know food and I don't even know what category to place it in. The bottom line is I need to think about it, because if I do this, I know I'll never get my money back."

"That is so harsh, Danielle."

"It's honest Lani. Would you rather I lied?"

She heard a disgruntled sigh. "No."

"I'm glad, because it's riskier than when I decided to invest in you for the total do-over on Monroe's." She heard another sigh and murmur of agreement, which was enough. Danielle didn't need to push the point any further. "Send me the paperwork and I'll take a look, just in case I'm wrong."

Danielle planned on spending Saturday afternoon with Layda, who had offered to show her the best local sources for meats, cheeses and breads. On the way out of the house, Danielle paused to capture a photo of Monroe sitting in the crook of Georgy's elbow.

"My little granddaughter is going to sit right here with me and watch old war movies," Georgy announced.

Layda's expression was one of long suffering. "He loves those choppy black and white films from the States. He can sit there watching them for hours."

Danielle and Layda took their time, driving to different districts, sampling meats, picking up ham hocks and pates, cheeses and breads. Danielle loved the ability to purchase fresh goods and enjoyed being with her knowledgeable mother-in-law.

"I really do like you calling me that."

"I know. I like saying it. Just like my favorite father-in-law." When they returned and Danielle had retired to bed, she heard a soft knock at the door. Layda peered around the corner.

"Danielle," Layda whispered, "Lars is downstairs. He'd like to see you." Layda's expression of concern was evident, and it took more than a second for her to register Danielle's hesitation. "Shall I say you are already asleep?" Danielle bit her lip, nodding. She went into the bathroom and turned on the bath where she stayed for another thirty minutes. When she felt more in control of herself, she put on her bathrobe and made her way to Layda's bedroom. The door was open and she saw the light on.

"Layda?" she called, quietly.

"I'm here. Come in."

Danielle stepped onto an oriental carpet, the plush fabric of light hues making up a scene from the Jade Palace. The fringe stopped at the end of the sitting area in front of Layda's bed. Layda invited her over, and Danielle sat on the edge, drawing one leg under the other. It had been many years since her mother passed away, and she'd not had a mother daughter conversation since then.

"I'm sorry you had to deal with that," she began, holding her hands in her lap. "I never expected him to show up here."

"He was very eager to speak with you."

"Was he nice?"

Layda nodded, her eyes full of concern. "Always. He's been consistent throughout all these years, but he's worried Danielle. Honestly, so are we. Do you want to talk about it?"

Danielle rubbed her thumbs. "I don't want to hurt you unnecessarily, Layda. It's not fair."

A rueful smile lifted the corner of Layda's lips. "Fair stopped applying months ago."

Danielle closed her eyes and spoke of the last three weeks. Her fears, worries and concerns. "There is something else," Danielle continued. She lifted her left hand to show Layda the eternity band on her finger. "This was from Lars, given to me before my father's death."

"I notice you never take it off."

"It was a symbol of all we once had," she said sadly, the word as painful as pressing on a bruise not yet healed. "The fear is like a cancer, growing inside me. The more I try and make it go away, the faster it grows."

"Taking over the love?" Danielle nodded.

"I want to tell you something now," Layda said, exhibiting a sentiment Danielle had never seen before. Shame, Danielle thought. That's what it was. "For months, each time you went to work, I worried about the metro crashing or you getting hit and

306

dying. Every time I knew you were driving with Monroe, I worried. When you went out at night, I had anxiety attacks, thinking about your safety. Even when I knew you were at work, I worried something would happen to you, or Monroe. Every waking moment I thought about the different terrible things that could happen."

"I had no idea," Danielle murmured. Layda nodded and inhaled deeply, her shoulders rising and falling. "How did you get over it?"

"I've been taking anxiety medication," Layda revealed. "Georgy tells me it's normal to be depressed, but I thought I was stronger than that." She pressed her eyes closed then opened them wide. "I'm not. So, I'm doing my best to let go. Georgy is different than me. I understand men tend to be fatalistic, as in, what will happen will happen. Us women typically like to think we can control things."

"Which we can't," Danielle interjected.

"I don't believe taking drugs in your position is helpful, and it would make me worry more."

"Layda, if this…resolves itself, would you be okay with having Lars in my life, and by association, yours too?"

"Danielle, you didn't have to wear that ring on your finger for Georgy and I to understand that he holds a special place in your heart." Layda glanced down at her hands. "It pains me to say this, but I need to share my true feelings on the matter." Layda raised her gaze, the blue of her eyes lighter than Andre's, but just as expressive. "In so many ways, Lars has been there for you, through everything, strong and steady. It seems like he was, and is, the man destined for you."

Danielle went to bed with those words ringing in her ears. The next day was Sunday, she called Lars. After a few rings, it went to voice mail. She apologized for not being able to see him the previous evening and invited him over for brunch.

"If that doesn't work, dinner is also an option. My place, if that's okay." She sent a follow-up text and expected to hear back from him within the hour. After all, he loved her, just as she loved him. He had to know she was struggling and trying to work through her issues, and now, she was taking the first tentative, yet significant steps towards him.

Throughout the afternoon and evening, she waited for his reply. It never came.

CHAPTER 53

Danielle sent Glenda a note requesting a meeting with Lars at his earliest convenience. She informed Danielle that Lars was gone for the week in Geneva.

"Would you like me to schedule a conference call?" she asked. Danielle said yes and thanked her. Not long afterward, Glenda gave her the update. "His assistant can't find a slot on his calendar until next week. Is it urgent? Can I set something up with Ulrich or one of the other partners?"

"No, it can wait." Seven or ten *days*? He was now either going through his own time of self-reflection or he was getting back at for how she'd treated him. She called every day for five days without a response. On the evening of the sixth day, she chose a different approach.

"I gather you aren't speaking to me, which I can understand after the way I've acted. Even so, I could really use your advice, and well, you did promise you'd always take my phone calls."

Five minutes later, she got a call. "Thank you," she began.

"You are right. I promised." Danielle cleared her throat and told him about Lani's situation.

"You won't talk about us, but you will talk about a woman who left her husband and career and now wants money from you so she can lose it too?" Lars asked, incredulous.

"I...yes, I suppose," she started, then came clean. "No, actually, that's not true. I said I needed advice and invoked your promise because I guessed that was the only way I was going to get you to return my phone call."

"Then your ploy worked. Congratulations." She'd never heard him use that tone of voice with her. "Do you actually want my thoughts on investing with Lani, or can you guess what I'm going to say?"

She felt her small balloon of confidence deflating. "You are going to tell me not to invest."

"Correct." Worried he was going to hang up on her, Danielle spoke quickly.

"Lars, I'd like to speak with you in person, if I may. I'm willing to come to your apartment, right now, if need be."

"That won't be necessary. The phone works just fine."

"But you came here, why can't I come there?"

"Quite honestly? Because I have company." Danielle felt her heart implode. Her mouth went dry and she could barely breathe.

"Company?"

"Yes. So, as you think about that, I'd like you to ruminate on one additional thing. When I told you that I'd be patient and wait, I never said you could treat me poorly. Not when you were with Andre, or when I found out about the pregnancy or even losing you the first time around did I stoop to the behavior you have been exhibiting."

"I never thought…" she began, words failing her.

"You never thought what? Are you like Lani, who never believed Stephen would find another person after her, but that he, too, would wait until she figured it out?"

"Lars, it's only been a couple of weeks, almost a month. You injured your hand," she stammered, still reeling from his disclosure. "You don't think my response is normal?"

"Yes, all of that is true, and *normal* would indicate the maturity of at least speaking with your partner, your *boyfriend*."

"I'm sorry," she said quietly.

"Do you know what it's like to have a child's bedroom in your own house with no child? To have started a new life, believing I could reclaim what I once lost only to have it ripped away?" he continued, the fierceness of his words like sparks shooting out from a growing fire. "You are not the only one with hopes and dreams, and expectations and feelings, Danielle. But instead of talking to me, which is all I ever wanted, you evaded me for weeks then refused to see me. I could handle you having concerns and trying to address them but not running away from something so important."

Danielle had been prepared to acknowledge all he said, admit to it, apologize and beg for a second chance right up until that last statement. "You speak of running? At least I didn't run into the arms of another man, unlike you, with a woman who is now at your home."

She heard Lars' breathing grow intense, and she imagined his face contorted with anger, the way it had been in his office the one time she'd seen him nearly lose his temper.

"For your edification, Stephen is in the other room, along with Eva. We were planning a surprise birthday party for your thirtieth." His voice stretched taut like a high-wire. "Your incorrect assumption proves your inability to give me the credit I have earned, and very much deserve."

Danielle closed her eyes in remorse. Why couldn't she have stopped while she was ahead. "Lars, I'm—"

"No. Please stop. And if you would be so kind, please don't wear the ring I gave you any longer. I have loved you for nearly two years, Danielle, and this proves it wasn't enough. I can't give you any more of myself."

"Please," she begged. "Please don't say that."

"I didn't do this, Danielle. You did."

CHAPTER 54

Danielle sobbed until the muscles between her shoulder blades had a spasm.

He couldn't do this—*wouldn't* do this. As she wiped her eyes, she self-talked her way through Lars' rejection and request to stop wearing his ring. He was hurt, she got that. But to just walk away?

One hour and three extra strength Tylenol tablets later, Danielle was lying in bed, her head aching even with an ice pack on one side. The emptiness in her core was surrounded by a thick layer of regret. Sleep was the only remedy for her state, and eventually it came.

Monday morning, Danielle pulled her hair back from her face, leaving several curls to frame her cheeks. She purposefully selected an outfit that would give her the appearance of confidence and optimism, classy yet controlled, everything she didn't feel. The two-piece knit Celine ensemble, her pearls and silver pumps were the start. To that, she added the watch Lars had given her, wearing it on her left hand, the coloring a perfect match for her light blue outfit. She completely ignored Lars' request to remove the ring. If she was going to go down in flames, she was going to make sure it was a meteor hitting the Earth.

Live life to the fullest, her late father had always counseled. And that meant taking control when she needed to, or taking control back, in this case.

At the mandatory Monday morning meeting, she took the third

seat from the front, her back to the lake, just as she'd done those first months at the firm. She was sure Lars would notice. It was her way of sending the signal she was not going to let him leave her that easily.

Once the traders were assembled, Lars led the meeting. He wasn't wearing the brace this morning, but it wouldn't have mattered. She was set on her emotional agenda. As he spoke, she allowed herself to take in his appearance, his silver-hued shirt, his black onyx and mother of pearl cufflinks contrasting perfectly with the black speckled charcoal tie. He was as appealing and magnetic to her as he'd been twenty-four months prior.

The room was full of the standard MRD team, with the addition of Jacob, Georgiana and Margaret as well as two others whom she didn't know. Lars announced the downstairs offices were now complete, and over the next six months would be fully staffed with another dozen traders. He talked of mentoring the other traders and how the effort should lessen over the next thirty days.

"I expect your efforts to be more peer-to-peer and less mentoring over time." He made eye contact with her as he did the others, but somehow, she felt he was looking through her, not at her. Jacob had a question regarding methodologies and Lars answered it was trader-dependent.

"We don't have a set process for our traders. They have the freedom to choose their own ways and means."

"Then how will we get the best tribal knowledge?" Georgiana asked.

"The traders will be paired with those in their relevant area, or the one most closely aligned. Margaret will be working with the desk leads on that pairing."

The meeting adjourned and Danielle was trading on her

computer when she heard a two-tap at her door. She looked up, expectant yet composed.

"Would you please see me in my office when your day is done? Four or four-thirty would be preferable if you can arrange it at home."

"I'll double check and let you know." His gaze was fierce, but at least he'd spoken with her. The door had cracked open, just a little, but she would squeeze through it.

Danielle called Emma and received confirmation she could stay late. She called Lars back and left him a voice message she'd be at his office at 4:30 unless he specified otherwise. Given the expected nature of their conversation, it would be ideal to have the floor vacant.

She hung up the phone and saw the light blinking on her voice message system. She listened to a voice mail from her attorney. He'd reviewed the contract for Lani and had his recommendation.

She called him back. "This is not a good contract," he said. "You are being asked to approve the use of your name, image, likeness and words etc., for the purposes of marketing."

"Isn't some of that typical?"

"Generally, quotes are considered normal, but these other requests aren't typical and open you to risk. If the restaurant fails, is sued or loses its license due to poor health conditions, your reputation will be indelibly tied to this entity."

"Can't we simply strike those terms?"

"No." He'd taken the liberty of contacting Lani's counsel and had been told the contract was non-negotiable. "He said it's all in with the terms or not at all." Danielle was sure Lani would rather have the money than use her image and couldn't imagine this was a deal breaker. She'd double check to make sure. But at present, she wanted the counsel she was paying for.

"Your advice?"

"Don't do it. The risk is not worth the potential upside."

She tried to imagine what Lars would say. She was sure he'd be even more against moving forward than the attorney.

Danielle waited until noon then went out for a walk. The benches were covered in wet snow, so she stood, hovering in the quiet. Glancing at her beautiful watch, she took a deep breath for courage and called Lani.

"Hey!" Lani greeted enthusiastically. Her friend expected good news, not rejection.

"Lani, hey, I stepped out of the office for lunch and wanted to give you a call."

"Great! Did you get the paperwork?"

"Yes, along with my attorney's recommendation. Lani, I'll be direct. I want to support you financially, really I do, but I can't sign this contract. It needs to be modified if you want me to sign."

"What do you mean?"

Danielle relayed the concerns of the attorney. "If we can strike that section, I can still invest."

"Hold on," Lani said, muting the phone. "Max says no. The restaurant needs it." Danielle stretched her neck, as if she could make the stress go away.

"What it needs is a lot of customers, not my name or likeness or quotes."

A moment passed before Lani spoke, and Danielle wondered if Max was eavesdropping on the conversation. "You don't think I'm going to make it, do you?"

"I hope and pray every day you will."

"Answer the question Danielle."

"Lani, I told you not to do this. That was me as your business partner and friend talking to you."

"And I thought my friend would help me out."

"I'm trying to Lani. Just strike that section and I'll do the paperwork today."

"I told you no, we can't do that."

"Well, if you change your mind, let me know."

"What kind of friend doesn't believe in me?" Lani asked, her voice belligerent. "I've done all the right things in perfect order, and now you take away your offer to support me? That's not how friends operate, Danielle."

Danielle's fragile but determined state of mind went from a ripple on top of the lake to a white-capped wave. Still, she pushed her mental ballast down, deep into the water, trying to keep herself steady and calm.

"*Friends,*" she said, emphasizing the word, "don't leave their investors, partners and friends when they become successful. *Friends* understand and respect one another's decisions, like I did you. And *friends* don't guilt trip friends into an open-ended contract when they need to be bailed out."

"Are you really talking to me this way? This is monumental."

"No Lani. It's a restaurant. It's not a life and death situation."

"Oh, please, Danielle. It is for me. How can you even say that?"

Danielle felt herself tilting as the waves underneath her grew in strength. Her voice was smooth and cold when she spoke. "Easy. You experience the death of a loved one and realize how inconsequential everything else becomes."

"I can't believe your using a line about Andre on me."

Danielle was dumbfounded. "Using a *line?*" she repeated in disgust. "You know what Lani? You are a beautiful woman who got literally everything she wanted in life. A restaurant without having to pay a dime, more profits that she ever imagined, a gorgeous man who is intelligent and was completely and *is still* utterly devoted to you, despite the way you treated him. Then what? Your dreams of success were realized and you changed. You turned away from every value you ever held dear."

"I became true to myself," Lani shouted back.

"Does true to yourself mean being with a man who wants casual sex and treats you like any other woman on the street? Does being true to yourself mean you owning a restaurant that's as austere and boring as the first one you started?" she continued, knowing her comments had become personal and cutting. "So if you being true to yourself means being alone and broke and guiding your life without moral principles, then congratulations, you've succeeded." *Crap.* She'd just used nearly the same phrase Lars had used with her.

"You are a complete bitch, you know that?"

"Perhaps, but at least I have my integrity intact and my focus clear."

"Right," Lani sneered. "Just because Andre was killed you think you have some moral high ground? You have been treating Lars like shit because you are scared and expect sympathy from everyone. You'll drive him away just as I did with Stephen and then you'll be alone. You watch."

Danielle grit her teeth. "I don't have to watch, Lani. It's already happened. So, you can now congratulate yourself on being correct about my inadequacies. Feel better now?" Her chest was heaving and in the silence that followed, she glanced over her shoulders, hoping no one had heard her outbursts.

"No. I don't," Lani said, haltingly. "I'm sorry."

Danielle's pulse rate started to drop. "Don't be. I shouldn't be taking out the mess I've made of my life at you. I...frankly, I deserve it. You said nothing more than the truth. I was brutal and I apologize."

"Maybe we should take a break."

Danielle watched the sun bounce from the top of one cresting wave to another. "Maybe we should."

Never in their dozen years of friendship had they had such a fight, much less a nuclear blow-up. At least the Earth beneath their feet hadn't been entirely scorched. In time, the grass might grow back.

Danielle slowly made her way back to the office. Her next appointment was going to be with Lars, her managing director and boyfriend. Or was it *former boyfriend?* She wasn't sure if the day could get much worse, but she'd soon find out.

CHAPTER 55

She rang the buzzer outside his door, it clicked and she walked in. The offices were dark and the hallways were quiet, confirmation they were likely alone.

Lars was sitting behind his desk and didn't look up from his computer screen as he asked her to sit. Danielle went to the sitting area. "I'd prefer to have you across from me," he said, this time, glancing at her.

"Unless this is a disciplinary conversation, I'd prefer to sit here." She waited a split second to see his response, then took her usual place on the high-backed leather chair adjacent to the couch. She crossed her legs, placed her hands in her lap and checked the email on her phone while she waited for him to join her.

He eventually came over and sat on the couch, his arm resting on the end, the ends of his fingers curled on the leather. His position and manner all business.

"Although this conversation is not disciplinary in nature, it does have to do with your employment here. I've spoken with Noel and we are wondering if you'd like to be let out of your contract."

A burst of warmth shot from her belly to her legs, the kind that only came when she got angry.

"That came out of nowhere." Lars ignored the comment, his forefinger moving slightly as he waited for her response. "You may relay to Noel that I'm happy and committed where I am."

"I don't expect that to continue, and I've told him as much."

Danielle raised an eyebrow. "Then you will have tell him that for once in your perfectly managed life, you have miscalculated."

His eyes were so hard and focused she imagined them cutting steel. As he remained silent, she continued.

"And you've had this conversation with Noel because you don't want a relationship with me any longer?" His fingers began tapping on the leather. "Let's cover a few vital details, just as we did the first day of my employment. First, you want me to leave but I won't. You will have to fire me. I'll sue and you will lose, because my numbers will stand up in any arbitration and we both know it. However, given the small chance that you succeed in forcing me out of here, you will need to prepare yourself for a potential lawsuit from Margaret and the Velocity team over the decreased value of MRD, since my staying added a lot of value for the business. The millions of dollars you would have made in generated fees and the billions of dollars under my management will be gone, following me anywhere I go, since firing me releases any contractual bond we have. Lastly, I'm not taking off the ring you gave me," she said, raising her hand, "nor am I returning the watch. They were given with love and I still return that love. Fiercely."

When he finally spoke, his voice was as monotone as his eyes. "I don't believe you, Danielle, nor do I believe you will be unaffected by us no longer dating."

She leaned forward on her elbow. "How and when does *belief* enter the equation? I didn't want you to change your habits because of me."

"I never said I would," he replied calmly.

For a moment, she was stymied. "But you said you would compromise."

"I said I'd talk about a comprise," he clarified. "And while you were wondering if you could handle your fears of being with me, I've been questioning if I can really give up my life-long activities or if I'd turn resentful at doing so over the years."

Danielle had no response. It was a perfectly rational concern, and rose above the immediate here and now of simply being with one another.

"In other words, we could stay together for some period and end up apart anyway."

Lars now leaned forward, the distance between then shortening. "Yes. That was one thing I considered. The other is I realize you can't handle all the love I can give you." He looked as though he were going to say more, but she wasn't going to let that comment go without a response.

"And what I realized is that you have never had someone love you so much that they were willing to walk away from you *because* they loved you. So, who loves the other person more?" She challenged.

"That's subjective and unanswerable," he said. With each exchange of words, the intensity behind their emotions had increased even as their voices lowered to keep the conversation contained within the four walls of the room.

"Have you?" she asked, her voice soft.

"Have I what?"

"Been loved by someone as much as I love you?" It was not a question she thought she'd ever ask him, or anyone before now. All that he'd ever said and conveyed seemed to lead up that simple truth. She inched towards him now, out of genuine desire to be close to him.

"I was, and am, still afraid of you getting hurt or dying," she admitted, trying to replicate Layda's humility at the admission. "Layda confided to me she takes pills because she has the same worry about me and Monroe. Every time we leave the house. When we are in the car. Even when we are asleep at home. Anything, anytime, anywhere." Danielle dropped her hand down in front of her, stretching it out from her elbow, almost touching his fingers, but not quite. "I thought the biggest show of my love was to let you live life, in the most fulfilling way possible, like my father advised me to do. And if that meant stepping away from you, as my father also said, so be it."

Lars dropped his head, then looked back up. "I've admired many things your late father said, but not that. Stepping forward, into me, into my arms, was what you needed to do."

His eyes softened for the first time, his glance like a rope being extended to a climber clinging to the side of a mountain. She extended her forefinger and touched the skin on the top of his hand.

"I am immature in the ways of a real relationship. Lani told me so in the worst of ways but she was right. So are you. And if history is any guide, and if I don't change in a fundamental way, I'll keep falling into the same emotional pit." Lars held his hand still as Danielle moved her finger along his skin, an inch at a time. "Lars, please believe me when I tell you this. I love you more than any person, or thing in my life, save Monroe, and even that is different. She is my daughter. You are the love of my life."

He slowly turned his palm over, a silent invitation for her to continue. She kept her fingertip on his skin, slowly caressing the center of his hand.

"Can you see it if from my perspective," she asked quietly. "Even a little?"

Lars curled up his fingers, enclosing hers. The action drew her to him, infinitesimally. He lifted her hand to his mouth, placing a kiss in the center of her palm. She felt a spread of warmth through her body and up to her throat as he sensually moved his lips in a circle before guiding her hand to his cheek. Her hand slid into his hair as though she were touching a ghost that might dissipate.

"This is my perspective," he murmured, his thumb holding her cheek as his fingers gripped the back of her neck.

She felt his breath in her mouth as she opened her lips, drawing him in. "Lars," she murmured. "This office isn't all that discrete."

"I don't give a damn about that word anymore." His hard, full lips pressed on hers so completely she was prevented from emitting any sounds other than groans of pleasure. His arms went around her, pulling her onto the couch. "Why did you pursue me when I told you to leave me alone?

"Because only a person madly in love pursues a person who acts uninterested. And I believed it was an act, not reality."

Lars responded to her comment by gliding his mouth up to her ear, pausing. "After all we have gone through, I can't make any more promises."

She nodded, feeling him pull her closer, like a net lifting her up from the dark water. "I don't expect or deserve promises," she murmured, "but I am hoping for a life time of tomorrow's."

The arms around her wrapped tighter, the bind close and comforting. One day at a time was all he could give. She closed her eyes, nodding. It was enough…for now.

ABOUT THE AUTHOR

Before she began writing novels, Sarah Gerdes established herself as an internationally recognized expert in the areas of business management and consulting. Her nineteen books are published in over 100 countries and three languages.

BOOKS IN PRINT BY
Sarah Gerdes

Contemporary Fiction

Global Deadline

In a Moment

Danielle Grant Series

    Made for Me (book 1)

    Destined for You (book 2)

    Meant to Be (book 3)

A Convenient Date

Fiction: Action- Adventure

Chambers Series

    Chambers (book 1)

    Chambers: The Spirit Warrior (book 2)

Incarnation Series

    Incarnation (book 1)

Non-Fiction

Author Straight Talk: The Possibilities, Pitfalls, how-to's and Tribal Knowledge From Someone who Knows

Sue Kim: The Authorized biography

The Overlooked Expert: Turning your skills into a Profitable Consulting Company- 10th Anniversary Edition

Navigating the Partnership Maze: Creating Alliances that Work

Social Media

Instagram: sarahgerdes_author

Facebook: Sarah Gerdes author

www.sarahgerdes.com

ACKNOWLEDGEMENTS

A special thanks to Chuck P., who was the first (and only) person to read this manuscript as it went off to the editor. His timely and insightful perspective bettered the book, especially the ending. May his "man-card" always remain intact.